THE LON
PAST O

During a fierce air battle against the Germans, Reed McGurn collided with an enemy plane and was sent plummeting toward earth. But just before a horrendous crash and a bloody death, Reed McGurn passed out. When he came to, he found no severe injuries; and, amazingly, he was nowhere near Germany! He set out on foot and came upon a scene straight from the history books—a woman dressed in animal skins, a Cro-Magnon warrior, and a great jungle cat ready to attack! Before long, McGurn discovered that he had been thrust back in time. Back to a time when savage beasts and fierce cavemen roamed much of the Earth. Back to a time when the lost kingdom of Atlantis flourished in all its splendor. There would soon be a vicious clash between this advanced civilization and a vicious brute from a savage jungle realm. And Reed McGurn found himself marked for death in this brilliant novel of lost worlds and lost races, penned by science fiction veteran Howard Browne.

CAST OF CHARACTERS

LT. REED MCGURN

This ace WWII pilot crashed in an unknown land, finding strangers who wanted to kill him and beautiful women who wanted to mate!

ATHORA

This stunning beauty was the royal princess of Atland—but she found herself smitten with a commoner from another time.

SAR-GATH

With a network of spies to keep him informed, this high priest was filled with much more than religious fervor.

CLAT-RON

As High Priest of Atland he thought he was going to rule the kingdom someday…with the beautiful Athora by his side.

LUA

Taken captive by a Clyrusian spy, her hopes of being rescued were slim, retaining her virtue even slimmer…

FARGOLT

He was supposed to be loyal to Atland and its royalty, but were his intensions truly noble?

MENTANEK

He was King of Clyrus, a depraved ruler whose ruthless ambition was to take over Atland, crush its king, and reap the bounty!

ASHTOTH

As the King of Atland his only hope of retaining rule over the kingdom lay in the recovery of a priceless statue.

FORGOTTEN WORLDS

Special Illustrated Edition

(Lost World-Lost Race Classics #2)

By
HOWARD BROWNE

Illustrated by
Robert Gibson Jones

ARMCHAIR FICTION
PO Box 4369, Medford, Oregon 97504

The original text of this novel was first published by Ziff-Davis Publishing Company.

Cover art by Robert Gibson Jones

For more information about Armchair Books and products, visit our website at…

www.armchairfiction.com

Or email us at…

armchairfiction@yahoo.com

CHAPTER ONE

One of Our Planets is Missing

LIEUTENANT REED McGURN, sole American member of the Pursuit Squadron, Royal Air Force, was on his way home from a solo reconnaissance flight over southern Germany. Judging from his instruments he should be close to the Rhine by this time, with his objective, a French aerodrome, a few miles beyond.

At peace with the world was the square-faced, dark-haired, handsome young lieutenant on this sun-freshened morning of an October day in 1939—at peace with the world as long as no Nazi plane rose to challenge his present position over the *Vaterland.*

Ten thousand feet below unrolled a vista of rugged countryside dotted with tiny villages and crisscrossed with ribbon-like roads. Nothing there to indicate that a few miles to the west two mighty armies lay firmly entrenched on either side of a great river, each awaiting the word that would send it against the sunken and theoretically impenetrable fortifications of the other.

The single-seater Spitfire purred steadily westward. McGurn's strong jaws moved rhythmically against a wad of gum as he hummed softly to himself above the muted roar of the Rolls Royce motors.

And then the English music hall tune ended abruptly in mid-air. Rising steeply against the western horizon were several tiny dots—dots that rapidly formed into a single, evenly spaced line.

"Messerschmitt…" muttered the lieutenant, his narrowed blue eyes studying the approaching planes, "—five of 'em!"

Nothing to do, he decided quickly, but meet the five head on, then attempt to out-maneuver the lot. Once past that line and the Messerschmitts could never overtake him.

Deliberately Reed McGurn permitted the Nazi ships to gain in altitude. Through the glass of his enclosed cockpit he could see them poised to streak down and blast him from the sky.

The distance between hunters and hunted quickly narrowed. Suddenly orange flames slanted from the wings of the German

When we look around at our world
today and see the wonders of modern
civilization we feel justly proud---
but what of the long forgotten past in
which this planet Earth played a part?

FORGOTTEN WORLDS
by LAWRENCE CHANDLER

planes and a stream of bullets tore through the glass near McGurn's head. Then everywhere about him were the sounds of roaring motors, the stutter of guns, and the eerie whine of diving planes.

The British craft seemed to stagger in mid-air under the deluge of German bullets. Not until then did McGurn shove the nose of his Spitfire downward, power-diving in a seemingly desperate effort to shake off those five Hun war-birds.

Instantly the Messerschmitts streaked earthward in mad pursuit, pouring lead into the tail of the lone fugitive.

And then, a grim smile tugging at the corners of his mouth, the wily lieutenant thrust hard against the control stick and sent his plane into an inside loop that whirled him from under the Nazi guns. Head downward he gyrated through space, climbed steeply again, then dived once more. But now the former picture was reversed; the pursued had become the pursuer; it was McGurn now who loosed eight streams of blazing death from the muzzles of Browning guns.

Two of the Messerschmitts, their pilots dead at the controls, spun earthward in flames, voicing the awful scream that a doomed plane gives in futile protest against its fate.

THE remaining Germans scattered before the hail of lead from McGurn's wings, then pulled out of their dives and turned to engage him. Now the battle became one of maneuver, of rolls and spins and dives and loops.

But the odds were still too great. Bullets poured into the cockpit of the dancing Spitfire, shattering the instrument panel and driving bits of metal and particles of glass into McGurn's face and body. Partially blinded, the lieutenant sought to turn his plane aside to escape the blast; and at that moment an enemy ship drew alongside to attack that flank.

McGurn saw that a crash was inevitable. Desperately he fought to pull his plane's nose above the bulk in his path. In the instant before the impact he caught a vivid impression of the fear-twisted countenance of the enemy pilot, then the two planes came together with terrible force.

McGurn felt himself torn bodily from his seat, the side of his head banged heavily against the wheel in his hands, and through the fog of pain and noise he was dimly aware that the Spitfire was falling. Helpless to lift a hand he sagged limply forward and watched the level ground, far below, rise with incredible swiftness to meet him.

While even more swiftly raced his thoughts. This was the payoff. Today's official British communiqué would list the loss of a plane over enemy territory. McGurn was suddenly glad that he hadn't married that New York blonde last year; she would have hated being a widow. And one nice thing about being an orphan: no parents would have their hearts torn by his death.

Death? Hell, he wasn't dead—yet. Too much to be had from living to go so soon. His head was clearing rapidly, and he reached out to grasp the threshing control stick. The ground was very near by this time, with wide green fields leaping upward to enfold him.

Suddenly the land below was blotted out by a great gray cloud, which had materialized from nothingness; and even as McGurn wondered wildly how it had gotten there, dank mist closed about him and the falling plane and shut out the sky and the earth.

What caused the miracle that followed, Lieutenant Reed McGurn was destined never to know. But abruptly the broken Spitfire was no longer plunging furiously to destruction; instead the plane, nose still almost vertical, was sinking gently through the gray cloud like some damaged liner in a calm sea.

Eyes popping with amazement, McGurn tugged frantically at the wheel, seeking to force up the plane's nose and set the ship into a glide. His strength seemed gone, however, and the wounded Spitfire continued to settle deeper within the gray opacity.

Then sunshine once more enveloped him, the cloud was gone, and with it had vanished the wide fields and rugged terrain of southern Germany. Less than a hundred feet beneath the aircraft lay a mighty forest that appeared to cover the entire countryside.

Only a glimpse of this was given McGurn; for the plane, as though released by some giant hand, plummeted downward again. The high flung branches of a great tree reached greedily for the Spitfire, there was the ugly sound of rending metal, something smote the lieutenant across the forehead with stunning force and then darkness…

LIEUTENANT REED McGURN came slowly back to the world he had so narrowly missed leaving. For a long time he lay motionless while his stunned brain fought to shake off the effects of a numbing blow. At last the blue eyes fluttered up, swam momentarily, then focused on the broad limbs of a great tree.

It was only after three efforts to sit erect had failed that the young flier was able to draw himself into an erect position, and even then it required almost superhuman control to keep him there while searing pain hammered at his temples. Weakly he lifted a hand to his aching head, felt tenderly of an extensive lump along the hairline above his left ear, then lowered the hand to stare with bewilderment at his now bloodstained fingers.

Everything came back to him now: the terrible dogfight across the sky, the collision with the Nazi plane, which had wrecked his own craft, the strange gray cloud that had seemingly broken the long fall to earth, and, lastly, the endless expanse of forest, which magically had appeared where no forest could possibly be.

Slowly Reed McGurn turned his battered head and gazed about him. What he saw served not at all to dissipate his complete mystification. Apparently he had been plunged into the heart of a wilderness of growing things—a wilderness of semi-tropical jungle and trees as untamed and primeval as that of any in darkest Africa. About him towered tremendous jungle patriarchs, their huge boughs laden with creepers and vines, their boles so close together as to make it almost impossible for a human to pass between them. So dense was the foliage, so tangled the masses of leaves and flamboyant blossoms that the ground beneath must remain in perpetual twilight, denied the direct rays of the sun.

"I don't get it," said McGurn, aloud. Sounds came to him now: the discordant voices of birds, the hum of myriad insects, the rustle of vegetation in the path of humid jungle breezes.

"No sir. I don't get it." He repeated the words, more for the sake of hearing some familiar sound than anything else. Mechanically he extracted a stick of gum from the pocket of his uniform blouse and placed it in his mouth. The act of chewing caused his head to increase its painful throbbing; but somehow the exercise of a long established habit helped in orienting himself to the strange surroundings.

With an effort he managed to gain some control of his shaken mind. Some freak of climate, he told himself resolutely, had created a bit of tropics forty degrees north of the equator. This was southern Germany, or perhaps some deep valley in Switzerland. First he must locate a clearing and, using the sun as a guide, gain some idea of direction before setting out for civilization. He wouldn't be the first flier who had walked back from a ride.

He rose gingerly to his feet, hesitated long enough to overcome the wave of nausea and dizziness that spun his head like a whirling propeller, then sighting a gap in the circle of trees, walked slowly toward it.

Pushing through a tangled mass of undergrowth, he stepped out into a tiny natural sun-drenched clearing.

There, battered and ripped into an almost unrecognizable pile of wreckage, lay the remains of the Spitfire.

Voicing a cry of relief that was more nearly a sob, Lieutenant Reed McGurn stumbled to the side of the broken hulk and ran his fingers caressingly over the twisted fuselage. From the standpoint of practical value the plane was worthless; no amount of mechanical ingenuity could put together that shattered bulk and splintered motor. Even if by some miracle repairs were possible, the pilot wasn't born who could have lifted a ship over the wall of trees about the clearing.

But it was not what the plane could do for him that had caused McGurn's cry of mingled relief and thanksgiving; it was the sight of a familiar object, some link with the known world of uniforms and orders and the military life.

From a compartment in the twisted cockpit, he found four unbroken packs of American-made cigarettes, a handful of book matches each imprinted with advertising for an American brand of beer, and the standard .455 Webley service revolver together with nearly sixty rounds of ammunition. All these, in addition to a small, powerful flashlight, which in some way had survived the crash undamaged, McGurn distributed among his pockets.

Ready now to brave this alien world in search of one more nearly familiar, the young American descended to the ground and set about selecting the direction in which he meant to travel.

The sun stood almost directly overhead, indicating the time as noon, or nearly so. Evidently he had lain unconscious for close to four hours. He wondered at the nearness of the sun to the Earth. It seemed larger, somehow, than he last remembered it. Larger and hotter; he was aware of perspiration running like tiny rivulets over his skin and soaking into his clothing. He was strongly tempted to remove the woolen blouse and let the light breeze cool him, but decided against it. One simply couldn't stroll into the normal chill of October in Germany while stripped to the waist.

A break in the wall of foliage caught his eye. Upon investigation he found it to be the mouth of a game trail that led toward what he decided was the northwest. The Allied lines, McGurn reasoned, lay roughly in that direction.

And so, with a light shrug of his broad shoulders, he set out along the narrow path.

TWO hours later the disheveled figure of Lieutenant Reed McGurn, naked to the waist, skin covered with scratches and the angry welts of insect bites, coated with dust and bathed in sweat, dropped wearily to the ground beneath the wide branches of a mighty tree and buried his head in his arms.

Where was he? Into what uncharted corner of the earth had fate tossed him? Since leaving the vicinity of the fallen Spitfire, he had seen things that had no business existing outside the cages of a zoological garden. Monkeys, entire tribes of them, chattering at him from the middle terraces of the wild and tangled labyrinth of trees, birds whose plumage and size were beyond anything he had come across in school textbooks; even a great snake—a python he judged—desending in slimy coils from a mossy branch above the trail.

If such as these were about, was it not probable that more dangerous things filled this God-forsaken place? Where there were monkeys and giant snakes, there were most likely lions and tigers and leopards. What could he hope to do if attacked by any one of such beasts?

Reed McGurn admitted to himself that he was frightened. Most of his fear seemed to stem from not knowing where he was—that paralyzing sense of being completely lost, which can send the strongest into blind panic.

His fingers were trembling as he lighted a cigarette. How tired he was. The heat beat at him like a whip of many lashes. What he would have given for a long drink of cold water. With all this vegetation there was bound to be streams in the vicinity. Yet not the tiniest brook had he found in the past two hours. Somewhere he had heard that all wilderness trails began and ended at running water.

After resting for a few minutes he would push on. Surely this green purgatory could not cover the entire earth. Somewhere men like him sat telling tall tales over mugs of cold beer and ale. Yes, he would wait long enough to get back some of his strength, then rise and go on again.

Wearily he slumped back against the broad bole of the tree, the cigarette dropped from his fingers and sleep overwhelmed him…

He awoke with a start…and found that twilight had come down upon the jungle. Getting stiffly to his feet, he lifted his arms to stretch cramped muscles, only to freeze in that position as the rustle of disturbed leaves from across the trail came to his ears. Straining his better than average eyes against the fading light he was able to make out the shadowy outlines of some huge object flattened behind the curtain of vines at that point.

Cold beads of perspiration sprang out on the lieutenant's forehead. His hand stole cautiously into a pocket and closed about the butt of his service revolver. The Webley's compact weight stayed fading confidence.

The amorphous figure beyond the cloaking foliage did not move. McGurn took a deep breath. Had his imagination tricked him? Was he menaced by a grass-covered stump or fallen log?

Carefully McGurn essayed a backward step, and, as nothing happened, another. It was a log, then! At this rate he would soon be fleeing madly from his own shadow…

With a mountainous sigh of relief, McGurn let his tense muscles relax and he turned away, his fingers releasing their hold on the gun.

And at that moment the silence of the jungle was ripped apart by the terrifying scream of a charging animal. McGurn, his scalp crawling with terror, wheeled sharply, revolver in hand, as a sleekly sinuous shape shot from the depths of vegetation and rose in a swift, silent spring at the half-crouching lieutenant.

Four times the angry crack of a gun split the jungle quiet, the powder flashes weirdly disclosing the snarling face and back laid ears of a giant cat.

A tremendous weight crashed against McGurn's body, driving him heavily to the earth. His head struck some hard object with terrific force, a hundred pinwheels spun before his eyes; a sharp, agonizing pain tore into his chest, and for the third time that day Reed McGurn lost consciousness.

CHAPTER TWO
Now You Are Mine!

BITOG, a warrior of the Cro-Magnon tribe of Mosat, squatted on his muscular, sun-tanned haunches at the entrance to his caves and fed mental fuel to the blazing anger raging within him. For hours he had sat there, while the customary activity in the clearing below gradually lessened and the tribal members sought their caves and sleep as dusk deepened into night.

As the swollen disk of a full moon rose higher in the night sky, the sheer cliff containing the caves of Mosat's tribe lost its curtain of shadows and stood out, bold and forbidding, in the brilliant rays.

Behind the cliff, stretching endlessly in all directions, were broad plateaus covered with towering trees and lush jungle, cut with deep ravines and marked with wide ribbons of grassland teeming with zebra and deer and the wild horse. Countless small streams and many wide rivers coursed through the vast territory, many of them emptying their waters into a shoreless sea far to the west.

From beyond the towering ramparts of semi-tropical forest bordering the clearing at the base of Mosat's cliff, came the long-familiar voices of the night: the coughing grunt of a hunting lion, the shrill scream of a panther, the staccato barkings of a jackal pack.

Bitog, however, was blind and deaf to all this. He was in another world…a hell of hatred and wrath and wounded pride. The sullen, brooding anger within him was reflected in the twisted lines of his heavy-featured face and the manner in which the thick knuckled fingers of his powerful hands knotted convulsively as though tightening about the throat of some invisible enemy.

He, Bitog, mighty hunter and fighter, feared and respected by all, even unto Mosat himself, had been humbled and degraded in the eyes of his people. And the one who had done this to him was a woman.

Woman? Lua was no woman. She was barely more than a child—almost young enough to be his own daughter. Yet, woman or child, she had said things to him that no other in all the tribe of Mosat would have dared to utter.

It had happened that same afternoon. He had come down from his cave, and approached Lua, daughter of Yortak, where she knelt at her task of scraping a deerskin. Pausing beside her, he placed a strangely tender hand on one of her softly rounded shoulders. And when she looked questioningly up at him, half awed by his splendid, great thewed body naked except for the tanned pelt of Kraga, the lion, about his middle, he told her in an oddly thickened voice that he wanted her to be his mate—that he had tired of living alone in his cave and from this day on she was to make his food and tend his wants and warm him with her nearness during the long cold nights of the rainy season.

Lua, the lovely golden-tanned oval of her face suddenly flushed with mingled astonishment and loathing, had risen to her feet with swift grace.

"Mate with *you?*" she cried, tossing back the soft fragrant strands of honey-colored hair with a haughty gesture. "Sooner would I put myself within the coils of Sinu, the snake! You are old—old and mean! Two suns ago I saw you strike Alea's little child because he stood in your way. Everyone hates you. Go away from me—beater of children…"

Other women of the tribe, working at their endless tasks nearby, had heard the scornful words and made no attempt to hide their pleasure at seeing the despised Bitog put in his place.

He should have struck her down, Bitog told himself now. But he had been too dazed by the unexpected rebuff to do more than slink away, as Cretah, the hyena, slinks from the path of Kraga, the lion. How the other warriors of Mosat's tribe must have laughed when they learned from the gossiping tongues of their women how mighty Bitog had turned in flight before the bite of a girl's words…

As Bitog squatted there on the stone ledge outside his cave, his seething mind conjuring up distorted pictures of revenge, he was suddenly electrified by the sight of a girl's slender form emerging from the mouth of a cave almost directly below where he was sitting. Puzzled, he watched her inch carefully down the sheer escarpment toward the level ground at its base. The bright rays of Mua, the moon, picked out her untamed wealth of yellow hair and the sleek pelt of Tarka, the panther, covering the softly rounded perfection of a lithe figure.

"It is Lua," he muttered wonderingly. Rising to his feet for a better view he watched her drop lightly into the clearing and without a backward glance race across the open ground toward the mouth of a game trail in the wall of verdure marking the forest edge.

Once there, Lua turned for a fleeting glance at the cave-dotted cliff…then she was gone as though the earth had opened to swallow her up.

BITOG ran a bewildered hand through his heavy shock of black hair, his rage of a moment before replaced by a gnawing curiosity. Whatever, he asked himself, had possessed Lua to enter, alone and unarmed, the lurking place of savage, bloodthirsty jungle animals? Even Bitog, experienced hunter and mighty fighter though he was, would have thought twice—and twice again—before venturing alone into a night-shrouded forest.

But the prod of curiosity was far stronger than inherent caution; and Bitog was on the point of descending the cliff to follow the golden-haired girl, when a glimpse of a second figure, stealing stealthily down the scarp, froze him into statuesque immobility.

Recognition was immediate: it was Azar, youngest son of Mosat, the tribal chief. He was no more than seventeen—a tall, slender youth whose body had not yet put on the sinews of manhood.

Bitog, like a good many others of Mosat's tribe, was rather contemptuous of Azar. He displayed little interest in the hunt or in learning the art of becoming a great fighting man. Instead the slim-bodied youth spent long hours in painting scenes of Cro-Magnon life on the walls of the tribal caves, his medium the ocherous clays to be found near mountain streams.

It was not until Azar had crossed the clearing and was entering the forest that full realization dawned on Bitog as to the reason behind these nocturnal prowlings. But as he saw the chief's son melt among the Stygian shadows cloaking the same jungle path Lua had taken, he suddenly understood; and once more consuming anger flamed within him, fed to still greater heat by the tinder of jealousy.

Hesitating no longer, Bitog slid recklessly down the almost vertical slope and raced with bounding strides toward the mouth of that game trail.

And as he stepped among the grotesque shadows there, he became as one of them: silent, sure-footed, cunning—a hunter stalking wary prey.

Brilliant shafts of moonlight occasionally lanced through breaks in the ceiling of tangled branches, leaves, creepers, and vines, dappling the pathway with pools of silver. Always, Bitog was careful to skirt those patches of light lest his human quarry catch sight of him. His movements were quick, certain, controlled. And though many twigs and broken branches and dead leaves littered the winding trail, not once did a thoughtless step betray his passing.

He had covered perhaps a hundred yards in this fashion before he caught a glimpse of those he sought. They were standing together at the edge of a small natural clearing, the man with an arm passed about the girl's waist, talking in low tones.

Fingers of flame closed about Bitog's heart and the blood pounded wildly at his temples. His first impulse was to leap into the open, tear the girl from Azar's embrace, and fasten his powerful hands around the young man's throat.

But mingled caution and curiosity tempered his wrath and he continued to slink stealthily ahead, crouching at last behind the bole of a large tree no more than a few feet from where the boy and the girl were standing.

Together they formed an unforgettable and appealing picture—the First Man and his Mate, in the setting of a primeval forest. Azar's slender supple body, straight as a spear shaft, was clothed only in a loincloth fashioned from the sun-cured skin of Tarka, the panther. Thrust within its folds was a keen-bladed knife of flint, his sole weapon. A heavy growth of thick brown hair, rudely hacked away at earlobe length, topped a handsome sensitive face and a high rounded forehead that told of both imagination and intelligence.

The girl, too, wore a garment of panther skin; it covered her from shoulder to well above the knee, following the lithesome curves of her form with breath-taking results.

To the burly Cro-Magnon warrior who had followed them here, however, all this was as nothing. He saw only that the girl he had chosen as his mate was in the arms of a rival—a rival whose physical prowess was non-existent when compared with his own. To his mind, no other qualifications were worthy of consideration.

And so it was that Bitog remained hidden within the jungle shadows, waiting until he tired of his role of eavesdropper.

"I am afraid of him, Azar," Lua was saying, her voice troubled. "He will not forget that I refused him while the women listened. Had you seen his face and eyes as I saw them, you would know why I am afraid."

SECRETLY Azar was as much troubled by the incident as was Lua, for he fully realized they had not heard the last of it. Bitog would be more determined than ever to have her, if for no other reason than to soothe his pride and still gossiping tongues. But when he spoke, his tone reflected none of his worry.

"If he bothers you again," he said calmly. "I will make him leave you alone. I will tell him that you belong to me—that I am to claim you as soon as I have won the right to do so."

She looked up at his set face in quick alarm. "No Azar...you must not tell him that. He would seek some excuse for killing you."

"I cannot spend the rest of my life being afraid of Bitog," Azar said grimly. "And he might not find me so easy to kill."

Lua's expression was one of mingled pride and exasperation. "You know perfectly well you could do nothing against him, Azar. He is a great fighter. It is said that no warrior of any tribe within many marches would dare to challenge Bitog. Alone, with nothing more than a spear, he has slain Kraga; the lion."

Azar scowled. "If you think so much of him, why not become his mate?"

"Because I hate him," the girl retorted hotly. "If you don't want me there are plenty of others who do."

The cave youth laughed softly as he drew her closer within his arms. "I've been warned about you. They say a man might as well mate with Shanda, the leopard; that you are stubborn and proud and will never learn to obey. It would serve you right if I let Bitog have you."

Behind the tree's cloaking verdure, Bitog drew the stone knife from the folds of lion skin and took a slow, cautious step toward the couple in the clearing.

Lua, stung by the young man's words, sought to pull away from his embrace; but he only laughed again and bent his head to fasten his lips firmly against the girl's lovely mouth. For a moment she continued to struggle, then her bare arms crept around his neck and almost fiercely she returned his caresses.

Finally they drew apart, both panting a little, their expressions solemn and a little tender. "As if I would let another have you," declared Azar. "Since it is the custom of our tribe that a warrior must alone track down and kill his food before he is permitted to take a mate, I will go *now* to hunt. Tomorrow the right to claim you shall be mine, and Bitog will have to look elsewhere for a woman…"

In sudden panic Lua caught hold of his arms. "No…not at night! Not while the great cats are hunting!"

As though to emphasize her protest the thunderous challenge of Kraga, the lion, came faintly to their ears, followed by the shrill scream of a leopard.

Despite himself, Azar shivered. "Rather than worry you, I will wait until morning," he said soberly.

He did not see the tender smile of understanding on the girl's lips as her arms went once more about his neck and drew his mouth to hers.

As the two figures merged, a red haze of fury swam before the slitted eyes of the man lurking in the undergrowth behind them. Snarling like a wounded beast, Bitog burst into the clearing and charged straight at Azar as the astonished youth, warned by the crashing foliage, whirled to face him.

In the brief moment before Bitog was upon him Azar had no opportunity to draw his own knife. Thrusting Lua aside he crouched under the descending blade and swung his bare fist into the madman's face.

The blow, with only a boy's undeveloped strength behind it, served but to increase Bitog's insane hatred. Again he slashed out with his knife, and again Azar avoided the thrust. But this time Bitog was close enough to reach out with his free hand and fasten fingers of steel about the youngster's throat.

Azar, seeing only death in the narrowed blazing eyes above him, struck out wildly, the knife at his side forgotten; but Bitog, ignoring the flailing fists, slowly lifted his own knife, savoring the terror in the boy's eyes.

Once, twice, thrice—the long blade plunged into the unprotected chest of Azar, son of Mosat, the blood spouting forth to stain the murderer's skin. And as the slender body crumpled lifelessly to the ground, a small clawing, biting hurricane burst upon the slayer!

SO UNEXPECTED was Lua's attack that Bitog, despite his superior size and strength, fell back, lifting his bloodied hands to protect his face and eyes against those tearing nails. Before he could recover he felt the knife ripped from his hand, and had not its loss suddenly torn away his confusion as he awoke to the actual danger now threatening him, Azar would have been avenged before his blood had stopped flowing.

With a quick twist of his body Bitog managed to partially avoid the stabbing thrust, the flint tearing a long furrow in his side. The sobbing, screaming girl slipped and fell to her knees from the impetus of her swing; and before she was able to regain her feet Bitog was upon her.

It was one thing to get his hands on the girl, but keeping them there was another. Time and again only Bitog's agility kept the knife from finding him and his arms and chest were streaked with red welts where Lua's nails had gone home. But at last the man's superior strength prevailed and Lua lay panting in his grasp, her knife surrendered to its owner.

"You laughed at me," growled Bitog. "'Rather the coils of Sinu,' you said, than the arms of Bitog. Now your lover is dead and soon you will be dead beside him. Let Tugah, the jackal, pick your bones."

If he expected her to beg for mercy, to plead for her life, he was doomed to disappointment. Her eyes blazed at him and her lips curled back in a gesture of hatred that was almost animal in its intensity. Across his arm fell the wealth of her golden hair and he could see a tiny pulse pumping in her throat.

Even as Bitog lifted his knife to kill her, his desire for this beautiful girl fought to restrain his hand. But even more than he wanted Lua did Bitog want to live. He had slain one of his own tribe—slain not in self-defense or to protect something that was rightfully his, but wantonly and without adequate cause. In such matters the tribal law was simple and direct: quick death to the guilty.

With Lua dead, however, there would be no voice raised to name him a murderer. When the clean-picked bones of Lua and Azar were discovered on the following day, who could say how they died? Kraga or Conta, Shanda or Tarka—any one of the great cats could have surprised the couple in their sylvan rendezvous.

Lua saw the red-rimmed eyes narrow and felt the rippling muscles of the mighty body tense preparatory to the knife stroke that must take her life. With the sudden strength of terror she twisted from his embrace and sunk her teeth in the tanned forearm that had been holding her. Uttering a startled cry of pain Bitog fell back a step and Lua ducked beneath his clutching hands and raced across the glade, her goal the mouth of the path leading away from the caves of Mosat.

Bitog recovered instantly. With great bounding strides he bore down upon the girl, striving to close the gap before she could reach the possible safety of inky jungle.

While from the depths of cloaking underbrush at the very point they were nearing, two baleful yellow eyes were fixed with unblinking attention upon the two members of Mosat's tribe.

CHAPTER THREE
This is a God!

AS LIEUTENANT REED McGURN came slowly back to consciousness he was first aware of a great weight pressing heavily against his legs and chest. For several moments he lay unmoving, his hurt mind striving to fight off shock sufficiently to recall where he was and what had happened.

And then full realization swept over him, and with a low moan of terror McGurn shoved frantically at the dead weight holding him pinned to earth. The formless bulk of animal weight gave slowly under the man's frantic efforts and Reed McGurn rose shakily to his feet and stared down at the lifeless hulk of a giant panther.

It was not until the young American had bent and discovered two closely spaced holes in the cat's sharply receding forehead that he understood what had killed it. Only then did he become aware of the Webley still clutched in his right hand.

The reaction set in and McGurn trembled so that he was barely able to stand. Weakly he leaned against a nearby tree and laid a cheek against the moss-covered bark until the paroxysm of shivering had ceased, then straightened again and fell to examining himself to learn what damage, if any, the cat had inflicted before it died.

Beyond a few bruises and three parallel scratches high up on the right side of his naked chest, he appeared little the worse for wear. The scratches were undoubtedly left there by the panther's claws when McGurn was first bowled over, and probably accounted for the sharp pain he had felt just before he lost consciousness.

He lighted a cigarette; and while the first lungful set his head to spinning again, the sensation passed quickly and he felt like his old self again. Bringing out the small flashlight he played its powerful beam along the length of the panther, marveling at his almost incredible luck in killing it with the flurry of wildly aimed shots.

As he stood there congratulating himself, the shrill cry of a woman came suddenly to his ears.

McGurn's first reaction was pure relief at the sound of a human voice—the first indication since being unaccountably plunged into this mad world that he was not its only mortal. He was on the point of plunging madly along the path toward the source of the sound, when sudden caution stayed him.

There had been a note of fear and horror in that cry. Would he be running into some new danger? A miracle had saved him a moment ago; but two miracles in one night were hardly likely. Or was it a human voice he had heard after all? The sound had not been repeated. Perhaps one of the impossible colored birds…

Quickly reloading his revolver, McGurn set off along the trail, moving slowly and with infinite care. The light from his small torch picked out a sharp bend in the trail some thirty feet ahead; and as he reached it he winked out the flashlight beam and, his gun barrel leveled at his hip, made the turn.

He was in time to see the slender figure of an almost naked girl racing across a fairly large, moon-flooded clearing toward him, closely pursued by the most magnificently built man McGurn had ever seen.

The girl was only a few steps from the trail's mouth, but her pursuer was so close that Reed knew instantly she would be caught short of her goal. Without waiting to debate the wisdom of interfering the American lifted the Webley and took quick aim.

At that instant the girl's flying feet tripped and she fell headlong. The man behind her voiced a single shout of exultation…and the undergrowth burst apart and a great black-maned lion sprang through.

Bitog skidded to a halt, an almost ludicrous expression of astonishment and fear twisting his face. Kraga, the lion, had stopped his charge, too—not knowing whether to attack the prone girl only inches short of his mighty claws or to drive away the two-legged animal a foot or two beyond her.

For the space of several heartbeats the grim tableau endured. Then Kraga threw back his large head and roared out his thunderous challenge.

It was then that Bitog made his choice. With a lithe bound he rose high in the air and caught a low-hanging branch, swinging himself across it and scuttling upward like a monkey.

Kraga, satisfied at having outbluffed the competition, bent his head toward the paralyzed figure of the girl. As the hot stench of the animal's breath beat against her exposed face, Lua closed her eyes and waited for the horrible death she knew was to be hers.

Reed McGurn fired three shots at the exposed flank of the lion.

Even as the lieutenant pulled the trigger he knew he was not going to kill so huge a beast with his Webley. The combination of bad light, intervening foliage, and a case of nerves made hitting his target a major problem, let alone inflicting a fatal wound.

As it was, one of the bullets creased Kraga's back, another removed neatly the tip of a back laid ear, while the third missed him entirely. But the thunderclaps of exploding powder and the eye-searing flashes of fire were more effective than bullets could possibly have been.

KRAGA voiced a startled growl that was more nearly a squeal, wheeled about to face the author of those terrifying sounds, reared high on his back legs…then turned and vanished into the surrounding jungle.

As the powerful brute disappeared, Lieutenant Reed McGurn felt the muscles of his legs turn to water and he dropped weakly to his knees, the breath whistling in his nostrils. When he opened his eyes again, he saw the girl lying at the clearing's edge where she had first fallen.

Regaining his feet McGurn walked slowly toward her, the gun lowered but ready for instant use. Halting beside her he knelt and took hold of one soft, naked shoulder and shook it lightly.

"How about it, sister? Are you all right?"

The sound of gunfire still rang in Lua's ears—a noise infinitely more horrible than Kraga's voice could ever be. Half-conscious, she was dimly aware of the gentle fingers against her skin, of the strange sounds in an unfamiliar human voice.

A strong arm passed beneath her and she felt herself being turned until she was lying face upward. She trembled, waiting for some horrible thing to happen, but all she heard was the continued sound of unfamiliar words.

"Come on, kid. Open your eyes. You're all right."

The strange words meant nothing to her but the tone in which they were uttered was vaguely reassuring. Slowly the long dark lashes swept up, reveling a round pair of the bluest eyes Reed McGurn had ever seen—and the loveliest.

"That's better," he said, his voice shaking a little. "How about getting on your feet? Here, I'll give you a hand."

She obeyed the lifting pressure under her shoulders and rose unsteadily to her feet. She swayed there and McGurn slipped his arm soothingly about her waist.

"It was close, all right," McGurn said, smiling. "But luckily lions can be scared like anything else. He's probably still running."

So frank and compelling was this strange being's grin that Lua's own lips began to curl in reply. And then a sudden thought brought terror back to her eyes.

"Bitog!" she gasped. "Where is he? We must run away or he will kill us both!"

Lieutenant Reed McGurn felt a wave of disappointment so intense it hardly could be endured. More than anything else during the long afternoon and evening he had desired human companionship. Now that he had found it, they were separated by having no common basis of understanding, for her words were as unintelligible to him as he could see his were to her. Even deeper, the realization came that her words were like no others he had ever heard; almost—he shuddered at the thought—as though they were uttered by a being from another planet.

Yet, even in the dim light, he could see that she was a human as himself—and very beautiful. The last observation came to him unbidden…and was forgotten as the girl took a tight hold on one of his arms, and with a clearly frightened glance about her, sought to pull him back the way he had come.

He hung back surprised at the strength in her slender arm. "Wait a minute," he protested. "There's nothing for us in that direction. I just spent a lot of time finding that out."

She tugged at him frantically. "Hurry," she cried. "Bitog must not find us here!"

Her actions if not her words were clear enough and McGurn smiled wryly. "I guess you know what you're doing," he said. "I'm the stranger around here—not you."

Meekly he set out, following the girl quickly along the pathway. Twice she outdistanced him in the utter blackness and he called out to her, fearful that she had left him entirely. Each time she hurried to shut off his calls with firm pressure of her small hand against his mouth before continuing onward.

It began to dawn on the American that the girl was fleeing from something, and he remembered the giant man who had been chasing her when the lion put an end to the matter. That, he decided, must be the answer. Could he have but made her understand, he would have told her she had nothing to fear; that the Webley he carried made him the equal of any man of her world, no matter how mighty.

Abruptly the girl came to a halt in the center of the trail, her head lifted as though she was listening intently. A moment passed this way, then she again took McGurn by the hand, and turning at right angles to the path, plunged into the impassable jungle.

ON THEY WENT while McGurn floundered helplessly through an ocean of plant life, bouncing against unseen tree boles, tripping on vines and creepers, trampling through thorn-covered bushes. By this time his trousers were torn and ripped in many places and his naked chest and shoulders crisscrossed with blood-dotted scratches. Giant mosquitoes and other insects swarmed about him, attacking his sensitive skin.

While on and on they went for what to the tiring aviator seemed many days. He gritted his teeth and bent his head for protection against whipping branches and razor-sharp brambles and staggered ahead, determined that he should not be the one to suggest resting.

Suddenly the forest and jungle ended and McGurn saw they had reached a strip of open ground at the base of a low, almost perpendicular cliff dotted with a number of black spots, which he rightly suspected as being cave entrances. Motioning her companion to remain standing where he was, Lua moved cautiously about the clearing, head bent, eyes searching the ground with the aid of the moon's rays. To Reed McGurn her actions were completely without meaning; but Lua was looking for some trace that the caves above her were inhabited.

There were sufficient signs to satisfy her that this was a deserted village. The rank jungle grass was everywhere because a long time had passed since the passage of many bare feet had beaten it down; no ashes of fires were evident; no earthen pots were stacked at the cliff base.

Lua crossed to a far corner of the clearing and knelt beside a small spring bubbling there. She drank of the cold water and as she raised her head a soft sound at her back brought her up and about like a startled deer.

"You intend drinking it all, sister?" said Lieutenant Reed McGurn…

He sat back finally and smiled at her, the water dripping from his chin and falling to his chest to trace tiny crooked paths through the coating of grime and sweat. For a long minute they stared deep into each other's eyes before Lua lowered her gaze, a wave of red rising into her cheeks.

McGurn stretched his arms mightily and yawned. "What do we do now?" he asked.

Lua glanced up at him and shook her head. So much had happened, so much that was horrible and mad, that there had been no time to think, to wonder at this strange apparition beside her. Compared to the men of her tribe he was frail indeed, and the strange fur clothing him from the waist to his toes was like nothing in her limited experience. Yet it was he who had uttered the loud noises that had sent mighty Kraga running into the jungle noises mixed with Aka, the lightning! In spite of being able to do such terrible things, and the strange way he spoke, he was very handsome. It was hard to be afraid of a being so handsome…

The sudden memory of what Old Mentak had said one night around the cave fires came to her. A great storm was raging outside at the time, mixing torrential rain with crashing thunder and vivid lightning flashes that made the night brighter than midday.

"There are many gods," declared Mentak who was very old and much wiser than all the rest of Mosat's tribe put together. "Some are angry gods who throw Aka at the earth below, crying out with great rage the while. These gods live in Oru, the sun, and hate us. Were it not for the kind gods who lead us to fresh game that we may feed our bellies and who fight against the wicked gods we would be dead a long time ago."

A great fear took sudden hold of the girl. "This is a god…" she thought. "He has come down from his home on Oru for some reason, perhaps in search of a mate."

The last thought filled her with dread, and she shrank back a little from him. Yet mixed with her sudden fear was a strange breathless thrill, which with quick anger she beat down. The memory then of Azar, her beloved, crumpling beneath Bitog's knife flooded into her mind and suddenly she bent her head and began to cry with a silent intensity that shook the man seated beside her.

"Hey…" said Reed McGurn. "What's the matter with you?"

His words did nothing toward stopping the flow of hidden tears. He stared at her bent head and wondered helplessly how he could talk her out of this storm of grief when there was no common bond of language between them. He had seen girls cry before and there were ways to snap them out of it—not necessarily by talking. But he didn't know this one well enough to use any method other than speech.

The bright rays of Mua picked out with almost startling clarity the slender roundness of her limbs and body accentuated rather than concealed by the soft folds of panther skin. The cloud of curling blonde hair would have been the envy of any woman of his world and he felt an almost insurmountable desire to put out a hand and stroke it.

Come to think of it, he told himself, that might not be a bad idea. The poor kid was scared and was crying because she needed comforting. Being chased by a wild man and having a lion practically sitting in your lap would give anybody the screaming meemies.

AND SO REED McGURN reached out one hand and placed it comfortingly about the bare shoulders of the sobbing girl. He felt her body stiffen slightly but not too much and the storm of sobs lessened a little. Thus encouraged, the lieutenant sought to draw her gently closer that she might lay her head upon his shoulder. Long experience had taught the American that a man's shoulder ranked high with all girls as a place for female heads.

But he had not counted on the high degree of superstitious fears in primitive man. Lua, daughter of Yortak, was conscious only of paralyzing fear as the arm of this strange being had slipped about her shoulders—a paralysis which abruptly snapped as she felt the pressure of that arm as it attempted to bring her closer within its grasp.

With a single lithe movement she was free of his embrace; and before the astounded lieutenant realized what was happening, the half-naked girl was on her feet and running swiftly toward the towering, cave-dotted cliff.

The thought of being left alone in this wilderness was more than McGurn could bear. Even inarticulate companionship was better than none at all. Shouting for the girl to stop, he jumped to his feet and raced after her.

But the escarpment was close, so that before he had taken more than a few strides the girl was swarming up the sheer slope with all the nimbleness of a monkey. By the time McGurn had reached the foot of the cliff, his quarry was thirty feet above him, her naked feet and grasping fingers finding holds where it appeared no holds existed.

Three times Reed McGurn tried to scale that cliff and each time he slipped helplessly back to earth after lifting himself only a few feet. The unyielding leather of his shoes was unable to take hold of the rock and his fingers became sore and bleeding. When, after the third attempt, he looked up at the sixty or seventy feet of almost vertical stone he saw that the girl had completely disappeared. Whether she had scaled the heights and faded into the distance beyond, or had holed up in one of the caves, he could not know.

With a muttered curse he abandoned his efforts and turned away. A few yards from where he stood was the wall of jungle and trees. The thought of entering that horrible place of moving shadows and eerie rustlings made the hair lift on the nape of his neck.

As he stood there debating his next move, the fingers of his right hand toying with the butt of the Webley, the distant roar of a lion came to his ears, followed by the shrill scream of a panther. McGurn shivered a little, not alone because of the chill air against his naked back.

Holding the Webley ready in his hand he walked slowly toward the towering rampart of trees, every sense alert for some lurking danger amid the stygian gloom. And while there were many small rustlings there, nothing showed itself to threaten him. Pausing beneath the spreading, vine-cloaked limbs of a jungle patriarch, Lieutenant Reed McGurn slipped the revolver into a pocket and drew himself into the branches. A flurry of movement among the leaves above him set his heart to pounding and brought his gun out ready for use. But whatever was responsible ceased to be a danger as the man's ears followed it into a neighboring tree.

A monkey, thought McGurn grimly. Slowly he drew himself higher into the tree until, high above the ground, he found two limbs extending horizontally and on the same plane. Here he paused to sit down with his back against the bole and his legs stretched along the two branches. He weighed the wisdom of loosening one of the strong vines and binding himself to the trunk that he might not topple into the depths beneath while sleeping. But doing so, he realized, would prevent escape were he attacked by some jungle dweller; and he decided to risk a fall rather than so handicap his movements.

Seconds later he was sound asleep, while the hunting cries of a savage world rose and fell about him like the surf of an angry sea.

CHAPTER FOUR
The Golden God

A VAR-AK, seventh ritual priest to the omniscient and omnipresent Ammon-Re, Creator of all Life, Lord of Destiny, Ruler of the Twelve Triangles of the Universe, once more put down the oars of the small boat and stood up to stare westward across the empty wastes of ocean.

Other than the gray expanse of rolling waves nothing was visible to his searching eyes. Not since the shores of Atland had faded into the western horizon had he seen any sign of the people he had betrayed. No swift *petrix* cutting the ocean waters in search of him; not a single *dyark* splitting the air overhead.

Yes, Avar-Ak had triumphed. For all the boasted cleverness of Clat-Ron, the High Priest, Avar-Ak had outwitted him. Let him and his followers scour the ocean between Atland and neighboring Clyrus to the south. Whatever they found in those waters would be of small use to them. Eventually Avar-Ak would make that journey, bearing with him the one thing that would make him the most powerful man in Clyrus instead of a despised underling in Clat-Ron's service.

It was unfortunate that he must wait a moon or two before he could take over his rightful place in the world. But an attempt to reach Clyrus now would never have succeeded. Were he able to operate a dyark he could have landed triumphantly in Clyrus even before the priests of Ammon-Re had learned of his theft and flight. Even a petrix might have done the job and it he could have handled easily, so simple were such boats to control. But there had been no time to locate one along the wharfs.

A thin smile twisting his narrow lips Avar-Ak took up his oars again and pulled once more for the shores of Afrota, now a low bulk against the eastern horizon. Thin were Avar-Ak's shoulders under the pale blue tunic, like slender reeds were his arms and legs. But in his gaunt frame was a wiry strength past all belief, in his cunning mind a shrewdness that should have been employed to more worthy and honorable ends.

Twice the sun had risen and set since Avar-Ak fled by small boat from Atland. His tiny store of food was almost gone and not in ten hours had water passed his lips. Yet ambition and avarice, so intense in this small-bodied, middle-aged man as to border on madness, drove his muscles untiringly on while blisters formed on his soft hands under the pull of the oars—blisters that broke to expose raw flesh beneath.

Two hours short of sundown the slender, high-gunwaled, white-metal boat entered a tiny landlocked harbor on the western coast of Afrota. With renewed strength Avar-Ak sent the light craft skimming across the harbor's smooth waters; and soon he was drawing the boat high up on the white sands beyond the reach of the tide.

Beyond the beach rose a dense jungle and impenetrable forest, dim and shadowy beneath the slanting rays of the sun. Monkeys raced and scolded among the branches and brilliantly plumed birds rivaled the gorgeous blooms spilling in riotous color everywhere.

Once, long ages ago, Atland had been just such a wilderness of jungle-choked forest over much of its surface. But inland were mountain ranges supporting vast plateaus high above the sea's level where temperatures were much cooler and far less humid than their surrounding terrain. Except for a few seaports Atland's cities were nestled in on the tableland, and only the most adventurous of their inhabitants ever ventured into the animal-infested lowlands.

As a result Avar-Ak knew little or nothing of the jungle or its denizens. His hastily formed plans called for a landing on Afrota, the erection of some sort of shelter where he could spend a moon or two, hunting his food with the powerful weapons he had filched from Clat-Ron's own private arsenal.

But at sight of the grimly beautiful land before him now, Avar-Ak felt a sudden foreboding. There was beauty here—but behind that beauty was the primitive law of survival of the fittest, the rule of kill or be killed, and a choice of but two roles: hunter or hunted. Avar-Ak ran an uncertain hand through his straggling locks of gray hair and looked thoughtfully down at his boat.

The sight of a large, cloth-wrapped bundle lying between the thwarts dispelled his doubts, however. Dragging it out he managed to hoist it to one narrow shoulder; then he set out with resolute steps toward the forest's edge.

There was no break in the wall of foliage at the point he reached, and so he turned at right angles to it and trudged ahead, searching for a pathway to lead him toward the distant hills dimly visible like great purple clouds to the east.

Once, his sandaled feet and bare legs passed within inches of a small snake hidden among the tall grasses—a snake whose fangs held poison enough to take the lives of fifty men. But the snake did not strike as, completely oblivious to his peril, Avar-Ak plodded by.

Darkness found the priest still skirting the jungle's edge. By means of vines he hoisted his closely guarded burden high into a tree, and close beside it through the long, chill night Avar-Ak waited impatiently for the sun to come again.

Morning found him on the move again, and it was not long afterward when he came upon a break in the wall of underbrush marking the entrance to an elephant path. After resting for a few minutes, Avar-Ak reshouldered his pack and disappeared from view.

THE hot rays of an early morning sun pouring through an open space in the ceiling of foliage awakened Lieutenant Reed McGurn. Stiffly he lowered himself to the ground, caution forgotten under a gnawing thirst that led him directly to the small spring where he and the strange wild girl had drank deeply the night before.

When he had taken his fill of the cool water, Reed McGurn spent the next quarter hour searching for some sort of primitive ladder built into the side of the cliff; for despite the agile ease with which the girl had scaled those heights is seemed impossible there was no easier route to the caves. But he found nothing beyond various roughened spots and shallow niches, which gave an illusion of possible use, but certainly were useless to the flyer.

Several times he shouted aloud in hopes of bringing the golden head of his former companion into view at one of the caves. But not once did he see a sign of life, and so reluctantly he concluded that the girl had fled into unknown country beyond the cliff top.

His belly reminded him sharply that he had not eaten in almost twenty-four hours and his thoughts turned to a method of rectifying the matter. More than anything else, perhaps, hunger brought home to him the complete change in his life during the past day. Getting a square meal had passed the simple method of strolling into Officers' Mess and lazily consulting a menu while an attentive non-com awaited his order.

How, he wondered, would the cave girl act in this situation? Probably she was able to track down a deer or zebra, or whatever grass eaters inhabited this tropical world, and strangle it with her bare hands. Of all the people in the world, why must she have been the one for him to get mixed up with?

It was then the sobering thought struck him that perhaps there were no other kind in this world…

What kind of damn-fool thinking is that, he asked himself impatiently. This was the year nineteen hundred and thirty nine and he was Lieutenant Reed McGurn who had been born in Winnetka, Illinois, on the fifteenth day of April, twenty-two years before. Yesterday he was flying a Spitfire over Germany; a Heinie had sent him crashing down into some lost valley far enough below sea level to maintain a tropical climate and all that went with it. Civilization had passed it by, leaving the inhabitants where mankind had been twenty centuries before. Eventually he would find the valley boundaries and get back to his job of winning the war.

Yes sir, it was all so nice and sensible and logical. And he didn't believe a word of it.

But he *had* to believe it. What other explanation was there? Except maybe that he had died and this was Heaven. Still, it hardly seemed likely that a man could take his plane to Heaven with him. Too, the scratches and welts and insect bites were smarting and it seemed out of place to be plagued by such things in the Hereafter.

Reed McGurn scratched his head and looked at his fingers, which were shaking a little and felt the sun on his bare shoulders and was aware of hunger pains under his belt. Standing here twisting his brains solved nothing. He took out the Webley and replaced the cartridges expended on scaring the lion from the softly rounded figure of his girl acquaintance from the caves. He dug out one of his remaining seven sticks of Wrigley's Spearmint, stripped away the wrapping, and tucked the gum into his cheek. Then he set out on a hunt for food.

The game trail he found leading into the jungle was not the same one by which he and the girl had entered the clearing the night before. This one was narrower and wound around more. He walked slowly along, sweat standing out in glistening globules on his chest, back, and face from the humid air. The Webley he held ready in one hand, his ears and eyes searched constantly the walls of foliage and the creepers, vines and leaves hanging in great loops and whorls from the trees.

Monkeys raced and chattered and grimaced their wise little faces at him from the safety of the broad branches. McGurn weighed the advisability of shooting one of them but abandoned the idea promptly. He would have to be a lot hungrier before dining on monkey meat.

But the little man-like beasts had their use. In passing a small, bush-like tree bordering the path, he saw several monkeys pluck some of the red, orange-sized fruit growing there and devour them rind and all. The lieutenant picked one of them, flicked away a spider the size of a shilling piece, and sunk his teeth into the pulp.

The juice, he discovered, tasted a great deal like an over sweet grapefruit, but the rest was too tough and stringy for consumption. He sucked several of them dry and, greatly refreshed but still ravenous, went on.

A TURN in the trail brought him unexpectedly to the edge of a long, narrow stretch of grassland completely surrounded by jungle and forest. Even as he left the path he saw, a hundred yards in the distance, a herd of small deer grazing peacefully amid the lush grasses.

McGurn's mouth watered. He pictured a hunk of venison held above open flames, with drippings of fat hissing as they splattered into the fire. The distance, while not considerable, was too far to risk stampeding the herd by a bad shot. While he had never hunted game of any sort, he called upon whatever knowledge of the subject reading had given him. The wind against his face was enough to tell him there was no danger of his scent being caught by the herd. The grass was quite long, certainly enough to hide him while he wriggled nearer those venison steaks.

Letting himself carefully down on his belly, Lieutenant McGurn of His Majesty's Air Force, began to drag the feeding family of deer. Clutched in one hand was the Webley, and as he moved he sought to measure the distance he covered. Fifty yards should be enough. At that distance he could hardly fail to place a bullet in a vital part of his living target.

As he forged steadily ahead the thought came to him that thus had some hairy progenitor stalked down his food—an ancestor who carried only the rude weapons of the prehistoric past instead of a mighty engine of destruction such as a Webley .455. Yet he had succeeded in wresting food from his world as was evidenced by the fact that Reed McGurn was alive today.

On went the lieutenant, while the hot sun beat down on his back and the tall grass parted to let him through. Finally when he was confident that the distance was narrowed sufficiently for his purpose, he cautiously raised his head until his eyes were above the level of grass tops.

To his chagrin he learned he was still a good seventy-five yards from the herd, having crawled in a rude half circle instead of the straight line he intended. The flanks of the animals were more exposed, however, and at any moment a shift in the wind might send his quarry thundering out of range.

With great care and deliberateness McGurn brought up the Webley's barrel and trained it at a point behind the left shoulder of a plump doe feeding a little apart from the others. Slowly his finger contracted on the trigger, there was a loud, ringing report, the stricken doe bounded high, her muzzle twisting in an effort to bite where the bullet had torn into her side.

As the deer collapsed, legs threshing in agony, the balance of the herd broke wildly and ran for safety. McGurn was already on his feet, and shouting aloud with pure exultation, raced headlong toward his kill.

Suddenly the grass erupted almost under his feet. As he slid to an involuntary halt, a startled cry on his lips, the immense bulk of a rhinoceros lumbered to its short, stocky legs and, lowering its massive head, charged the astonished man…

Lieutenant Reed McGurn knew even less of rhinoceri than he did of lions. But a single glance at the ugly head with its long horn aimed squarely at his middle and bearing down upon him with express-train speed was enough to galvanize him into action.

With a single bound he cleared a full six feet of grassland to one side of his former position, and as his feet came to earth, he ran with all the speed he could muster for the safety of the forest. Not once did he glance back over his shoulder to learn whether the rhino was gaining on him; and the nearest branch of the first tree became his haven.

Shivering, his muscles suddenly weak with the passing of peril, McGurn looked out in the direction from which he had come. To his complete surprise, the rhino had completely disappeared, nor was he able to locate where the body of the deer lay concealed by the long grass.

Now what? He thought. The prospect of exploring the small ocean of grass in search of the dead deer was made doubly unpleasant by the thought of the rhinoceros lurking out there somewhere. Yet it might be a long time before he could make another kill and his hunger was growing with the passing minutes.

"You big coward!" McGurn said aloud. "Get down out of this tree and find that pile of steaks. You're not going to let a little old rhino scare you out of a meal, are you?"

THE whine of insects and two monkeys quarreling in the next tree were the only answer he received. McGurn lowered himself by the hands and dropped to the ground. He took a few minutes to line up the probable location of the deer he had shot, and to give the rhinoceros an opportunity to show itself. But nothing stirred in all that expanse of swaying grasses, and so he set determinedly out.

Within fifteen minutes he found the limp carcass, its heart blasted apart by the Webley's heavy slug. Here was his food; all that remained was to hack off a few steaks, kindle a fire, and start eating.

And then came the realization that he had nothing with which he *could* hack off those steaks... Hastily he emptied his pockets, finding at last a small penknife—a prize won at a ring toss game at a village fair the month before. With this, and by dint of much hacking and sawing, he was able to cut away five or six slabs of meat from the exposed flank, getting himself pretty well covered with the animal's blood by his efforts.

Now came the problem of transporting the raw, dripping flesh to the place where he could build a fire. There was nothing in which to wrap the results of his clumsy butchering; and so he was forced to place the pieces in the crook of one arm, his free hand holding his revolver ready in case of sudden attack by some jungle dweller drawn by the scent of blood.

After giving the matter some thought, McGurn decided to return to the cliffside where the wild girl had led him the night before. There he would build a fire beside the spring, cook and eat his meat, then enjoy a cigarette and a few hours sleep within one of the caves.

By the time he was back to the spring, the sun stood directly overhead, its heat like a great soft hand covering his mouth and nose. The shadow of the cliff furnished some protection from the heat, and here he gathered together a sizable heap of dead branches and twigs. Hordes of huge black flies covered the meat by the time the young lieutenant was finished making the fire ready and some of his appetite faded at the sight.

But after washing the meat and placing several of the pieces on pointed sticks over the flames a savory odor rose to McGurn's nostrils and his hunger returned three fold. Because he had seen enough blood for one day, he waited until the steaks were thoroughly grilled before placing them on a leaf-covered slab of stone.

Never before in his life had McGurn sat down to a table with keener anticipation. This time there was no gleaming cutlery other than a cheap pocketknife, and six broad green leaves on a rough gray stone replaced snowy napery over polished wood. In lieu of a chair he squatted on his haunches and there were more flies hovering about than he had found in most restaurants.

As he reached an eager hand for the first steak, a small stone flew past his ear, struck full upon his stone plate, and sent his food flying into the still glowing embers of the fire.

CHAPTER FIVE
The Princess Athora

DEEP within the inner gardens of the palace of Ashtoth, three men waited beside an azure pool set amid a scene of indescribable beauty. Wide, winding paths of gleaming white crushed stone led between banks of cleverly blended flowers and fountains where concealed jets flung shimmering veils of water in graceful patterns. Carefully tended and pruned trees and bushes dotted the landscaped grounds in symmetrical designs—combining riotous color with a soft overtone of green to both please and soothe the eye.

But to the three men standing near one of the gracefully shaped benches lining the pool, all this beauty was wasted. While they differed greatly in size and general build, all had the strong hawk noses, piercing black eyes, lean olive-skinned faces and stern, self-righteous expressions that marked them as the aristocrats and leaders of their kind. This latter designation was made evident by the harsh red color of their knee-length tunics and the gem-encrusted belts of solid gold at their waists.

One of the men, whose dress differed from the others only in that the design of gems in his belt was worked into the form of twelve glistening triangles, was addressing the others, his tone soft and conspiratorial.

"We shall be running this very close," he said. "It is possible my spy has not yet been able to get his message to Clat-Ron, high priest here in Atlantis and the second most powerful man in all Atland. But we dare wait no longer, for they may capture Avar-Ak, the treacherous under priest who stole the Golden God—capture him at any moment. Once we have driven our bargain with Ashtoth and we have his word…then it matters not whether they catch Avar-Ak, for Atland's king is a man of principle and honor who would give up his kingdom before breaking his oath."

One of the others made an impatient gesture. "We know all that, Sar-Gath. But what of this man Clat-Ron? It is common knowledge that he desires the hand of the Princess Athora that he may someday take over the rule of all Atland. Will he calmly and meekly stand aside and permit the betrothal of Athora and our own king?"

"Think a moment, my good Balimak," said Sar-Gath, his tone pointing out that he was humoring a fool. "Don't you see that, as high priest, Clat-Ron will not dare raise an objection? To the contrary, he will be placed in the painful role of backing our cause—of urging the union of the woman he desires with the man he hates. For let word reach the people of Atland that their Holy of Holies is in possession of their neighbors to the south and the blood of Atland's ruling class and priests would run red in the streets of every city in the land."

"Would that not suit our purpose as well?" asked the third of the group. "With Atland's ruling class driven from power and only a leaderless mob in control, what would prevent our armies from invading and taking Atland over, palace and hovel?"

"No, Zondarc," replied Sar-Gath promptly. "Even leaderless Atland's armies so outnumber our own that it would be a long, difficult war with the result very much in doubt. But her armies would not be lacking a leader; there would be Mathlane the Mighty, probably the greatest warrior and leader of fighting men in all the world. Compared to him the warlords of our own beloved Clyrus are as infants in the strategy of waging war.

"My way is best," he continued. "Why lay two countries to waste when both can belong to us intact and free of hatred? The world is not for the strong but the wise; brute force is always helpless in the hands of the cunning."

Balimak nodded resignedly. "Very well, Sar-Gath. We agreed to do this your way, and your way it shall be. As High Priest of all Clyrus, you should know what effect the loss of Atland's Golden God will have on her king and her own high priest. But let this scheme end in disaster for Clyrus and not even Ammon-Re, Ruler of the Twelve Triangles, will be able to spare your life..."

THE noble Zondarc glanced at the dial of the *leton* strapped to his wrist. "We have been waiting over twenty *yads,*" he complained. "What manner is this in which to treat three noble visitors from Clyrus?"

"It is Ashtoth's way of letting us know our proper place," Sar-Gath observed. "Why should the king of mighty Atland, surrounded by the splendor of his court, ringed about by the magnificent city of Atlantis, hurry to an audience with representatives from so weak and poverty-stricken a country as Clyrus?"

"Once he hears what we have to say," said Balimak, "and I'll wager his manners will improve."

Sar-Gath held up a cautioning hand. "Beware of letting him see so much as a spark of triumph in our eyes. Any untoward act or word on the part of anyone of us could undo all our careful planning. Ashtoth is a proud man, from a long line of proud men; and should he get the idea we are dictating what he must and must not do…well, Golden God or no Golden God war will follow…"

"We shall let you do the talking, Sar-Gath," said one of the others. "You may regard that as a tribute to your penchant for intrigue."

As a compliment, the remark left much to be desired and a dull red crept into the High Priest's cheeks. That the others held him in almost open contempt was no secret to the wily Sar-Gath; for they were men of noble birth and great wealth, while his, were humble beginnings and he was tolerated only because of his hard-won position as head of Clyrus' religion. Not that the ruling classes of either Clyrus or Atland were at all devout; it was simply that the worship of Ammon-Re through elaborate rites was the most powerful method of holding in subjugation the masses in both countries. For that reason alone high priests were admitted to the inner circle of kings and nobles.

The measured tread of sandaled feet on crushed stone reached the ears of the three men from around a bend of a garden path.

"They come…" whispered Sar-Gath. "Weigh every word during this interview, for the future history of both countries will depend on what is said during the next few yads."

First into view came six soldiers of Atland, members of Ashtoth's own private guard, tall, spear-straight, muscular men clad in tunics of purple and white—the personal colors of Ashtoth's own household. At their belts swung the pistol-shaped huars, whose needle-sized muzzles could emit rays that were able to dissolve whatever they touched—be it stone or wood or human flesh. In each brawny right hand was a slender spear, tipped with an alloy of gold and creonum, the white metal that served as the basic material for the civilized world.

Striding behind his guard, majestic in carriage and bearing, came Ashtoth, Atland's king. Fully four inches beyond six feet he stood, broad of shoulder and narrow of hip, his narrow unlined face and high forehead topped with a wealth of reddish-gold hair clipped short to fight its tendency to wave. Blue eyes given to mirroring his every mood surveyed the three visitors with an imperious dignity and there was a stiff cast to the set of his smooth shaven jaws and unsmiling lips that told of the masked enmity he held for any and all citizens of Clyrus.

Yet when he spoke, words and tone were courteous, albeit reserved, and his finger traced the outline of a triangle in the air before him, the standard sign of peace and friendship when men of Atland meet.

Each of the visitors made the same sign and, as host, Ashtoth was the first to speak.

"Welcome, men of Clyrus, to Atlantis and the gardens of my palace. Sit you down on yonder bench and slaves shall bring you food and drink."

He gestured and several female slaves, young and very beautiful, came forward bearing large platters of gold containing dishes of rare delicacies and goblets of gem-studded gold filled with heady *ato,* the fermented grape drink common in both Clyrus and Atland. Kneeling before the visitors the slaves presented their platters and the men of Clyrus tasted of the food and drank of the wine, for to refuse would have been a studied insult to Ashtoth himself.

Like any perfect host, Atland's king waited until his visitors were served before partaking of the refreshments. He barely nibbled at the contents of the dishes and only moistened his lips with ato, for he was a man who prided himself on his physical condition and practiced moderation in all things.

With the social amenities out of the way, Ashtoth got matters down to the business at hand. Waving away all slaves except one, a lovely, dark-haired girl in a diaphanous purple and white tunic which revealed much of her slender form, whose duty it was to keep the visitors' goblets filled with ato, Atland's king seated himself across from the others and said:

"What urgent matter has brought you from Clyrus to seek this audience?"

THE words, while courteous in tone, were more abrupt and to the point than was usual when heads of state came together in peace. More than that, however, Atland's ruler had not inquired after the health and well-being of Clyrus's king—an omission that did not pass unnoticed by the others.

As spokesman for the visitors, Sar-Gath made answer. "Mighty Ashtoth," he said humbly, "noble king of Atland, we came on a mission of friendship and peace, to weld still closer the traditional ties of amity which have always existed between our countries."

A shade of annoyance crossed Ashtoth's aristocratic features. "Then there is no special reason for your seeking this audience?" he asked crisply.

"A very special reason, noble Ashtoth," Sar-Gath said hastily. He was seeking desperately to probe behind that smooth expressionless face, to find some indication that Atland's king was aware of the true reason behind this meeting. It could hardly be otherwise, of course; for the coincidence of the Golden God's theft and a request for an audience with Ashtoth by three of Clyrus's high-ranking officials was too strong to be a coincidence. The one factor that could upset everything was the possibility that Atland's ruler was not aware of Avar-Ak's earthshaking act of thievery. It seemed hardly credible that Clat-Ron would keep the information from his king, for Atland's high priest could not help but realize only concentrated action by all could succeed in regaining possession of the Holy of Holies before irreparable harm was done. And Clat-Ron would keep secret the fact only if he hoped to regain the Golden God before it fell into unfriendly hands. It was to end that hope which had prompted Sar-Gath to attempt to get word to Atland's high priest that the Golden God was now in the hands of Clyrus's rulers.

"You have my complete attention, Sar-Gath," Ashtoth said shortly.

"In recent years," the High Priest or Clyrus began, choosing his words with extreme care, "the country of Atland has grown in power and wealth while Clyrus has slipped deeper into poverty. Ours is not a land of rich resources and a large population such as is yours. Consequently Clyrus must look to her mighty neighbor to the north…or suffer eventual extinction."

"All this is well known," observed Ashtoth quietly.

"Of course. And because it is well known many groups in both countries seek ways to change that picture. Unfortunately there are those who see in Clyrus's weakness a chance to hasten her extinction as a sovereign state—a situation that we realize you deplore as deeply as do we of Clyrus.

"Because we understand fully that your sympathies lie with those less fortunate, it is my feeling—and that of these two noblemen of Clyrus who are with me here today with the backing and complete confidence of Mentanek, our king—that you will welcome a plan by which Clyrus may be restored to a position of strength and respect in the world. For ours is a common heritage, our language and customs the same, in our veins flows the same blood."

Ashtoth's face was impassive. "You have such a plan?"

Before replying Sar-Gath drained his cup of ato and held it out for the hovering slave girl to refill. "Yes, Lord of Atland, we have a plan—one which, if acted favorably upon, will bring together in lasting peace and friendship the rulers and peoples of our two countries."

"The details of the plan." Ashtoth's voice was bland.

The moment was at hand. Both Balimak and Zondarc, their lean, hawk-like faces tense with strain, bent forward tautly.

"A plan as simple as it is strong," cried Sar-Gath, his voice rising slightly under the excitement within him. "What could bind our two nations closer together than a union between our two ruling houses?"

In an excess of enthusiasm the Clyrusian high priest bounded to his feet, flung aside his goblet of ato, and made the sign of the triangle with broad sweeping strokes of one hand. "Let the union of our two nations be marked by the union of two of their noblest people—Mentanek, king of Clyrus, and the loveliest daughter of all Atland—Athora, princess of Atland..."

OTHER than a wave of angry blood that darkened his face, Ashtoth showed no reaction to the high priest's frenzied words. He was aware of the burning eyes of the two Clyrusian nobles watching him, and it required almost a physical effort for him to beat back the hot words that leaped to his tongue.

Sar-Gath, his wave of enthusiasm spent, sank back onto the bench and accepted another goblet of ato from the slave girl. He drank part of its contents, and then said. "What say you, noble Ashtoth? Does not our plan seem one to sweep aside the barrier of hatred and distrust now building between our nations? May I take back word to my waiting king that you have given consent to the union we have proposed?"

Ashtoth had not been king of Atland for thirty years without learning his job and learning it well. He knew Mentanek of Clyrus would not have sanctioned this move unless he held high cards; for otherwise he would never have dared to incur the wrath of his powerful neighbor. At the moment Ashtoth could think of nothing Mentanek might have with which to back himself up, but that did not mean he had nothing. Ashtoth's proper course, then, was to learn exactly what it was that gave Clyrus's king the courage to make such a proposal.

"This has come to me as a great surprise, Sar-Gath," he said slowly. "There are obstacles in the path of such a union—not insurmountable, of course, but there nevertheless. I shall need time to think it over."

This clear attempt at evasion pleased neither Sar-Gath nor the two nobles of Clyrus. Had the Golden God been firmly in their hands it would have been a different story; then Ashtoth might have taken his time in accepting the inevitable. But Avar-Ak's whereabouts were unknown, and it was entirely possible the thieving under priest and the holy object he had taken would be captured by the Atlands before the Clyrusians could find him.

No, Sar-Gath could not wait. He must have Ashtoth's promise that the union would take place—and he must have it at once, today.

"Naturally," the high priest began smoothly, "the noble Ashtoth is surprised by our proposal. Was it not that my king is impatiently awaiting a favorable answer, I should be glad to return to Clyrus and acquaint him with your desire for time to think it over. However, I dislike risking his displeasure by offering him no more than that. If the Lord of Atland would inform me of the nature of those obstacles he mentioned, I should be pleased to explain them to Clyrus's king."

Ashtoth bit his lip. His first impulse was to order the high priest and his two hawk-nosed companions out of Atland and back to Clyrus—hastening them with an ultimatum of death if they delayed leaving by so much as a single yad. But first he must know what newfound strength they were counting upon to back them up in their demands.

"The obstacles are these," he said harshly. "I have neither the power nor the wish to betroth my daughter as lightly as I would give away a palace slave. Too, Clat-Ron, high priest to Ammon-Re, has sued for her hand—an honor not to be refused should my daughter express her willingness to accept him as mate."

With an effort Sar-Gath managed to fight back a smile of triumph. "And were Clat-Ron to agree to withdraw in favor of Mentanek of Clyru. Would you be willing to urge the lovely Athora to wed him?"

Now indeed was Atland's king taken aback. Clat-Ron he knew was completely smitten by the blonde beauty of the princess—so smitten that nothing could conceivably force him to give her up to another. What, then, lay behind Sar-Gath's question?

He smiled stiffly. "Let us see what Clat-Ron has to say about that," he said flatly. Beckoning to one of the members of his personal guard stationed well out of earshot of the conference, he sent the fellow to ask Atland's high priest to join them.

A FEW minutes later the tall broad-shouldered figure of Clat-Ron came toward them across the gardens. His knee-length tunic, common among all Atlands, was white and about his middle was a broad golden belt containing hundreds of gems worked into the pattern of twelve triangles marking his high office.

He came up to the group on the benches, greeting his king and the visitors with the familiar tracing of a triangle in the air with one forefinger.

"You sent for me, my king?" he said in his deep resonant voice when introductions were made—introductions he acknowledged with reserved courtesy, for, like most of Atland's ruling class, he bore little respect and no liking for any Clyrusian.

"Our noble guests," Ashtoth said tonelessly, "have come here at the behest of their king, seeking to repair relations between their country and ours. To insure a better relationship they have suggested the union of Mentanek and my daughter...the princess Athora."

There...it was out... Ashtoth leaned back and took a goblet of ato from the slave girl. Clat-Ron's reaction was certain to be heated—so heated, in fact, the result might well be war. The power of Atland's high priests were, by long established precedent, second only to its kings—in fact many kings in its long noble history were former Voices or Ammon-Re—and Clat-Ron need ask no permission to so answer Mentanek's emissaries that an open break between the two nations would be inevitable. Certainly there could be no greater provocation for such an answer than the knowledge that the lovely Athora was desired by Clyrus's ruler.

Then Clat-Ron spoke—and such was his reply that Ashtoth jerked erect, staring at the high priest in openmouthed astonishment.

"The suggestion is a worthy one, noble Sar-Gath," he said humbly, "—one that honors us and the people of Atland."

"But—but, Clat-Ron," sputtered his king. "You yourself have asked—"

A warning pressure of the fingers Clat-Ron had dropped absently on his shoulder cut him off before he could say more. "You may return to the noble Mentanek," the high priest continued urbanely, "and inform him that our reply to his gracious offer will reach him within a few days."

This openly conciliatory attitude told Sar-Gath all he wanted to know. Avar-Ak's theft of the Golden God was known to Atland's high priest, and he had interpreted this demand for Athora as unquestioned evidence that the Holy of Holies was now in Clyrusian hands.

With this knowledge bolstering his courage Sar-Gath instantly decided to push his advantage to the utmost. "Only because my king is understandably anxious for a favorable decision do I ask for the privilege of placing before the princess Athora herself his pledge of undying love and to request from her an expression that his attentions are not unwelcome."

Ashtoth was tiring of these flowery speeches and diplomatic exchanges. Clat-Ron for some inexplicable reason had let him down badly and he wanted to know why. And so, disregarding the bite of the high priest's fingers, he broke in on the conversation.

"Unfortunately," he said, a steel edge creeping into his tone, "the princess is unable to receive visitors at this time. Clat-Ron has told you our answer will be given to your king shortly. That is our last word."

What Sar-Gath's reply was to have been was not known, for Clat-Ron stepped quickly into the breech. "As my king has pointed out," he said smoothly, "the princess Athora is indisposed and can see no one just now. However she may be able to receive you tomorrow and if you will return to the palace in the morning…"

Sar-Gath was satisfied. More than satisfied in fact. The spy he had sent to Atlantis had been able to get word to Clat-Ron that the Golden God was in Clyrus—thus explaining the high priest's anxiety to keep the peace. Clearly Ashtoth was not yet aware of the true state of affairs—a matter which would be attended to just as soon as the visitors were gone.

HE rose to his feet, now, followed by Balimak and Zondarc, to signify he was accepting the dismissal in Clat-Ron's final sentence. "Until tomorrow," he said, and if there was an undercurrent of threat to his words it appeared to pass unnoticed by the Atlands.

As an act of royal courtesy Ashtoth sent several members of his own guard to escort the Clyrusians from the palace grounds. When they were gone, the tall stern-faced king dismissed the slave girl and the others of his hovering retinue and turned to the high priest.

"I am waiting," he said coldly, "for an explanation for the sandal-licking treatment you afforded those men. Has your blood turned to water, your bones to dust that you bow humbly before Clyrusians?"

Troubled was the noble countenance of Clat-Ron, but nothing of cowering in his attitude. He was at least fifteen years Ashtoth's junior, being no more than forty—handsome and intelligent and a noble in his own right. His fine gray eyes were clouded with pain as he lifted his gaze to meet the king's half-puzzled and completely angry stare.

"I have not told you this, my lord," he said, "for I hoped to undo the evil that has fallen upon us—undo it before it was necessary to inform you of what has happened."

Ashtoth, appalled by the lifeless timbre in the voice of a man he could have sworn nothing could ever unnerve, grasped the high priest roughly by an arm. "What are you trying to say? What has happened to make you this way?"

"The golden god," said the other tonelessly. "It is gone."

"Gone!" cried Ashtoth, his face suddenly ashen. "Are you completely mad? Gone where?"

"Stolen—stolen by a traitorous under priest—one Avar-Ak, seventh ritual priest of the temple. How it happened no one knows—but two days ago one of the guards to the inner sanctum discovered all six of the bars to the only door were—severed. He called me and I entered, only to learn that the creonum casket had been forced and the golden god taken.

"I allayed the guard's suspicions by telling him the holy image had not been disturbed and ordered the lock restored. When I began questioning the other priests it was learned that Avar-Ak could not be found. Only then did I begin to recall certain actions and attitudes the seventh ritual priest recently displayed. He is an old man who never managed to rise high in the ranks of his chosen profession—a condition which must have made him do this awful thing as an act of revenge for fancied wrongs."

Atland's king seemed to have aged ten years in as many seconds. For several yads he sat there, his face buried in his hands, his broad shoulders bowed in mute suffering. Finally he raised his head to meet the agony reflected in Clat-Ron's eyes.

"Mentanek of Clyrus has it now," he said brokenly. "There could be no other answer to the attitude of those who called here a few yads ago. Why has he not let the people of Atland know it is gone from our country, so that they would turn upon us and kill us all?"

CLAT-RON was silent for a long moment, thinking. "Only two reasons are possible. Either he does not want all Atland destroyed by mobs of its own citizens, thereby lessening its value to him when finally he ascends your throne—or the golden god is not in his hands at all…"

"But that last is impossible," cried Ashtoth. "He would not dare send messengers with such a proposal as was made to us unless he had complete power to sustain him."

"Perhaps not," agreed Clat-Ron. He was thinking quickly now, putting his thoughts into words as they came to him. "Wily and shrewd is Clyrus's high priest—he is the master mind of that country and its real king—not ease-loving Mentanek. In your court—even within the temple of Ammon-Re—are hundreds of his spies. One or more of them may have learned of Avar-Ak's act and relayed word to Sar-Gath. Seeking a way to turn the information to some use, he hit on forcing a promise from you that the princess Athora would be given in marriage to his king. There are no higher stakes. Why, that alone would be indication enough, he may have reasoned, to prove he held the golden god…"

"As well he may," Ashtoth remarked bitterly.

"Perhaps not," Clat-Ron said slowly. "He made one slip—a minor error—so minor that it may be no slip at all. Still it may be strong enough for us to hang our hopes on."

"Don't sit there mumbling to yourself," exclaimed the ruler. "What is this mistake that is no mistake?"

"Why," said Clat-Ron, gesturing with one finger for emphasis, "was Sar-Gath in such a hurry to seal the betrothal? With the golden god in his hands he could afford to wait weeks, playing with us like a jungle cat with prey. Instead he practically threw diplomacy to the winds in urging a promise from us that the marriage would take place. Why?"

"Perhaps he thinks we may succeed in getting the golden god away from them, the same way it came into their hands."

"Hardly likely," retorted the high priest. "If they do have it, nothing could be more carefully guarded... No, Ashtoth, the golden god is still somewhere with Avar-Ak. We must find that worthless priest before he falls into the wrong hands..."

"But we have no time to hunt for him," protested Ashtoth. "Sar-Gath and those two Clyrusian nobles will be here tomorrow to see Athora. They mean to have an answer from us then; how dare we say no, since the golden god actually may be in their possession?"

Clat-Ron nodded thoughtfully. "We must find a way to put them off without risking an open break. We have until morning to hit on something. I will get word to you should some plan occur to me."

The two men rose, and with troubled hearts went their separate ways. Neither noticed the slave girl as she rose from where she had been listening behind a rose bush and hurry toward one of the palace wings.

CHAPTER SIX

The Dilemma of Reed McGurn

AS THE flying stone struck the savory deer meat into fire, Reed McGurn was transformed from a suave and polished officer into a beast whose dinner has been snatched from its jaws. Voicing a muffled curse that was more nearly a snarl he bounded to his feet and whirled to fall upon the author of this new outrage. Even were fifty heavily armed cave men responsible it would not have prevented him, probably, from charging them with the utter ferocity of a starving lion.

But there were no fifty cavemen—nor one. Instead the lithe, sweetly rounded figure of Lua, his erstwhile companion, was slipping lightly down the cliffside toward him.

Catching up one of the several sticks on which he had been grilling his dinner, McGurn began frantically to rake the steaks from the fire before they could be completely ruined. By the time he managed to rescue them they were covered with dust and ashes, and about as appetizing in appearance as the soles of his boots.

A soft hand touched his elbow and he wheeled to find the blonde and lovely girl of the caves smiling up at him, her warm blue eyes sparkling, the golden lengths of bare legs and arms glowing under the sun's burning rays. She was saying something in her outlandish language, the softly musical voice adding charm if not lucidity to the strange words.

With utter cheerfulness Reed McGurn could have raised his strong right hand and dealt her a tooth-shaking slap. But a heritage of good breeding and the unquestioning acceptance of society's edict that no gentleman strikes a lady made this impossible.

And so the young American lieutenant gathered the lovely Lua into his arms and kissed her again and again—kissed her full warm red lips with all the concentrated savagery that he would have put behind the open-handed blow she deserved for her act of vandalism.

For a brief moment the cave girl struggled mightily to push those bruising lips from her own. She was aware that her heart was pounding wildly—with fear, she knew—and then suddenly Lua realized there was no fear within her, but another emotion no less breathtaking. Her struggling ceased and almost of their own volition her arms came up and around the neck of Lieutenant Reed McGurn.

His anger abruptly cooled, the flyer released his hold and attempted to step back, only to discover he was firmly held in a soft embrace and being soundly kissed in a fashion that brought the hot blood to his cheeks. With clumsy gentleness he broke the girl's hold and stepped back.

"W-wait a minute," he stammered. "Don't get me wrong. I—"

Suddenly Lua turned her back on the bewildered man and burying her face in her hands began to cry bitterly. The face and figure of another had risen unbidden before her mind's eye—those of a young handsome cave youth whose straining chest was receiving thrust after thrust of a stone knife from the hand of Bitog. How could she welcome the kisses of a strange man when less than a sun was gone since the boy she loved had been foully slain? The memory of his smile and brave words to her only a brief moment before he lay dead in that small clearing tore at her with pain heightened by the act of disloyalty to him by accepting the caresses of another.

McGurn scratched his head and shifted his weight from one foot to the other. The girl's storm of grief was as unintelligible to him as had been her kisses of a moment earlier—at least as far as the reasons behind both.

He put out an uncertain hand and tapped her on the shoulder. "Listen," he said unhappily. "I'm sorry if I upset you. I didn't mean anything by—by kissing you that way. You made me mad by ruining that meat is all."

The girl ignored both the prodding finger and the plea in his voice.

"Aw, hell with it," muttered McGurn and went back to his dust-covered dinner.

By thoroughly washing the strips of venison in the spring's cold water and restoring them to the pointed sticks above the fire, he managed to bring the meat back to an edible condition once more. This done, he placed half his supply on a thin, leaf-covered rock and turned to offer it to the cave girl.

SHE was standing a short distance away, watching him. As he approached her holding out the rock and its savory contents, she turned a fiery red and lowered her eyes but made no move to avoid him.

"Let's start all over," said McGurn winningly. "We both made a mistake and it won't happen again. Now dig into this; you must be hungry. God knows I am."

The words meant nothing to Lua but the gesture and the appetizing odor of freshly cooked meat meant a great deal. She smiled breathtakingly at the young American, accepted the food he was proffering and followed him back to the fire.

They sat on rocks facing each other and ate, confining their attention to the venison. When the last of it had disappeared, McGurn put out the fire and went back to join his companion.

The time had come, the American told himself, either to teach this girl his language or learn her own. The latter sounded more reasonable; surely whatever tongue she spoke would be simpler than the King's English.

As he seated himself, the girl looked up with a smile. McGurn smiled back; then, pointing to himself, he said. "Reed McGurn. Reed McGurn. Reed McGurn."

A tiny frown marred the smooth, golden-tanned forehead of the girl and she stared at him wonderingly. Again McGurn repeated his full name over and over, each time tapping himself vigorously on the chest. Finally realization dawned in the girl's eyes and she nodded her head understandingly.

"Reedmcgurn," she cried, pointing a slim forefinger at him and laughing with excited pleasure. "*Edo dn* Reedmcgurn!"

Even run together that way his name never had sounded better, McGurn decided. The prefix she placed in front of it possibly was the cave people's equivalent of *you are.* And so he pointed his finger at her, this time, lifted his eyebrows questioningly and said, "*Edo dn—? Edo dn—?*"

"Lua," she said animatedly. "*Ke na* Lua!" And then followed a string of firecracker syllables completely without meaning to McGurn. He halted the flow of words with an uplifted hand.

"Okay, okay," he said, grinning. "One thing at a time. I'm Reed McGurn and you're Lua something or another. Now let's take it from there."

And so they "took it from there." The hours sped by, the annoyances of heat, humidity and insects forgotten as McGurn wrestled with the intricacies of the first human language in Earth's long history. By the time the long shadows of the neighboring forest fell across the clearing, he was able to speak many simple sentences in which nouns and verbs predominated. Finally the lieutenant glanced at the encroaching dusk and said, "The sun is gone. I am hungry. Are you hungry?"

"Yes," said Lua. "I, too, am hungry," and the man and the girl laughed with pleasure that they were able to talk with one another.

She showed him how to distinguish edible fruits of the jungle from the poisonous varieties, where to dig for succulent tubers and how to set traps for the smaller animals of the forest. And when night came down on the clearing she indicated where the almost invisible foot ledges were located on the sheer cliff containing the long abandoned caves. He was forced to remove his heavy soled service shoes to make use of the primitive staircase, and even then he cut a woeful figure in comparison to the agile ease with which Lua negotiated the almost vertical wall of rock.

The barrier of differences in culture and background between them formed by twenty two thousand years proved to be no barrier at all. Neither of them, in fact, knew such an obstacle existed; for to Reed McGurn this jungle-clad and beast-infested territory was in some forgotten corner of modern Europe; while Lua regarded this strange young man as one of those Gods who dwelt in the sun. Last night she had run from him because the stories told of those Gods pictured them as beings filled with cruelty and masters of torture. But that had been last night; and after the hours of loneliness that followed her running away, she had determined to rejoin him even if she must pay for a few hours of companionship by suffering countless indignities at his hands. The afternoon turned out to be so filled with laughter over her attempts to teach him her language that she quite forgot her earlier fears—all, that is, with the exception of those during the first few moments when this God had taken her roughly in his arms and smothered her lips with kisses. And as the afternoon waned she found herself hearkening back to the incident more and more often with a kind of mortified pleasure at the memory. But each time the handsome face of the dead Azar rose to shame her, bringing quick stinging tears to her eyes.

SHORTLY before darkness came again to the clearing, Lua aided McGurn in bringing a quantity of fresh tree limbs to one of the lower caves—boughs which he formed into a comfortable bed on the stone floor. It was when McGurn carried his first load of branches into the cave Lua selected for him that he received the greatest shock to his mind and nerves since his bullet-punctured plane first crashed into this incredible world some thirty hours before.

What he saw were vast murals decorating both side walls from floor to ceiling-murals of epic design and scope picturing the hunting of deer and antelope by war-like groups of men similar to the one who had been pursuing Lua at the time he rescued her from the lion. Other scenes in the murals showed parties of such men staging pitched battles, their arms, spears, and knives; while others depicted everyday life of cave dwellers. All figures, while crudely drawn, portrayed a sweep and power of execution that made them seem ready to step down from the walls themselves. Much of this lifelike character was due to the freshness and vivid hues of the colors used by the artist responsible.

McGurn threw down his burden of branches and stared long at the drawings, his expression one of mixed astonishment and consternation. "Who did those?" he demanded of the girl.

Lua shrugged, surprised at the question. "The *Leza* of the tribe who once lived here, I guess. Why?"

Leza was a new word to McGurn, who decided it meant "artist." He said, "How long ago was it…" He sought for a word that meant "painted" in his meager vocabulary of foreign words and could find none. "…made?" he concluded.

"I do not know," Lua said. She went close to the nearest wall and examined the brilliant colors. "Five summers ago, maybe."

"Five years!" said McGurn in English. His memory was digging back into the days when he had been pouring over schoolbooks at Winnetka High. There had been several blurred halftone cuts in one of those books—pictures reproducing in dull black and white scenes almost identical with those before him now. It was the recollection of the text accompanying those cuts that set his heart pounding with dull horror. The text had appeared in the first section of a book entitled, *Ancient History,* and explained that such paintings decorated the caves of the first race of *Homo Sapiens*—Cro-Magnon Man, who, the text had gone on to say, disappeared from Earth some twenty thousand years before!

"There's no *sense* to this," cried the young American in his native tongue. "Are you trying to tell me this part of the world is where the Cro-Magnons ended up at? That they haven't changed any in twenty thousand years?"

Lua stood silent, aghast at the flow of angry and, to her, completely unintelligible words. It was her stricken, lovely face that brought Reed McGurn abruptly back to an even keel.

"Sorry," he said ruefully; then, in the girl's language, "I will bring more branches."

He turned and fled back to the dusk-filled glade. As he crossed the open ground he looked up into the sky, noting the first stars of early evening. It was then he first observed the stars themselves were not where his courses in aerial navigation had said they were. Wildly he closed his eyes to shut out the heavens themselves, bowed his head, and plunged into the forest to gather another armload of leaf-covered boughs.

Later that evening Reed McGurn and Lua, daughter of Yortak, sat side by side on the tiny ledge outside the cave and looked out over the dark expanse of primeval forest and jungle. The awesome challenge of a hunting lion came faintly to their ears, answered by the shrill scream of Shanda, the leopard.

"What is there, Lua," asked the flier soberly, "beyond this land of trees and grass and hills?"

Lua, whose thoughts were a jumble of misery and contentment—misery at the separation from her people and her father, as well as the nagging worry that Bitog might eventually succeed in tracking her down—and a contentment she was unable to analyze clearly except that the frail figure of this god beside her figured in it in some manner—looked up from her reverie as the question fell on her ears.

"Beyond this?" she asked, waving a softly rounded arm at the nocturnal scene. "Nothing that is different. Except," she added after a moment's pause. "I have heard there is a place of water so big no man knows what is beyond it. At times the water becomes angry and runs far up on the land as if to eat it up, making a great roaring noise as it does so. This I have not seen with my own eyes, but men of the tribe have told us about it."

A "place of water" that large, reflected McGurn, could mean either a lake or even the ocean itself. This latter possibility seemed remote, however, since all territory in the vicinity of the earth's oceans was known by the men of his world. He said. "And are tribes such as yours the only people you have ever seen or heard of?"

LUA shifted restlessly on the stone ledge. She found the man's questions uninteresting to the point of boredom. A tiny voice in the back of her mind asked why he did not put his arms around her and talk of other things—of whispered intimate things every woman at many times in her life wants the man beside her to say. But again the memory of Azar pushed away that tiny voice and forced her to listen coolly to the stranger's words.

"Other people?" she said in reply to McGurn's last question. "There are no others. I have seen none, nor has anyone else of our tribe. Of course, there are many stories…"

"Yes?" prompted McGurn eagerly. "What stories, Lua?"

"Oh, they are doubtless lies. It is said that once, long beyond the memory of the oldest man of our tribe, a great flying bird carrying strange men fell into the jungles around here, A few of the men lived after the fall and they bore terrible killing sticks which took the lives of our warriors."

McGurn felt elation flood through him. Other men like him had blundered into this long-forgotten corner of the world, and where men could enter he could leave. "…And what happened to the men from the flying bird?" he asked.

"The stories do not tell that," Lua said impatiently. "Is not Mua, the moon, very pretty tonight? I do not remember seeing her look so lovely."

"Yes, the moon is pretty," McGurn said absently. "Tell me more of those old stories, Lua."

"I have forgotten them," she said shortly; then seeing his expression of disappointment, relented. "I have not heard them since I was a little girl. But they tell of a strange land far out on the place of water where people live in huge caves built with their hands from stone-people who do not wear the skins of Shanda and Tarka as we do, but funny white stuff covers their bodies from neck to knees. And on their feet they wear pieces of animal hide, and they cover themselves with pretty pieces of shiny rock, and they move about on the water between their land and ours on strange trees that go very fast."

As a description it left much to be desired, for the girl used only the words McGurn understood in her language. The business of covering themselves with pieces of rock and moving on the water on strange trees made little sense to him. But it was something, no matter how nebulous, to base his hopes on and his spirit soared.

Some day, when he was more acclimated to this new life, he would build himself a boat and cross the waters to this legendary land.

Now that he had arrived at a decision McGurn was suddenly aware that he was very tired. The upper half of his body, naked since abandoning his uniform blouse the day before, was smarting with a case of sunburn. Also, his feet were sore and bruised from climbing about the cliffside and crossing the clearing without shoes. His face could use a razor and his teeth a good brushing—matters he would make an effort to care for on the following morning.

He glanced at the girl beside him. How beautiful she was… The wealth of untamed blonde hair framing the soft oval of her tanned face brought back memories of that blonde in New York—the one he had been within a few hours of marrying. And then he thought of how he had seized in anger this girl beside him when the stone she had thrown playfully at him upset his dinner into the fire—seized her and covered her face with kisses, only to draw away when he discovered his caresses were being returned with an ardor that matched his own.

Why not take this wild girl into the cave with him? She probably knew nothing of such civilized refinements as a code of morals and the marriage ceremony—although, he was quick to admit in all fairness, neither did a lot of her civilized sisters!

Reed McGurn was lonely and puzzled and more than a little afraid—a combination of emotions which had driven men through the ages to seek forgetfulness in the arms of women. And so he half turned toward Lua with the intention of making love to her…and then abruptly he got to his feet.

"I am tired," he said stiffly. "I shall sleep now. Go to your own cave, Lua; in the morning we shall talk again."

Even as he spoke he realized how cold and stilted the words sounded. Much of this lay in the fact that the language used was not his own. But more than that was sharp revulsion at what he had been on the point of attempting. Reed McGurn was a long haul from saintliness, but neither was he an unprincipled rogue.

To Lua, daughter of Yortak, however, the man's chill words were a sharp rebuff of the friendly attitude she had adopted toward him…a sharpness intensified by the fact that she did not understand what lay behind it. And so she rose from her sitting position, gave him a haughty toss of her head that would have done credit to an insulted princess and left him standing there. A moment later she disappeared into the mouth of a cave above his own.

McGurn rubbed the back of his neck with a newly blistered palm and grinned ruefully. He had been given what he deserved and he would have liked to repair the breech. Well, perhaps in the morning…

He turned and entered the gloomy interior of his cave and removed his shoes and socks before stretching his weary frame upon the couch of leafy branches. For a little while he turned and twisted on his by no means downy bed, then weariness pushed aside all sensation of discomfort and he fell sound asleep.

While less than a half day's march to the west, a frail-bodied; middle-aged man wearing sandals and a travel-stained tunic, drew himself and his heavy pack into the branches of a huge tree for the night.

CHAPTER SEVEN
Flight from Atlantis

DEEP within a wing of the palace of Ashtoth, king of Atland, a slave girl crossed a luxuriously appointed room to where a heavy guard stood at rigid attention before the carved panels of a heavy door.

As she tame up to the guard he leveled the haft of his spear across his body, barring the way and bringing the slave girl to a sudden halt.

"Who are you, slave?" he said sternly, "and what brings you to the rooms of Athora, princess of Atland?"

The girl cringed under the sharp words, for she was only a slave, while this mighty warrior was a free man and a member of Ashtoth's own guard. But her voice was steady and its tone urgent as she made reply.

"I must speak with the princess," she said. "Tell her Clomia, the cup bearer, has urgent news for her ears alone."

"The princess has no time for the gossip of slaves," said the guard. "Go away lest you bring her anger against both of us."

"I will not go without seeing her," Clomia said firmly. "Always she has been kind to me and I now have the opportunity of repaying that kindness."

There was that in the slave girl's words and actions which impressed the guard and he hesitated to order her again to leave. "What is this news that is so urgent?" he asked curiously.

"It is not for you to hear," said Clomia, sensing his indecision and quick to follow it up. "Go at once and tell the princess I am here."

For a long moment the guard stared at her, uncertainty evident in his expression. Finally he said. "Wait here. I will tell the princess Athora that you are demanding she see you. How she acts after that will be on your head."

He turned, opened the door, and passed within, closing the portal at his back. Clomia, alone, began to be afraid of the step she had taken; for the information she brought had been gleaned from eavesdropping upon a conversation between Atland's supreme ruler and his guests.

At last the heavy door swung silently open once more, disclosing the guard and a beautiful woman near middle age who wore the purple-bordered tunic of the royal household.

"I am Rhodia, handmaiden to Athora," she said, smiling reassuringly at the trembling slave girl. "Come with me; the princess will see you."

Nervously, Clomia followed the woman through several lavishly furnished chambers filled with gracefully designed furniture covered with richly colored materials woven by the hands of slaves. Along tastefully decorated corridors they moved, their feet soundless on thick-piled carpeting, finally entering a daintily appointed boudoir, its pastel walls lined with drapes of silk and its narrow windows open to overlook the gardens below. Vases of flowers were everywhere, filling the room with their lovely scent.

Seated on the overstuffed surface of a fragile bench was Athora, rightly regarded by every human in Atland, slave and noble alike, as the world's most beautiful woman. A soft cloud of hair, black almost to the point of blueness, framed a narrow face and its delicately chiseled features. Her forehead was broad and smooth, her cheekbones high with a tiny hollow beneath each, her nose a trifle small but straight and imperious, her lips slightly fuller than the face deserved, the chin rounded and more than faintly aggressive. Although she could have seen no more than nineteen or twenty years, here plainly was a girl who knew her mind and would speak it without hesitation—a woman who could be yielding or adamant as the occasion required—a woman who could be accompanied or who could lead, but one who could never be driven.

Her body, under the contour molding touch of her tunic's soft material, was perfection itself—small, firmly erect breasts, a narrow, supple waist, softly rounded hips, and long, beautifully tapered legs ending in small, high-arched feet covered with white-leather sandals.

This, then, was Athora, daughter of a long and honored line of kings—regal, fully aware of her noble heritage and place in the scheme of things, gracious and kindly by nature...and yet still a girl unawakened to love and passion and still untouched by life.

AS CLOMIA entered the room accompanied by Rhodia, the princess smiled sweetly to the slave girl and called her by name. "The guard tells me you have word for me, Clomia. Tell me what has sent you to seek me out."

The slave wet her lips nervously, and it was not until the third effort that she was able to speak. "Perhaps I have done wrong, O gracious Athora," she said haltingly. "But you must believe that what I did was only because you have always been kind to me and that I would give my life to serve you."

"I shall remember that if what you have done is wrong," Athora promised, smiling. "Now tell me everything."

"The king, your father, entertained three guests in the palace gardens less than two *lats* ago," began Clomia. "It was my duty to fill their cups with ato and I could not help overhearing what they said. It concerned you, O princess of the dark hair."

"Concerned *me?*" Athora repeated, her gray-green eyes narrowing with surprise. "In what way? Who were these three guests?"

"One they spoke of as Sar-Gath; the others were named Balimak and Zondarc. All were of Clyrus, O daughter of the Sun."

Whereupon Clomia repeated all that she had heard, including Clat-Ron's seeming support of the plan to marry Athora to Mentanek, king of Clyrus—an attitude later explained during the conversation between Ashtoth and Clat-Ron after the Clyrusians were gone.

At mention of the theft of the Golden God the faces of Athora and Rhodia, her handmaiden, blanched and the two women stared at each other with stricken eyes. "The Golden God," whispered the princess. "This is indeed an evil day for Atland..."

When Clomia finished repeating the conversations she had overheard in the palace gardens, the princess sat lost in troubled thought for several moments. Finally she nodded briskly as though having reached a decision and, turning to the slave girl, said:

"You have done me a great service, Clomia, and you shall find that the princess Athora knows how to express her gratitude. Before the new moon comes you shall have your freedom; you have my word for that."

Clomia, her comely face alight with pure joy, dropped to one knee before the seated princess and pressed her lips to the hem of her robe. "Kind, indeed, is the daughter of Ashtoth," she said, her voice choked with tears of happiness. "But my greatest reward is the knowledge that I have served you well."

Athora reached out to help the girl to her feet and sent her from the room. When the door was closed behind Clomia, Athora turned to her personal maid, worry flooding back into her lovely face.

"What shall I do, Rhodia?" she whispered, anguish plain in her voice. "How could Clat-Ron so turn against me as to agree that I should become the wife of Mentanek of Clyrus? While he has never said it in so many words, I know he—he loves me. He has even approached the king for permission to make his love known to me."

"And do you love him, Athora?" asked Rhodia gently.

The girl's eyes softened. "I do not know. He is very handsome and he knows how to make a woman feel she is the only woman in a room—or the world, for that matter. He is big and strong and kind and intelligent—any woman would be proud to be his mate. Certainly I know of no man in all Atland—or Clyrus—I would prefer to him. And yet…"

"…you do not love him," finished Rhodia, smiling a little.

The princess rose to her feet and began to pace the floor. "All that is no longer important," she said. "What is important is that Clat-Ron is ready to give me to a man I do not know—a man who is neither respected nor loved even by his own subjects. I know that my duty calls for me to give myself to him to restore to its rightful place the Golden God; for without it my father no longer could be king of Atland. But Clat-Ron himself has said Mentanek may not have the holy symbol of Ammon-Re—that the Clyrusians may be trying to force an agreement from us before we learn the Golden God is not in their possession."

"I—I do not know what to say—what to advise you," Rhodia said in troubled tones.

Athora continued to pace the floor, biting her lips in an intensity of concentration, while Rhodia watched her in troubled silence.

ABRUPTLY the princess halted in mid stride as a plan leapt, full-born, into her mind. She wheeled on the startled maid, determination and satisfaction shining in her gray-green eyes.

"Rhodia," she said rapidly, "there is but one way out of this thing. I must have help to do it."

"You have but to command me, my princess," the handmaiden said quietly.

"I know. But I must have another—a man who can handle a dyark. A man who would unquestioningly risk the displeasure of my father and who would be willing to stake his life on a chance to help me. Know you of such a man, my Rhodia?"

"There are doubtless hundreds who would lay their lives at your feet, daughter of Ashtoth."

Athora gestured impatiently. "But do you *know* just one? One I could be certain would not run to my father with my plan the moment I gave it to him?"

"There is a flier attached to your father's Air Fleet," Rhodia said musingly. "He has not been in that branch of the service long, but

I chanced to meet him and he is very much…interested in me. For that reason—if no other—I think he can be trusted. Too, he has often spoken admiringly of you—of your graciousness and charm and of how he would count himself fortunate to be in your service."

"Can you find him and bring him here—now?" asked Athora eagerly.

"I will try," said Rhodia, rising. "I know where he is quartered and he is not on duty at this hour."

"Hurry to him, then," the princess commanded, "and tell him I await him here."

Fargolt, pantar * in the Air Fleet of Atland's military machine was gambling with a group of his fellow officers in one of the barracks on the palace grounds. He was winning heavily and his round, rather heavy featured face was flushed with excitement and satisfaction. As he reached for the symbol-covered cubes preparatory to making another cast, an orderly came up behind him and tapped his shoulder lightly.

Fargolt, still in a squatting position, turned his head impatiently. "What do you want?" he growled.

"A woman is outside, asking for you, pantar. She would give no name."

Fargolt hesitated, torn between the desire to increase the pile of creonum coins in front of him and curiosity as to what woman would be seeking him out. "What does she look like?" he said.

"Her face is hidden by the folds of a cloak," the orderly replied. He winked heavily. "But her figure is excellent."

"Come, Fargolt," said one of the other players impatiently. "Either cast the stones or pass them on and go to your woman."

Reluctantly the pantar relinquished the gambling cubes and scooped up his winnings. "Show me where the woman is waiting," he ordered.

As Fargolt and the orderly came out of the barracks' gate, the slender figure of a woman, her face shadowed by the folds of a light cloak came into view.

---

*A military rank, equivalent to Lieutenant. -Ed.

Surprise and a shade of worry crossed the pantar's face as he recognized the visitor. "Rhodia!" he cried. "Why are you here? Is something wrong?"

The woman moved her head slightly towards the staring orderly, and Fargolt, understanding, said, "I won't need you," to the man.

When they were alone, the woman permitted the veiling collar of her cloak to drop to her shoulders, revealing her face. Fargolt noticed at once the strained lines that he had never seen there before and quick alarm stirred within him.

"Is something wrong, Rhodia?" he asked again.

"Fargolt," the woman said in a low voice, coming close to him, "you have often spoke of your admiration for the princess Athora, and how you would welcome an opportunity to serve her. Do you still feel so?"

"To the death," replied Fargolt promptly.

"Then come with me," Rhodia said. "The princess has sent me to bring you to her, for she has need of your help. But you must swear to me that, regardless of what the outcome of your talk with her, never will you breathe a word of the conversation you have with her."

"I swear it upon the sacred image of the Golden God," said Fargolt solemnly; and a calculating gleam appeared in his suddenly narrowed eyes as he saw a shadow of fear pass across the beautiful face of Athota's handmaiden.

SIDE by side they crossed the palace grounds, along the flower-bordered walks and past the gleaming fountains of white stone, turning at last into a half-hidden entrance to the palace wing sheltering the princess' apartment. After traversing long corridors and deserted rooms, Rhodia ushered the pantar into the boudoir where Athota impatiently waited.

As Rhodia presented the man to her mistress, Athora looked long into the coarse-featured face of the flier, seeking to learn what lay beyond the surface. It was all important that she be able to trust this man; and while there was nothing visible to distinguish him from any of a hundred fighting men in Atland's armies, Rhodia's recommendation tipped the scales in his favor.

"I need of you, Fargolt," the princess said at last, "to help me in reaching the land of Afrota."

"Afrota!" cried Fargolt and Rhodia in unison; and the handmaiden continued, "Surely, my princess, you would not enter so wild and terrible a place…"

"There is no other place for me while the chance remains of my becoming promised to Mentanek of Clyrus," Athora declared. She caught a glimpse of Fargolt's sagging jaw, and added, "There is much you do not understand, pantar, nor do I wish to make a lengthy explanation. If it is your desire to help me it must be given without question."

"You have but to command me, O glorious Athora," Fargolt said promptly.

"Thank you," She dazzled him with a smile. "Should all go well, your reward will not be small.

"Now," she continued soberly, "can you arrange to have a dyark waiting on the roof of my apartment at midnight tonight? A dyark large enough to carry seven, in addition to you and me, to Afrota?"

"I can manage to do so, daughter of Ashtoth."

"Good. I shall be waiting there for you, together with the seven warriors who form my personal guard."

"I shall accompany you, Athora," said Rhodia firmly. "I cannot allow you to be without the companionship of another woman in that terrible land."

The princess placed an affectionate hand on the handmaiden's arm. "I am glad, Rhodia. I had hoped you would say that, but I would never dream of ordering you into so dangerous an exile."

"Until midnight then, O princess of the dark hair," said Fargolt, the pantar. Tracing the figure of a triangle with one forefinger, he turned and left the apartment.

ASHTOTH of Atland slowly paced the floor of his private apartment, his forehead set in troubled lines. At his order all but one of the room's lights had been extinguished and his personal slaves withdrawn to permit him uninterrupted concentration on the problem he faced.

Through the broad openings in two walls the city lights were visible, dotting the deserted streets of Atlantis. From this room, three full floors above the palace grounds, he could see to the distant circular wall encompassing the entire city. Broken clouds filled the night sky, and through occasional rifts moonlight brought a ghostly radiance to the scene below.

For hours Ashtoth had been pacing thus, worry weighing within him like a heavy stone. The loss of the Golden God, was in itself a crushing blow—one which might very well cost him his throne, but even more oppressive was the knowledge that it might be necessary to sacrifice the happiness of his only child to keep secret word of that loss. Many times during those hours he was on the point of going to his daughter and laying before her the facts, ready to adopt whatever course she wished, no matter what the cost. But the hope that either he or Clat-Ron would come up with some saving idea before tomorrow's conference with the Clyrusians kept him silent.

A knock at the door and a slave's voice saying the noble Clat-Ron was here to see him brought him across the room with three swift strides. And when he flung open the door and detected the exultant expression on the high priest's handsome face, Ashtoth's spirits soared to heights comparable only to the depths of his earlier dejection.

With a hand that trembled slightly he caught Clat-Ron's arm and drew him into the room, closing the door in the slave's bewildered face. "You've found a way out, Clat-Ron," he declared before the other could speak. "I can see it in every line of your face."

"It is possible," admitted the high priest, his wide smile belying the caution in his voice. "It is a wild, perhaps a foolish plan, but in its very wildness is its greatest strength, I think."

"Tell it!" cried Ashtoth impatiently.

They sat down in chairs drawn in a facing position. "First," Clat-Ron said, "we must go to the princess Athora and tell her the entire story. We—"

Ashtoth was shaking his head. "I don't want to trouble her, Clat-Ron. She's still a child, actually, and these matters of intrigue are not pleasant."

"It will be a great deal more unpleasant for her," the high priest pointed out, "if she is forced into marriage with that hulking idiot Mentanek. And I think your fatherly affection for her has blinded you to the fact that Athora is intelligent and mature beyond her years. I was about to say that we must have her cooperation if my plan is to be used."

Atland's king sighed resignedly and leaned back in his chair. "Let's hear it, then."

"We will go to her now," the priest said, "and tell her what has happened. Then we must ask her to disappear—to run away. Tomorrow, when the Clyrusians call to see her, her personal slaves must say that during the night the princess and one of her personal guards took a dyark and left for some unknown destination, ordering the slaves to tell no one she was gone.

"Naturally we shall appear to be greatly surprised and shocked by the princess' flight. Our embarrassment must be evident but not overplayed. Instantly you must order a fleet of dyarks to take off in search of her.

"Of course, Sar-Gath and the nobles from Clyrus are going to suspect us of engineering the whole thing. But suspicion is one thing; proof another. They will not dare break with you, for the possibility will remain that Athora acted so without your knowledge."

"This will only delay the inevitable," Ashtoth pointed out, his expression again troubled. "Sooner or later Athora must return to Atlantis; then we'll be back where we are now."

"But in the meantime," Clat-Ron said, "we shall have gained time—time in which to hunt down that thieving Avar-Ak and regain possession of the Golden God. You may be sure that Clyrus's king will be hunting for him also; if he succeeds in finding Avar-Ak ahead of us…then we shall have no alternative but to call back the princess and surrender to Mentanek's power."

"You may be wrong in thinking the Golden God is not already in his hands," Ashtoth said gloomily.

"I'd stake my life it is not," the high priest declared. "However five of my spies in Clyrus are attempting to make sure of that at this moment. Two of them have managed to worm their way into the first ranks of Mentanek's inner circle and we should know the truth within a matter of days."

WITH a gesture of infinite weariness Ashtoth placed a hand across his eyes. "Where could the princess go, Clat-Ron. Everywhere in all Atland are spies in the pay of Mentanek—always the chance would be that one of them would locate her hiding place."

"I thought of that," admitted Clat-Ron, smiling a little. "For that reason she must go where there are no spies."

"But where—"

"To Afrota."

"Afrota!" Ashtoth jerked erect on his chair, his jaws hanging in complete astonishment. "Are you mad? Where in that horrible land of beasts and snakes and thick jungle is there a place for her? Would you have her sleep among the trees like a bird, Clat-Ron?"

"There is more to Afrota than the things you name," Clat-Ron said equably. "I remember hearing from one of the warriors attached to the temple guard a story about Afrota. It seems he spent many days there when a flier he was on crashed near its coast. He told of mountains not far inland, and among them were deserted caves abandoned by a race of naked savages as they moved further from the ocean and its fogs. Athora, with a guard of warriors and a slave girl or two, can take over a few of those caves for half a moon or so and give us a chance to straighten things out."

"If you think I'm going to allow my daughter to live like a wild sav—"

"There is no other way," Clat-Ron said impatiently. "At least, none I can think of. And there's no reason for her to live like a wild beast, as you put it. The jungle can offer nothing in the way of danger a huar or two can't take care of. She'll have guards to protect her and the slave girls to keep her company. Certainly such a life would be far superior to becoming Mentanek's queen."

Ashtoth said wearily. "Perhaps you are right. At any rate we'll put the plan up to Athora and see what she has to say about it. She may be sleeping but this is too important to bother about that. What time is it?"

The high priest glanced at the gold-and-creonum strapped to his wrist. "It lacks but a few yads of midnight."

The two men rose and, leaving the king's apartment, walked slowly along the corridors of the palace, their destination the wing containing the apartment of Athora, princess of Atland.

FARGOLT, pantar in Atland's dyark forces, was alone in his quarters at one end of the large barracks on the palace grounds. He was loading a good-sized deerskin bag with his personal possessions. Finishing, he placed the bag on the floor, seated himself on a stool near a table in the room's center, and unrolled a small strip of papyrus. A quill from a jungle bird served as a pen, and a small saucer of black liquid made from a solution of water and powdered ochre gave him ink. Writing rapidly and with complete concentration, he penned a brief note on the papyrus, folded it, and sealed the edges with wax from a candle standing near his elbow. While the wax was still soft, he dug a small bit of carved stone from a leather pouch at his belt and pressed it into the yielding substance, reproducing there its raised design. Rising, he took the letter to the outer room and, summoning an orderly lounging there, instructed that it be delivered to one Rotath, a pantar attached to the palace foot troops located in a barracks elsewhere on the grounds.

Once the orderly had left on his errand, Fargolt swung the leather bag to his shoulder, made sure the hand huar was at his waist, and set out across the palace gardens, keeping well within the shadows cast by the great trees. Twice he avoided guards on patrol by hiding in clumps of bush; and when he reached the palace itself, he entered by a secret door leading directly to the princess Athora's quarters.

Arriving at the closed door of Athora's boudoir, he glanced at the dial of his leton, noting that midnight was but a few yads away. A slow, satisfied smile curved his lips as he raised a hand and knocked lightly on the polished wood…

*   *   *

An armed guard dozed lightly on a bench behind the locked door of a two story building a stone's throw from Atlantis's protecting wall of stone. The other inhabitants of the place were long since asleep in the quarters located on the upper floor.

A muted knock at the outer door awakened the guard with it start. As the knock was repeated, he drew his small huar and came lightly to his feet. Crossing quickly to the door, huar held ready, the guard pulled back its bar and drew open the heavy portal an inch or two. The figure of a man, his face shadowed by the folds of a cloak, was standing there.

"Who are you?" the guard demanded, his voice surly, "and what do you want?"

"There are seven hills," said the man outside, his tone without inflection.

"Do the hills have names?"

"The first is called Men."

"And the second?"

"Tan."

"The third?"

"It has no name."

"The fourth?"

"Ek."

The guard stepped back and drew the door wide. "You may enter," he said.

But the man outside made no move to cross the threshold and for the space of a full yad neither of the two moved. Abruptly the stranger said. "Mentanek," the guard replaced the huar in his belt and the cloaked figure entered the hall.

In the dim light and with his cloak lowered and open, the stranger was revealed as a pantar of Atland's foot troops. To the waiting guard he said:

"I bring a message to Sar-Gath. Inform him at once that it is of urgent importance and I alone may hand it to him."

"Wait here," said the guard stiffly and left the room.

Within moments the guard reentered the hall, followed closely by Sar-Gath, his dark, lean-jawed face impassive. But for all his lack of expression, the Clyrusian high priest was worried. It showed in his eyes and in the tightness of his lips.

"I am Sar-Gath," he said tonelessly. "What is your message, pantar?"

The warrior thrust a hand within the folds of his tunic and brought forth a bit of folded parchment bearing a strange design in the white wax sealing its edges. "I was given this and a message of instruction to place it in your hands," he said.

SAR-GATHS fingers closed tightly about the bit of papyrus. "Wait," he said; then, ignoring both guard and pantar, ripped open the folded sheet and scanned its few lines of oddly shaped characters. From time to time, he frowned in deep concentration, for the message was in code and not easy to read.

Finally he raised his head, and the impassive expression was gone, replaced by a curious mixture of exultation and anger. "Go to the roof," he instructed the guard, "and order one of the larger dyarks made ready for a long flight. Select three of the guards there to prepare to accompany me. We shall take off within five yads."

"At once, Excellency," The guard made the sign of the triangle and was gone.

Sar-Gath pressed a creonum coin in the messenger's hand and dismissed him, then hurried to an upstairs sleeping room to arouse the two Clyrusian nobles who had accompanied him to the palace earlier in the day. When they were awake and listening, he said:

"The princess Athora has been told Mentanek desires her in marriage and is preparing to flee to Afrota. She leaves from a private landing stage on the palace roof at midnight." He glanced quickly at the leton on his wrist. "It is nearly midnight now. I shall follow her and learn the exact spot on Afrota she expects to land. Then, when her absence is discovered by Ashtoth, and a great hubbub is raised, we shall listen sympathetically to his apologies, offer our services in finding her...then manage to 'locate' the missing princess. By the time the Atland king has recovered from the shock, Athora will be pledged to wed Mentanek."

"It may be impossible to follow her dyark at night," Zondarc pointed out. "Should its pilot cruise without lights there would be no way to trail him without letting him learn of our presence."

"We need not concern ourselves about that," Sar-Gath replied, smiling. "The man at the controls of Athora's dyark is one of my spies. Over a moon ago I hired him to win the trust of someone close to the princess. He did well, too—Athora's own handmaiden has fallen in love with him!"

"Your success, Sar-Gath," Balimak said, "is largely due to your ability to hire rascals as cunning as their master."

The high priest's bow in acknowledgement of the dubious tribute hid the anger in his eyes. Straightening, he strapped a ray gun to his wrist, made the sign of the triangle in farewell, and left the room, his destination the roof landing stage.

A SLAVE girl opened the door in response to Ashtoth's knock. At sight of the king and the high priest, she fell back a step in alarm, her face turning suddenly pale.

"Inform the princess," Ashtoth commanded, "that her father wishes to speak with her at once."

The girl's efforts to speak resulted only in an unintelligible mumble and her feet seemed rooted to the carpeted floor.

"Well?" said Ashtoth sharply. "Why are you standing there?"

The words seemed to snap what little control the slave had left. She began to tremble violently and tears spilled from her wide, frightened eyes.

The king, astonished by this inexplicable behavior, reached out to take her by the arm; but Clat-Ron, his expression suddenly stern, was there before him. Roughly he shook the girl. "Speak!" he shouted in a terrible voice. "Where is Athora?"

"Oon-on t-t-the roof," the slave girl stammered.

"The roof?" Clat-Ron released her, his expression puzzled. "Why is she there? Answer me!" he thundered when the girl hesitated to reply.

"The princess did not tell me," she said tearfully. "All I know is that she and Rhodia went there with Fargolt. He is a pantar in the Air Fleet."

"Air Fleet?" repeated Clat-Ron. "What in the name of Ammon-Re would she be—"

And then understanding dawned on his face. Sweeping the slave aside with a thrust of his arm, he bounded across the room, shouting for Ashtoth to follow. Together they raced through the apartment, along a corridor and up three flights of winding stairs to the flat roof of the palace wing.

As the two men burst through the final doorway they saw in the cloud-diffused moonlight the bulk of a large dyark resting on the crushed rock surface of the roof. Already the pilot was at his controls at the stern of the bullet-shaped craft, while Athora and her handmaiden were strapped in their seats awaiting the take-off. Forward, near the bow, several members of the princess' guard were nearly finished with their task of loading a mound of supplies through the open hatch of a storage bin in the dyark's side.

"Stay where you are!" bellowed Ashtoth from the doorway. He drew his death-dealing huar from its place at his belt. "The first man to move dies..."

Athora's heart sank. She saw the warriors of her guard standing as though turned to stone. Her plan had failed; there was nothing left but to bow to the inevitable. Already her father and Clat-Ron were crossing the roof toward her, the stones crunching under their sandals.

"Shall I make a try for it, princess?"

The quiet whisper from behind her barely reached Athora's ears. It set her heart pounding as she warmed at this indication of the pantar's unswerving loyalty. Did she date order him to risk a take-off? And then a vision of Mentanek's gross body and idiot's face gave her the answer.

"Yes," she whispered, not turning her head.

Ashtoth, now but a few feet from the dyark's smooth metal side, called out to his daughter. "What madness is this, Athora? Why are you—?"

Suddenly the sleek-lined airship shot soundlessly into the night, rising vertically from the roof as though plucked into space by an invisible hand. So rapid was the rise that Athora's senses reeled momentarily; and by the time she was able to look down, the dyark was fully a hundred feet above the palace and rising swiftly.

In the moonlight she was able to make out the actions of those on the roof below. She saw two tiny figures that were her father and the high priest waving frantically at the dyark, probably shouting orders to return although the distance was too great by this time for the sound to carry to her. Then she saw one of the seven warriors move at a run toward the roof's single exit and disappear from sight, probably obeying some order given him by Ashtoth. Perhaps an order to the commander of Atland's Air Fleet, instructing him to take up the chase of her plane, reasoned Athora gloomily.

She was suddenly despondent at this stroke of bad luck. Who could have informed on her? She would have sworn none knew of her plans other than Rhodia and Fargolt, the dyark's pilot. The fact both were with her now was evidence neither was the traitor. Who else could have known? None of the seven members of her guard had been told of her plans, all of them having been with her constantly since she summoned them a lat before midnight.

The dyark ceased to climb and began to move southward, rushing with great speed through the night sky. Within a few yads they were passing Atland's coastline and continuing on over the dark waste of ocean far below. The dyark's passage was completely soundless due to the complete absence of moving parts in the simple mechanism furnishing its motive power. However the chill air at their present altitude made the cabin's interior increasingly, uncomfortable, and Athora pressed the tiny switch that lowered thin sheets of metal over the hull's opening. In the ceiling of the cabin a mesh of fine wires became incandescent, furnishing both light and heat to passengers and pilot.

FARGOLT was an old hand at handling a dyark. Although his position was at the stern, a crystal screen at his eye level reproduced perfectly what lay ahead of the speeding craft. His handling of the controls was more automatic than usual, however, for he was deep in thought.

What course of action should he take? The idea of landing himself and the princess on Afrota's jungle-ridden surface was horrible to contemplate. He did not know why she wished to go there in the first place, and his sending the note to Sar-Gath detailing the princess' plans was prompted solely by his belief any extraordinary act by a member of Atland's ruling house would be of interest to the Clyrusian high priest. He could not risk landing her at the capitol city of Clyrus; the news would be back to Ashtoth within a few lats and war would be bound to follow—a war Clyrus was ill equipped to wage.

He started guiltily as the princess, seated immediately ahead of him, turned to ask him a question.

"In what direction are we moving, Fargolt?"

"South, my princess."

"Afrota is to the east."

"I know. I am but attempting to mislead possible pursuers."

Athora smiled in relieved tribute to the man's cleverness. "I was fortunate to have found so intelligent a warrior. I shall not doubt you again."

"It is a privilege to serve you, O glorious princess," said Fargolt noncommittally.

His course of action was plain, Fargolt decided. He would land the princess on Afrota at whatever point she wished, then slip the dyark away at night and fly to Clyrus for further instructions.

Slowly he swung the dyark's nose eastward, then stepped up its power until the streamlined craft had attained its maximum speed.

A thousand feet higher and fairly well back, the pilot of a second dyark watched a pinpoint of light marking the princess' plane on its crystal screen. As the brilliant dot began to move faster across its surface, he moved a switch on the panel in front of him and his own craft leaped ahead in silent pursuit.

CHAPTER EIGHT
The Fate of Avar-Ak

WHEN Reed McGurn awakened, the sun was already high and pouring in at the entrance of his cave. Yawning mightily, he went to the narrow ledge outside and let his eyes run across the expanse of sheer rock between his and the cave Lua had entered the night before. There was no sign of her at its mouth, nor was she visible in the clearing below.

Returning to his own hole-in-the-wall, as he silently called it, he buckled the Webley about his narrow waist and picked up his shoes. Returning to the ledge he let the shoes slip down the slope to level ground, then very slowly and cautiously he followed. Squatting at the base of the cliff, he donned his shoes, lighted a cigarette, then rose and walked over to the tiny spring to quench his thirst.

He rubbed a thoughtful palm across his cheeks, the action reminding him that a shave was in order. Common sense told him a hairless face was probably the least important thing in this savage world, but habit was strong and he felt he could face the perils of this new life with more confidence after a clean shave.

He took out the small pocketknife used the previous day to hack steaks from the body of the deer and tested its single blade against the ball of one thumb. It was fairly sharp but not nearly keen enough for the purpose in mind. After a short search he found a bit of rock near the cliff, and against this he honed the knife blade to a fine edge. For a beard softener he used water from the spring while the pool itself served as an unsteady mirror. Fortunately shaving had never been a problem with him because of the texture of his skin and whiskers that usually gave up without a struggle.

It required almost half an hour of patient and careful whittling to remove the hairs, however, and two or three nicks drew blood. The cold spring water stung his scraped skin but left him feeling greatly refreshed.

There were several rips in the material of his service trousers where jungle thorns had taken their toll. But his shoes were still in excellent shape and though he was bare to the waist his sunburn was darkening to a deep tan and no longer smarted. Insect bites dotted his exposed chest and back, but they were a minor irritation and he ignored them.

By this time it was nearly noon, and still Lua had not put in an appearance. McGurn's belly was beginning to protest the absence of breakfast, and the young American decided to wait no longer before doing something about that. If the cave girl was still sulking over last night's incident, he'd be darned if he would crawl to soothe her ruffled feelings.

Drawing the Webley and holding it at his side, ready for instant use, McGurn walked slowly across the clearing toward the game trail entrance in the wall of jungle and forest. Before plunging into that green labyrinth he meant to make certain none of the great cats was lurking behind some bush or foliage clump. Reed McGurn was learning.

Other than a family of monkeys leaping among the higher branches and swearing at him amid the dappled light of the sun filtering through vines and leaves, and an enormous bird with very green plumage and a red bill, he could detect not a sign of life.

Moving his shoulders in a faint shrug, like a swimmer about to plunge into surf he knows is cold, the flyer vanished among the tangled fastness of growing things.

While from the entrance of a cave in the sheer wall of rock behind him, Lua watched him go and smiled a small, secretive smile—a smile of understanding and pride at the combination of ignorance and bravery that permitted this strange young man to walk thus calmly into so terrible a world.

FOR nearly an hour Reed McGurn moved slowly along the tortuous twistings of the elephant path. Not long before he had come to a fork in the path; and where yesterday he took the one to the right, today he chose the other in hopes it would bring him to a watering place or another section of prairie, either of which, he reasoned, would be the stamping grounds of grass eaters.

He was interested and faintly amazed to learn that his heart was not pounding as hard as on the day before and his nerves seemed more relaxed. The realization gave him a heady sense of exhilaration and power. He swaggered along, holstering the Webley carelessly while tearing the wrappings from a stick of gum with a flourish; and when, a short time later, he lighted a cigarette, it was with the easy insouciance of an airman home from a bombing raid unscathed by enemy fire.

While at the peak of this frame of mind Reed McGurn rounded a bend of the trail and came unexpectedly into a good-sized clearing. He took one step into open ground, then came to a sudden and involuntary halt, the popular air he was humming dying on his lips as his eyes took in the first stages of a grisly tableau—grisly but all too familiar to this savage world.

There was a lion and a man facing each other across a narrow space a few feet from the path's continuation across the clearing. Evidently McGurn had come upon the scene just at its inception, for the lion—a huge, tawny-maned beast—was still in the act of rising from a clump of long grasses forming a natural ambush, while the man's mouth hung open in the first shocked indication of surprise.

Here was the third human McGurn had seen since being plunged into this forgotten world, and one totally unlike the first two. He was too old and far too frail to be wandering about alone in a danger-infested wilderness. He wore a knee-length tunic of white cloth and sandals of brown leather. Scrawny gray hair straggled across his dome-like skull like seaweed on a beach boulder, and his skin was that soft dead-white hue that comes from too few hours outdoors.

McGurn, spellbound, expected the old man to scream in terror and run for the nearest tree. Evidently the lion was waiting for the same reaction, for it remained standing amid the grasses, its tail twitching in jerky undulations, its round yellow eyes fastened hypnotically on its intended prey.

But the old man neither screamed nor ran. While McGurn stared in mingled disbelief and admiration, he calmly lowered from his shoulder a cloth bound bundle, which he set on the ground at his feet. Disregarding the lion completely he bent and began to tug open the bundle with calm unhurried movements of his thin hands. It was so exactly like some clerk opening a parcel of shirts for a customer's inspection that McGurn, despite the impending horror he was about to witness, caught himself grinning.

The lion, curious as are all animals, watched with complete interest as the man rummaged through the bundle. It was not until he came up with a strange tube-like affair bent at one end to form a hand grip and started to level it that the beast decided his prey intended to defend himself. Its tail shot suddenly erect and, voicing a hideous roar, the lion sprang at the figure in its path.

The American's hand streaked for the Webley in what he knew was a hopeless effort to save the old man's life, but he never completed the draw.

The lion was in midair when the stranger succeeded in pointing the tube's business end at it. There was no explosion, no streak of fire, no sound.

No lion!

A strangled gasp of utter incredulity burst from McGurn's throat. He clapped his free hand to his eyes, rubbed them harshly, and looked again. The old man had bent again and was returning that deadly length of thin metal tubing to his bundle, his actions as unhurried and calm as before.

Had he paused for even a moment's reflection, Reed McGurn would never have gone blundering into the open the way he did now, shouting a welcome to that amazing old man who had obliterated a five hundred pound hunk of muscle, teeth and claws as if it were no more than chalk marks on a slate.

At sound of McGurn's hail, the tunic-clad figure took a single quick glance at the approaching airman, then bent to his bundle again and brought out the narrow tube. He was in the act of pointing it before the American realized his intentions. With a startled cry McGurn threw himself headlong. He heard the air crackle above him, the sound being barely more than audible. While still in a prone position he saw the old man lower the muzzle of his strange weapon to cover him. In another second, McGurn realized with a kind of blank astonishment, he was going to be dead—blasted into nothingness like that lion.

AFTER Reed McGurn disappeared from view along the elephant path, Lua came down from her cliffside aerie and went to the spring to quench her thirst. Rising, she let fall the skin of Tarka, the panther, which formed her only garment, and bathed herself in the clear, cold water. After a few minutes of this, she slipped the soft folds of panther hide back into place and went to the jungle's edge in search of fruit to break her fast.

Last night's anger at Reed McGurn's chill rebuff was mostly gone. She found herself smiling softly as she thought of him—of his stumbling attempts to learn to speak as she spoke, of his broad shoulders and those blue eyes that could be laughing and hurt and bewildered and angry to match his every mood. They could burn with a wild and heart-catching fire, too—as they burned when he caught her roughly in his arms the afternoon before. She remembered the crushing impact of his lips on hers and her cheeks blazed even with thinking of that.

Deliberately she made herself think of Azar—calling to mind the love she had held for him ever since they were children together. Tears stung her eyes as she relived the moment of his death...and even in the moment of her grief Reed McGurn's handsome face and stalwart figure obliterated that of the boy she had loved.

Shaking her blonde head in mingled anger and confusion, she entered the jungle trail and set out to follow her companion. She knew the forest was no place for her to be wandering, that the intelligent thing for her to do was to return to her cave and await the man's arrival. But an impulse she did not attempt to analyze drove her on at a swinging trot, although not once did she relax her attention to her savage surroundings.

At the point where the trail forked, she bent low to scan the earth, her woodcraft, woefully inadequate when compared to the hunters of her tribe, sufficiently developed to make out the marks of Reed McGurn's shoes. For—a short distance she moved slowly along the left-hand fork, picking out the marks to be sure he had not doubled back. Satisfied at last that he had continued on, she moved ahead, increasing her pace as the moment of reunion grew near.

She came into the clearing just in time to see Reed McGurn throw himself heavily to the ground as an old man wearing a strange white skin pointed an odd-looking branch at him. The old man's grim expression was enough to show her, beyond doubt, that he was intent on killing the other.

Nothing she could do would prevent her companion's death. Yet even as the knowledge came to her she was bounding across the grass toward him, preferring to die at his side rather than go on without him.

Avar-Ak half lowered the barrel of his xorth as the cave girl appeared at the opposite side of the clearing. Women such as this he had seen before, as tribes of cliff dwellers still living among a few of the unexplored mountain heights surrounding Atlantis. It was the man who had burst from cover a moment ahead of her that was strange to him and who he had been on the point of slaying.

From the corner of one eye he saw that the man was attempting stealthily to remove a small metal object from a bit of harness at his waist. Some sort of weapon, the priest decided, and once more he leveled the xorth at the figure on the ground.

Unknown to Avar-Ak were the ways of jungle denizens. Thus he did not know that where hunted Kraga, the lion, there too hunted Conta, his mate. And so it was that as his finger tightened on the tiny lever of his weapon, a tawny length of feline fury flew from the depths of jungle at his back, its scream rising high and clear on the humid air.

Old was Avar-Ak, but wily and quick-witted, too. Even as the first notes of Conta's cry fell on his ears he was whirling to meet her attack, xorth leveled to fire. But he had been completely ambushed. One flailing paw struck the weapon from his hand and Conta's full weight threw him heavily to his back.

Jaws widespread, saliva drooling from tongue and fangs, Conta lowered her head past the futilely striking arms; there was the awful sound of crunching bones and Avar-Ak, seventh ritual priest to Ammon-Re, was gone to his reward.

REED McGURN, still lying where he had thrown himself a moment before, threw off the spell of horror induced by the awesome sight of Conta making her kill. As he drew himself to his feet a half-naked vision of loveliness threw itself into his arms, blonde hair fell about his face as warm lips pressed wildly against his own.

"Reedmcgurn! Reedmcgurn!" sobbed the armful. "Did he hurt you? Are you dead?"

With as much gentleness as possible considering the circumstances, McGurn pushed the frantic girl away. "Take it easy, will you?" he begged. "There's a lioness over there. Do you want her to start on us next?"

She shrank away then, remembering.

Together, the man and the woman stood facing Conta, the lioness. The great cat stood motionless as a statue above the mangled body of her kill, her yellow eyes slitted in appraisal of the hated humans, low menacing growls rising from her cavernous chest.

"She is warning us away," Lua whispered. "Conta has made her kill; if we wait longer she may think we wish to take it from her, and charge us."

The American gripped the Webley tighter. "What do we do about it?"

"Back slowly away, watching Conta carefully. If she takes a single step toward us, turn and run for the trees."

"Gotcha."

The word was unfamiliar to Lua, but its tone told her he understood. And so the two of them began a cautious retreat. Conta watched them with unwavering attention until they disappeared within the jungle, then lowered her great weight across the body of her kill and began to feed.

Around a bend of the elephant path McGurn halted and mopped his forehead with an unsteady forearm. "Wow... They don't look that big in zoos."

Since he spoke in his own tongue Lua understood he was talking for his own benefit—a habit peculiar to men. She said. "Where were you going, Reedmcgurn?"

He smiled down at her. "To hunt for food. Meat."

"Good, I will go with you."

"What about that—what did you call it? Kraga?"

"No, this one was Conta. Kraga is her mate. Kraga always has a thick mane; Conta none at all. We will hunt in another direction."

Kraga, the lion. Conta, the lioness. A fine distinction but probably an important one. McGurn filed the information with his growing fund of cave people's words.

He said, "I'd still like to know what happened to Kraga. What kind of power was there in that tube to dissolve him completely?"

"What are you talking about?" Lua asked, bewildered. "Kraga was not there—only Conta."

"Don't tell me that," McGurn said flatly. "I saw it happen."

Whereupon he recounted the scene he had witnessed before Lua arrived. When he finished, she looked at him intently to learn if he were joking. "Such a thing is not possible," she declared with complete finality.

"That's what I keep telling myself," McGurn said ruefully. He ran a hand through his hair, his expression thoughtful. "Tell you what," he said. "I'm going back and get that—that weapon of his. Give England a few hundred like it and the war would be over in a week."

That last sentence meant nothing to Lua. But the first one did. "Conta would kill you. There is none in all the jungle who disturbs Conta when she feeds."

"There is now." McGurn made certain the Webley was in working order, then turned to his companion. "You stay here. I'll be back in a few moments."

Lua lowered her lashes meekly. "I will wait, Reedmcgurn."

He blinked at her bowed head. One thing about the cave men: they really knew how to train their women. Taught them to be—ah—submissive. That was the word. He patted her lightly on one bare shoulder, then turned and went toward the clearing.

At the edge of the cleared ground he paused to watch Conta, a hundred yards away, bolting pieces of the late Avar-Ak. The cloth-wrapped bundle lay where he had put it before blasting Kraga, the lion, into nothingness. Nearby, half-hidden among long grasses, was the section of tubing Reed McGurn wanted to get his hands on.

AFTER a moment's thought he decided to fire a shot or two over Conta's head in hopes the loud reports would scare her away. While he hated to waste ammunition, he figured acquiring that tube would more than repay its cost.

Aiming carefully at a point a few feet above the feeding cat, McGurn fired two rapid shots.

Reason told McGurn Conta's reaction would be either anger or fear; if the former, the cat would charge him, whereupon he would vault into the branches of a nearby tree; if the latter, Conta would run away, leaving the mysterious tube unguarded.

There was nothing wrong with McGurn's logic; but lions are not bound by the rules laid down by the logicians. Without rising from Avar-Ak's remains Conta turned her head, gave the American a long level stare…then turned back and resumed feeding.

McGurn muttered a word that had to do with Conta's parentage and replaced the two used cartridges from his dwindling supply. Since frightening the lioness away seemed impractical, he was left with the alternative of driving her from the vicinity by force. With great care he leveled the Webley, aiming at the juncture of shoulder and side. With infinite care he began to apply pressure to the trigger.

At that moment Conta rose to her feet and without a backward glance melted into the overhanging foliage.

Slowly McGurn let the unfired gun drop to his side and pent-up breath escaped his lips in a long sigh. Go figure out a lion! Evidently Conta had filled her belly, thus ending her interest in the corpse and McGurn and everything else in the neighborhood.

His lips curling in a wry grin, McGurn hurried across the clearing. Averting his eyes from Avar-Ak's grisly remains, he stooped and caught up the length of tubing, handling it with extreme care.

It was then that Conta, uttering a horrible scream, tore from the concealing undergrowth and charged upon the man in her path…

McGurn was completely trapped. No time to draw his gun and get home an effective shot. Blindly he swung up the length of tubing, his forefinger pressed frantically against a tiny knob set in one side…and Conta, the lioness, already at the peak of her final leap, vanished from sight.

The incredible weapon dropped from nerveless fingers as McGurn's knees gave beneath him, and the young flier crumpled to earth in a shaking heap of overwrought nerves. Dry sobs shook his broad shoulders and his nails bit deep in his palms as he sought to gain control of his twitching body.

A faint sound behind him brought him to his feet and around in a single rapid movement…to stare into the awed eyes of Lua, daughter of Yortak. At sight of her blonde beauty McGurn began to laugh uncontrollably.

She continued to watch him soberly until he was himself again. "I saw it," she said falteringly. "I saw Conta go into nothing at the moment she was about to tear you into little pieces. You are a powerful god from Oru, the sun, come down to find a mate, just as Old Mentak said. What will it be like to be the mate of a god? I am afraid."

"If you are afraid," McGurn said, straight-faced, "why did you not run away when you saw Conta vanish, thus proving me a god?"

A wave of red stained Lua's cheeks but her eyes never wavered from his. "I do not know," she whispered. "Unless it is because one cannot run away from a god."

But Reed McGurn knew the real reason and it set up a strange conflict within him. She was very beautiful and even more desirable, but she was also a savage—a cave-dwelling dame who probably would be fat and flabby in another few years, who probably had belonged to half a dozen wild men already. He had a brief, vivid picture of himself leading this untamed girl into Base and explaining to the Captain that this was the future Mrs. Reed McGurn… His shoulders rose slightly in an involuntary gesture of cringing.

"Forget it," he said, his voice almost harsh. Stooping, he caught up the length of metal tubing and held it out for the girl to see. "I'm no god, Lua. If anything is it's this thing. The poor old guy Conta killed had it first. Maybe he was a god."

"Conta could not kill a god," Lua said stiffly.

"Yeah. Yeah, I guess you're right," McGurn lowered his gaze to the strange object and he fell to examining it. It was fashioned of some unfamiliar grayish white metal, resembling somewhat an eighteenth-century pistol stripped of trigger, hammer, and all other moving parts. A panel set in the slightly curved grip caught McGurn's eye and he discovered it would slide back on tiny grooves. With the aid of his pocket flashlight he peered into the grip's interior, finding there a simple mechanism consisting of two marble-sized bits of golden-hued rock suspended on rods with a shielding slab of what appeared to be lead between them. A moment's experimentation showed McGurn that pressing the exterior knob raised the lead screen. Evidently exposing the two bits of rock set up some sort of reaction resulting in a release of disintegrating rays, McGurn, who was no scientist, gave up at this point. He did notice that the weapon was lined with a lead-like substance identical with that of the screen between the bits of stone. Another feature was the bell-shaped muzzle—so shaped probably to permit the rays a wider field of destruction.

IT WOULD have taken an unusual person to resist trying out this unique engine of destruction, and Reed McGurn laid no claim to such distinction. Leveling the flaring muzzle at a section of nearby jungle, he touched the release button. Instantly a circular section of bushes, vines, creepers and tree boles melted into thin air, leaving a smooth-lined tunnel six or eight feet in circumference and possibly one hundred and fifty feet in depth in the forest wall. This space endured for only a moment; then a rain of loosened foliage from above began to close the break…

"Run!" shouted McGurn, pointing wildly at the overhanging forest top.

Together, the American and his cave girl companion fled across the clearing while a great jungle patriarch, its base gone under the impact of those rays, toppled in slow majesty toward the open ground.

There was an awe-inspiring crash as it struck, its top branches missing by scarce a dozen feet the fleeing couple.

When it was evident no more trees were going to fall, McGurn and the girl retraced their steps. What was left of Avar-Ak was mercifully covered by a mound of broken branches and crushed greenery; and it required several minutes of squeamish prodding among the foliage before the young flier located the cloth-wrapped bundle he sought. Dragging it into the open, McGurn squatted down and plunged his hands into its interior.

He came up with three fresh tunics dyed a blue so light that at a distance it would appear white. "Too small for me," he said, grinning, "but I'll bet you'd be a knockout in one of 'em."

Lua shook her blonde head with puzzled exasperation as she usually did when he spoke to her in his strange sounding language, and reached past him to take a queerly shaped metal object from inside the bundle. Frowning, McGurn took it from her hand and fell to examining it.

Another weapon, he decided. It was shaped very much like his Webley Service revolver, with a round ball in place of a cylinder for bullets and a small button set on the inner curve of the butt. Evidently in grasping the weapon for use the fingers were spread to permit the button to emerge between two of them. Should the user wish to discharge it, he had only to shift one finger slightly to press that button. The whole works was of the same gray-white metal used in the ray gun, and, like the former, appeared to be much lighter in weight than its bulk indicated. Unlike the ray gun, however, there was no panel to permit entry to its interior. Either it was reloaded through its pinhole muzzle or did not require reloading at all.

McGurn drew a careful bead on a nearby sapling and pressed down on the button. As with the ray gun there was no sound, no streak of fire or gaseous discharge from igniting powder. But in the sapling's thin trunk appeared a tiny hole as clean and straight as though a hatpin had been thrust into it. The hole, McGurn found, went completely through the sapling, as well as through a six-foot tree trunk twenty feet behind it.

A smile twisting one corner of his lips McGurn thrust the weapon into the waistband of his trousers and returned to Avar-Ak's cloth-wrapped pack. From it he brought out a six-inch length of that same metal in the shape of a square tipped knife with a handle almost a foot long. The knife's cutting edge was remarkably sharp and almost at once McGurn recognized its function.

"A razor, by heavens! I'd rather have this than that ray gun!"

"What are you saying Reedmcgurn?" asked Lua, wonderingly. "Does the little knife please you so much?"

"You'll see," he said evasively. "What else is in there?"

"Some kind of bag," she said. "So heavy I cannot lift it."

HE pushed past her and, with an effort, brought to light a fair-sized cloth bag, its mouth drawn tight by a cord laced through the material, and from which issued a clanking sound as he let it drop to the ground.

"Sounds like a sack of washers," he observed. Releasing the cord, he reached in and brought out a handful of gilt pieces, each about the size of an American twenty-five-cent coin. Both sides of each bore raised figures: one was that of a nude, beautifully formed man; the other an intricate symbol unfamiliar to McGurn.

"Looks like some kind of money," muttered McGurn. "Wonder what he expected to spend it on in this Godforsaken place."

He tossed the coins back into the bag, closed it and reached once more into the bundle. All that was left was something very heavy, wrapped in many thicknesses of cloth. Removing them disclosed a statuette perhaps two feet in length, apparently carved from solid gold by a craftsman who possessed an uncanny skill in such work to judge from this example. It was a man's figure, with a face of extraordinary handsomeness, slender but muscular, arms folded across its chest.

But was it made of gold? The hue was clearly golden, but from the entire length of the figure emanated a strange glowing radiance, which seemed to pulse, to contract and expand at regular intervals. This gave to the figure an eerie appearance of life—as though the insensate metal were breathing. A strange prickling sensation flowed through McGurn's fingers as he touched the thing, causing him to release it hurriedly.

"I've seen this before someplace," McGurn told the girl. And then understanding dawned in his face. Quickly he reached into the bag of coins and brought one out. The man's figure on it was an exact replica of that luminous statuette!

Reed McGurn stared at the image for a long moment, then shrugged lightly, dismissing its importance—at least to him. "Not a bad haul," he said in the language Lua did not understand. He smiled at her baffled expression. "Let us take these things to our caves," he said in the tongue she had taught him. "It may be that some day they will be useful to us."

Refilling the bag he swung it to his shoulder and together Reed McGurn and Lua, daughter of Yortak, retraced their steps through the matted jungle.

And from the dark depths of foliage nearby, smoldering, deep-set eyes watched them go and a cunning brain plotted revenge.

CHAPTER NINE
Treachery

DAWN found the white metal dyark carrying the princess Athora drifting slowly due south along the uneven coast of Afrota. Here, near the juncture of water and land a high fog obscured the newly risen sun and enabled a second dyark, several thousand feet above and behind the first, to remain hidden from chance observance by anyone aboard the princess' craft.

Fargolt, at the controls placed behind Athora and her handmaiden, said, "There appears to be no landing place this near the water O princess of the dark hair. We should swing further inland."

Athora sighed. There were faint shadows beneath those lovely gray-green eyes—shadows left by a sleepless night and a wave of homesickness for the palace and its people, for her friends and for her father—a father who was willing to give her to a man an entire world hated…

"Yes," she said in answer to the pilot's question. "Turn into the east, Fargolt. If nothing else I shall not be forced to look longer at that hateful water."

The man's hands flipped two levers simultaneously and the long, low, bullet-shaped airship swung at a sharp angle to the left. Below a vast unbroken land of towering trees and impenetrable jungle began to unwind behind them like a limitless tapestry of many colors. Far to the east were towering dark masses of cloud-enshrouded mountain peaks like silent and forbidding sentinels.

An hour drifted by, seeming to move with the same low deliberation as that of the dyark, while the eyes of all within the cabin peered down through the unshuttered openings on either side. It was Rhodia's sharp eyes that saw it first.

"Look, my princess!" she exclaimed, pointing at something below and to the right. "A large plain. And there are animals of some kind that are grazing there."

"Tao, the deer, I think," Athora said, peering at the tiny dots below. "Land there, Fargolt; at least we shall be able to have our breakfast on solid ground."

Like a giant leaf settling to earth on a still day the dyark slipped gently downward in an almost vertical line. So perfectly controlled was the heavy ship that its keel sank to a stop among the long grasses without the slightest jar.

Fargolt hurried forward, swung open the release hatch, and followed the princess and her maid to the ground. In the distance were a score of bobbing heads that rapidly receded from view as a family of frightened deer bolted for safety.

Several hours passed before Athora signified she was ready to continue the journey. Once more the great dyark lifted into the sky—a sky cleared now of all clouds and morning haze as Oru, the sun, neared its zenith. The mountains to the east were clearly visible now, standing out bold and grim to bar their path.

Not long after they were back in the air, Athora uttered a low-voiced exclamation and pointed to something to her left. "A cliff!" she said happily. "With a cleared section of ground at its base. Perhaps we can find deserted caves there."

Instantly Fargolt changed the course and the ship raced in its new direction. This done, he said, "If there should be caves in that cliff, my princess, it is more than likely that they are inhabited by Klysan.* I suggest that, once we land, you and Rhodia remain in the cabin until I make sure you will be safe."

"A better way, Fargolt," Athora said, "would be to hover above the clearing for a while before landing. If we see any of the Klysan we can look elsewhere for shelter."

---

*Klysan—literally. "Beast-men."-Ed.

"But that might take days, my princess," the pilot protested. "With a single huar I can wipe out an entire tribe of them without danger to us."

The girl shook her head. "I have no wish to stay in a place surrounded by heaps of corpses. Please do as I say."

Fargolt flushed at her tone but offered no further remonstrance. Gradually the ship sank lower while its pilot cut its speed to hardly more than a crawl. Finally the dyark came to a complete stop less than fifty feet above the clearing at the base of the cliff, while three pairs of eyes scanned the open ground and the face of the almost vertical scarp.

"No sign of life," Fargolt announced at last. "We are in luck, my princess."

Athora's expression showed her relief. "You may land, Fargolt."

THE craft settled lightly to earth a short distance from the cliff. At his own suggestion Fargolt explored several of the caves while the women remained aboard. Finally he slid to level ground, slipped his sandals back on his feet and returned to the dyark.

"They have been empty for a long time," he said. "If you like, I can run a rope ladder to one of the larger caves and store our supplies in it."

Athora agreed to the suggestion and Fargolt fell to work while the two women wandered slowly about the stretch of open ground. Shortly thereafter they came upon a tiny spring not far from the cliff itself, and a moment later Rhodia uttered a sharp exclamation.

"Look, Athora," she said, pointing to a spot near the spring. "Ashes from a recent fire. This place isn't deserted after all..."

Fargolt, attracted by Rhodia's cry, came over quickly, his huar drawn and ready. At sight of the heap of ashes, he dropped to his knees and went over the neighboring ground with quick efficiency.

"Two people," he said. "One a girl; the marks of her bare feet show her to be one of the Klysan. The other marks, judging from their size, are from the feet of a man who wears some strange kind of sandal."

"Have they been here recently?" Athora asked.

"Within a few lats, I think." He rose to his feet. "I think it would be wise, my princess, for you and Rhodia to remain within the dyark until I have finished moving our supplies to your cave."

"I'm not going to stay hidden because of a single man and his woman," Athora said sharply. "Let me take one of your huars, Fargolt, and go on with your work. I can take care of myself and Rhodia."

"As you wish, O princess of the dark hair," Fargolt said, shrugging. He handed the weapon to her, then turned and went back to the dyark.

The two girls wandered slowly about the clearing, their steps leading them eventually to the mouth of a game trail that led into the dark forest. Rhodia shivered a little at sight of the miasmic place, but Athora's reaction was different.

"How beautiful it is," she murmured, her eyes roving about the tangle of vines and creepers laden with huge colorful blooms and fragile ferns. "Do you realize, Rhodia, that this is the first time I've been near a jungle even though most of Atland is nothing more than that? Whenever I've left Atlantis it has been by dyark, high above the forest. Let's follow this path for a little way."

"You mustn't, Athora," protested Rhodia, drawing back instinctively. "It is in such places that the big cats hunt their food, and there are great snakes as long as our dyark that could crush you in their folds, and the flying things whose sting means death. No, let us go back."

"Nothing's going to hurt us," Athora said impatiently. Her cheeks were glowing and her gray-green eyes flashing at the heady thought of adventure. "As long as I have this huar nothing can harm us. Are you coming with me or must I do it alone?"

Loyalty proved stronger than fear and, trembling visibly, Rhodia followed her mistress into the murky depths of the jungle. Above them chattered a family of long-tailed monkeys, birds screeched and rustled over their heads, a cloud of insects buzzed in their ears, and a huge scorpion scuttled unseen from under Athora's descending foot.

After covering perhaps a hundred yards and several turns in the winding trail, Rhodia's small store of courage was gone. "Let us turn back, Athora," she pleaded. "There is nothing to see that we have not seen already. Besides, Fargolt will miss us and be worried."

The princess, recognizing how much her companion was disturbed, relented. "Only as far as the next bend," she promised. "Then we'll go back."

Since it meant no more than a dozen yards, if that, Rhodia agreed, and the two girls went on.

It was at this point that Reed McGurn and Lua rounded the bend and came face to face with the Atlandian women.

Shocked surprise froze the four of them for an instant; then McGurn, unconsciously prepared for anything after three days of constant danger, regained control of his senses. Noticing the weapon hanging from a limp hand of the foremost woman, McGurn jerked the Webley from its holster and leveled it at her.

"Stick 'em, sister," he growled.

The words, spoken in English, meant nothing to either Athora or her companion. But there was no mistaking their meaning, and both shrank back in fear, the huar falling from Athora's nerveless fingers.

WITH a single, lithe movement McGurn stepped forward, scooped up the weapon, and drew back again. Now that he was master of the situation he took time to look over his captives.

Both were very beautiful, but the dark-haired one with a thin purple stripe at the border of her tunic-like dress was absolutely the most ravishing creature McGurn had met in a life replete with lovely creatures. Not only were her features and body beyond perfection, but the regal set to her slim shoulders and in the proud tilt of her head told him he was in the presence of royalty.

In English, McGurn said. "Who are you and where are you from?"

Athora, staring fixedly at him, felt fear flow from her. This square-faced, curly-haired, handsome young man was no Klysan, nor was he a native of Clyrus, the only two kinds of men she had reason to fear. The fact, all too evident in his speech, manner of dress and general appearance, that he was like no human she had ever heard of caused her a measure of uneasiness but nothing that bordered on panic. While the girl with him was obviously a

Klysan, it meant nothing; probably he had taken her by force far his own purposes.

The princess smiled breathtakingly. "I am Athora, daughter of Ashtoth," she said. "I have never seen a man like you before. Where is your country?"

Enough of her words were intelligible to the American to enable him to understand what she was saying; for she spoke in the same language Lua had taught him. There were minor differences; tricks of inflection to some of the words that made them seem strange to the ear even as they were being understood, while others were evidently expanded from root words of the cave dweller's language.

He said, "I have two names. The first is Reed; the second, McGurn. My friends call me Reed."

"I, too, will call you Reed," Athora said smiling again. "Where do you live? Are there others like you? Is this Klysan your mate? Or do you live with the Klysans? What is the strange thing you have in your hand? What are—?"

"One at a time," McGurn protested, laughing. "I'm from the U. S.—United States, that is. You know where that is, don't you?"

He knew what her answer would be before she made it. Some time back—whether an hour or a day before—Reed McGurn had come to the conclusion that he was in a world within a world—the first invisible and on a different plane from the second. As an explanation it made no sense whatsoever to him, but neither did this land of jungles and wild men and beautiful women.

Athora repeated the name of his native land with an awkwardness that lent it a peculiar charm. "I have never heard of such a country," she said. "There is no such place."

"I guess you're right," McGurn admitted ruefully. "Although I'd have sworn I was born and raised there. How about England or France or Germany? Europe, Africa, Asia? Those names mean anything to you?"

The princess was staring at him strangely. "Most of them do not. But two… Did you say Af-ri-ca?"

"Africa… Sure. What do you know about Africa?"

"The name is much like that of this land—Afrota."

McGurn scratched his head, frowning. "Africa is mostly jungles, too. Pretty strong coincidence. Any of those other names I gave you sound familiar?"

She nodded slowly. "There is an unexplored land far to the north of Afrota. It is called Uropa, although none of my people knows anything about it, other than it is very cold there."

"Uropa!" exclaimed McGurn aghast. "Why, that's the old name for Europe—a name nobody's used for thousands of years. And Europe is north of Africa."

Like a blinding light a theory had popped into his mind—a theory so utterly fantastic that his brain reeled under it. Had he, by some strange freak of fate, been thrown back into Time—back to the days of Cro-Magnon Man, as evidenced by those paintings on the cave walls? Both Lua and the half-naked man he had saved her from came close to fitting descriptions of that long-dead race…

HE CHANGED the subject abruptly, as though to escape from the forgotten world his thoughts were taking him to.

"Do you live around here, Athora? I mean, is Africa—Afrota—your country?"

The princess' expression became slightly haughty. "Do I look as though I were one of the Klysan? I am the daughter of Ashtoth—king of Atland."

"Is that good? I mean, where and what is Atland?"

"Atland," explained Athora, "is a land that lies west of Afrota. There is a great place of water between Afrota and Atland. In my land the people no longer live in caves as do the Klysan. We live in mighty cities and wear clothing instead of animal skins. We have learned how to make many things—things that place us far above the cave people. In our dyarks we cover in yads what the Klysan takes moons to travel. With our huars and xorths we can slay thousands of Klysans without being harmed ourselves. We are the children of Ammon-Re; the Klysans are beasts of the jungle compared to us."

It sounded very impressive, and Reed McGurn understood about half of it. But Lua, daughter of Yortak, understood it all. From the moment she and Reed McGurn had come upon these two strange women her anger had been growing. The beauty of the princess was as evident to her as it was to McGurn; and when she saw them laughing and talking together as though they were old friends, the milk of human kindness in her began to curdle. While she did not consciously shape the thought in her mind she felt that Reed McGurn was hers; and the sudden wave of anger that engulfed her at Athora's sneering reference to her people as "Klysan" was largely plain, old-fashioned jealousy.

With a lithe movement she was standing in front of Reed McGurn, and before the latter could grasp what was happening, she turned the full impact of her anger on the astonished princess.

"Go away," she cried. "We did not ask you to come here. This is my country and we do not need or want the things you talk about. Go away at once or I will call my people and they will kill you…"

Athora's reaction to the outburst changed from surprise to cold fury. "Beast-woman," she snarled. "How dare you speak so to Ashtoth's daughter? Let *this* teach you your place…"

With these words she brought up her hand and lashed a savage slap at the cave girl's cheek, the blow landing heavily before McGurn's instinctive lunge to stop it could succeed.

It took a couple of minutes and the cost of some of his own skin to keep the two girls apart. The tactics of both would have been in keeping with the best traditions of any New York nightclub brawl and, like any modern-day escort, McGurn bore the brunt of it all. Rhodia sought to help him, but he discovered most of her efforts were aimed ungently at driving Lua back and so he was forced to keep her away as well.

At last the melee ended, more from lack of breath than McGurn's efforts. The four of them stood there, silent and panting, angry and frustrated and, in McGurn's case, half amused. It was at this moment that Fargolt, alarmed at the absence of Athora and Rhodia, rounded the bend of the trail and came upon them.

At sight of the stranger facing Athora and her handmaid his huar came up, and Reed McGurn might have died at that moment had not the princess, warned by an expression of fear on Lua's face, whirled about and caught a glimpse of the leveled weapon.

"No, Fargolt!" she cried. "He is a friend."

The pantar lowered the huar's muzzle but kept it ready in his hand as he came toward the group. His chill eyes went over McGurn, noting his odd dress and the peculiar weapon at his belt. There was a huar thrust within the folds of his strange garment as well, and a bulging sack resting on the ground at his feet.

"There are no friends in the jungle, Athora," he said stiffly. "Stand aside that I may kill him."

His assumption that the stranger would not understand his words was based on the other's peculiar clothing and the obvious fact that he was of another race. He was completely unprepared, therefore, when McGurn whipped out his Webley and pointed it at him.

"If there's going to be any killing," the American said shortly. "I'll do it."

FARGOLT dropped the huar as though it was white hot and he fell back a pace in open fear. Lua darted forward before anyone realized what she was up to and caught up the fallen weapon. Without a second's hesitation she wheeled and, aiming squarely at Athora's swelling breast, fired!

McGurn's swinging arm was all that saved Ashtoth's daughter from instant death, flame from the deflected barrel passing a hand's breadth from her fear-stiffened figure. He tore the huar from Lua's fingers. "You little cat. Cut it out before I smack you one."

Lua did not understand his words but the tone was enough, and she drew back, hurt and humiliated. For a moment a strained silence hung over the five of them—a silence broken by the princess.

"I like you, Reed McGurn," she said with disarming frankness. "You shall come with us to Atlantis and live in my father's palace."

One of those words hit the young American like a thrown brick. "Atlantis!" he cried. "Atlantis… Are you from Atlantis?"

Athora gaped at him. "Of course. Then you know of my country?"

"Know of it? Listen, one of us is crazy and I'm beginning to think it's me. Atlantis sank into the Atlantic thousands of years ago…"

But even as he said the words he knew the incredible truth. He had gone back in Time—back to the days of Cro-Magnon Man and the contemporary people of fabled Atlantis. He stood there in the jungle path, confused and shaken, his mind washed clear of everything but the horror of what had happened to him.

As for Athora, she was no less shaken than the strange young man. From the first moment of their meeting she had been attracted to him—more so than for any man she had ever known. And now to learn that he was completely mad…

"Come," she said, placing a soft hand on his arm. "Come with us to the caves where we have camped. You need food and rest—a great deal of rest."

Her hand urged him gently along and he followed numbly, only dimly aware of what was going on. Rhodia and Fargolt followed, the latter already seeking to hit on some way of getting rid of this intruder.

Lua, forgotten by them all, stood forlornly in the trail and watched them go. A jagged lump seemed to form in her throat as she watched Reed McGurn being led away by another woman—a hateful, cruel, bad-tempered, *beautiful* woman. And he was going without a backward glance at the girl who had befriended him from loneliness…the girl he had taken in his arms and whose lips had welcomed his kisses.

A sudden rush of scalding tears filled her eyes and she turned blindly away, going she knew not where…

A pounding of feet along the trail behind her came to her ears and she wheeled just in time to be caught up in Reed McGurn's arms.

"What's got into you," he growled, "leaving me like this?"

Lua's smile was half tears. "Don't go with her, Reedmcgurn," she whispered. "Stay here in the jungle with me. We can be happy togeth—"

"You're not making sense," he said. "This place would get us both within a few suns. From what Athora says, her country is—" He stopped there, searching vainly for some word in her language that meant "civilized." "Listen," he concluded, "are you coming with me peacefully or do I have to carry you?"

"I will go with you, Reedmcgurn," she whispered; and the joy in her heart was strangely weighted with a foreboding of evil to come.

"Good. We must not keep them waiting."

They started off to join the three tunic-clad figures watching them in the trail ahead when Lua caught him by the arm. "Wait," she said, pointing. "Are you not going to take that with you?"

McGurn saw Avar-Ak's bag laying in the trail where he had dropped it when coming face to face with the Atlandian women. He nodded, took up the bag, and swung it across a shoulder. "Let's go," he said, leading the way.

A few moments after the party of five had passed from view, the bushes parted at one side of the trail and a half-naked, powerfully built cave man stepped soundlessly into the open. For a full minute he stood there as though turned to stone, head bent in a listening attitude, then slunk soundlessly along the path in guarded pursuit of the man he hated and the girl he knew he meant to have.

CHAPTER TEN
From Jungle Depths

NIGHT had come upon the jungle. From the distant depths of impenetrable wilderness came the fearsome challenge of hunting beasts, the notes reaching the ears of a group of five humans huddled about a roaring fire at the base of a towering cliff, its side dotted with cave openings. A short distance from where they sat, bulking huge and black in the light of the flickering fire, was the dyark that had brought three of them to this lonely spot.

Reed McGurn tossed into the fire the bone from which he had been gnawing the flesh of Bato, the zebra. He wiped his hands on a clump of jungle grasses and sighed with replete satisfaction. "No Soho supper club ever served a better dish," he said, smacking his lips.

Athora made a move of disapproval. "I do wish you wouldn't talk in that strange language," she complained. "What did you say?"

"Only that I never enjoyed food so much in my own country."

"Tell me about your country, Reed McGurn."

And so the square-faced young American told them of the Twentieth Century. They sat listening, enthralled by the picture he painted with words—swords that could not do justice to his subject because the language contained little to fit it.

Only as long as he spoke of customs and personalities was he able to hold their attention—at least as far as Lua was concerned. But when he began to talk of wonders of modern science it was Athora's turn to astound *him.*

"The airplanes you speak of," she said, smiling, "are poor things indeed when compared with the dyarks of Atland and Clyrus. You depend on whirling blades and a special kind of water for power. We use rays made inside the dyark by bringing into juxtaposition two pieces of rock. By the action of one rock on the other rays are formed which activate a small mechanism controlled by levers which the pilot operates. There is no need to stop for refueling; the power from those two rocks could keep a dyark in the air a man's lifetime without once descending.

"And the 'guns' you speak of. Are they more deadly than our huars? We have a weapon even more powerful and terrible than our huars, too—although I confess I have never seen one. It is called a xorth and fires a ray that turns into nothingness anything it touches. There are only a few in existence, since the metal ore used to create that deadly ray is very scarce. It is said the rulers of Clyrus do not have its secret and would give much to learn it, for were they to have many xorths they could conquer Atland with ease.

"Too, you tell about light made in your world—so powerful it turns night into the brightness of day. We have such light—but we need no wires to take if from one place to another. In the mountains of Atland and Clyrus is a great supply of ore, which gives off blinding light when treated in a certain water made by our learned men. This light endures for many lifetimes and cannot be 'turned off' during the day but must be covered while not in use.

"From what you have said, I believe our homes and public buildings are no less splendid than those you describe. True, in height ours are as nothing compared to yours but that seems unimportant. And where you have 'ships' to travel on water, we have petrix—again not so big as those you tell about but which can go much faster and are powered by the same rays used in our dyarks."

McGurn shrugged. "Yet with all these things," he said, "the people of Atland know little of the rest of the world. You have told me the land you call Uropa has not been explored, nor has Afrota. Since your dyarks may fly for what amounts to forever without stopping, why have the men of Atland not discovered what lies beyond your horizons?"

It was bad manners, to say the least, to answer a question put to Atland's princess. But Fargolt, who had been listening to McGurn's words with rapidly mounting anger, made reply.

"Why?" he repeated hotly. "I'll tell you why. Because it would mean death to do so. Think you that we know not what lays beyond the line where sky and water meet? That is where Oru, the sun, sleeps in a valley of fire. Were a dyark to fly over that valley's edge it would be swallowed up by huge tongues of flame. That we know because Ammon-Re has told us so. And that is why we know you are lying about a great land far to the east of Atland—a land you call America. There is no such land—unless it be the country we call Oruzal, where the fire monsters lair. It may even be that *you* are from Oruzal—come to tell of fabled lands so that the men of Atland and Clyrus will go out to hunt for them and be pulled down and destroyed by the fire monsters you serve..."

SO UNEXPECTED was Fargolt's outburst that the others, including McGurn, sat with open-mouthed astonishment while he ranted on. And at his closing remarks McGurn saw doubt begin to cloud the faces of Athora and Rhodia and unconsciously both women seemed to shrink from the American.

When the pantar fell silent, more from lack of breath than anything else, McGurn gave him a long, level stare. "It would seem..." he said, and there was little doubt but that he included Athora and Rhodia in what he was saying. "...it would seem that for all her splendor, Atland is peopled by fools. Whoever this Ammon-Re is who told you such stories, I say he's a bigger fool and a liar besides. Nobody could be that stu—"

He stopped there as Fargolt's fist struck him full in the face and knocked him sprawling from where he sat beside the fire. So rapidly had the pantar acted that McGurn was given no chance to block the blow, and an instant later the two men were rolling on the ground, Fargolt seeking to fasten powerful fingers around McGurn's throat.

"Fargolt!" cried Athora, leaping to her feet. "Stop it immediately. Stop it, I tell you!"

Even had the pantar heard the command, which is doubtful, he was no longer in position to obey. McGurn, while no world-beater at catch-as-catch-can fighting, possessed more knowledge in the art of self-defense than did Fargolt. With the aid of a wrestling hold he had picked up somewhere, he tossed the Atlandian aside and gained his feet before the other could scramble erect and charge him again.

McGurn cocked his good right fist, and as the pantar, face twisted with insane rage, bore down upon him he swung a short straight blow full into the hawk-beaked nose. There was a dull *splat,* and Fargolt reeled back and fell, a crimson flood gushing from his nostrils. Before he could rise, McGurn was standing over him, fists ready, his cold blue eyes like sunlight on ice.

"Try it again, brother," he said between clenched teeth, "and I'll put that pretty nose on the back of your head."

He spoke his native tongue but his bearing and tone left no doubt of his meaning in Fargolt's dazed brain.

Athora came up to the American and put a hand on one of McGurn's muscular forearms. "Let him up," she said quietly; and when the flier obeyed, she ordered Fargolt to his feet and back to his place at the fire. The others sat down again at the princess' half command, half request; and not until then did she speak again to McGurn.

"Reed McGurn," she said, and gone from her voice and expression was the friendliness so evident a few moments before, "only because there can be no doubt that you are strange to the customs of my people may I excuse the dreadful thing you have said. Nor can I blame Fargolt for attacking you; I would have done the same were I a man."

McGurn spread his hands helplessly. "What did I say that was so bad?" he grumbled.

"You spoke evil words about Ammon-Re. Why he did not strike you down with fire from the sky is something known only to him."

"Ammon-Re?"

"Ammon-Re," she repeated in hushed tones and made the sign of the holy triangle with one finger. "Creator of all Life, Master of Death, Lord of Destiny, Ruler of the Twelve Triangles of the Universe."

"Never heard of him."

"Yet he created you, Reed McGurn. You and every man and woman and child and animal and plant; the plains and the cliffs and the air we breathe."

LIGHT dawned on the American. "I get it. Ammon-Re is your…your…" He stopped there for he had not been given the Atlandian word for "God."

"—our Creator," Athora said solemnly.

"Ammon-Re," repeated McGurn slowly. "The word *does* seem familiar, come to think about it…" Suddenly his expression cleared. "Why, sure. The ancient Egyptians used to have a god by that name."

"Egyptians?" The princess frowned. "What are they?"

"You couldn't have heard of them," McGurn said ruefully. "They are people but they won't show up in history, so far as you're concerned, for another ten or fifteen thousand years…"

"Long ago," Athora said thoughtfully, "the high priest to Ammon-Re was called Egypus, the Holy. Many of our present rites of worship were given to us by him."

"There could be a connection," McGurn admitted, shrugging. "Tell me about Ammon-Re. I suppose you have priests and temples and such."

"Yes. But more than that is the Golden God."

"Golden God?"

"Yes. It is an image of Ammon-Re, made by his own hands and given into the keeping of Atland as a sign that its people are favored above all others of the earth."

"Mighty convenient," McGurn observed dryly, "for the people of Atland. How do you know your god made this golden statue?"

He gave the word "god" its English pronunciation, as he had all along, and Athora frowned at him now, not understanding. There followed a brief discussion before the matter was straightened out; that the English word "god" meant the same as the Atlandian "Aph." Thus Aph-Oru became "God of Gold" in its literal translation. This led to a fairly lengthy discussion along ecclesiastical lines, during which McGurn learned there were many gods to fill many roles, put only two that amounted to much. These were Ammon-Re, whose name was never mentioned aloud without the speaker making the sign of the triangle with one forefinger; and Set, who, McGurn discovered, compared almost exactly with Christianity's Lucifer—the Devil.

The others about the fire were frankly bored long before the discussion was ended. To Fargolt and Rhodia this was a matter taught them from childhood; while Lua found the subject too involved to follow. The cave girl sat with her back against the cliff, her mind filled with hatred of Athora. She had not forgotten the slap dealt her by Atland's princess, nor would she ever forget. Truth of the matter was that her hatred for Athora was based on something far deeper than the indignity of a slapped face, although she did not consciously realize that. All she did know was that the longer Reed McGurn talked to Athora, the stronger his interest in her became, the deeper that insulting slap burned into Lua's memory.

As for Athora, encouraged by McGurn's complete interest and ready sympathy, she was pouring out the story of why she was in this savage land. After swearing the now aroused Fargolt to secrecy, she told of Avar-Ak's theft of the Golden God, of the fear that the holy image was now in Clyrusian hands, of Mentanek's use of it as a threat to Atland's king and high priest to force a marriage between Clyrus's king and Atland's princess, and of her own flight to prevent the match.

Fargolt, listening, fell to scheming how to turn this information to his own best interests. He saw now that it might have been better had he not taken Athora away, since conceivably his doing so had upset Sar-Gath's plans for a showdown with Ashtoth. He blessed the impulse that had caused him to send a message to the Clyrusian high priest telling of Athora's intention to flee from

Atland. Possibly a dyark had followed the princess' party to this forsaken spot on Afrota. If that were true a searching party should "find" Athora within a few hours and no harm done.

BUT a fresh problem had arisen since he landed the dyark here—a personal problem. It involved Lua, whose beauty had struck home to Fargolt's heart with stunning force. Since the moment he first laid eyes on her lovely face and softly curved form Fargolt had been torn between desire and tradition—a tradition that no human worthy of the name would mate with a member of the Klysan—the beast people who dwelt in caves and wore animal skins. Not that there was much chance of winning this one to his arms; she was clearly in love with this man from another land. Still, even that might be turned to his own advantage; for it was quite evident Athora was greatly taken by Reed McGurn—and he with her. In fact McGurn would have been a fool not to have responded, for in all the world was no woman whose love was more to be desired than that of Athora of Atland. And because the fires of jealousy were blazing in Lua's eyes, Fargolt saw his hope to win on the rebound—should the chance present itself.

"This Golden God," McGurn said, when Athora had finished her story, "have you ever seen it yourself?"

"Why yes," admitted the princess, puzzled by the question. "Once each year it is displayed during rites honoring Ammon-Re."

"Is this Golden God about so tall?" McGurn continued, spreading his hands about two feet apart. "And does it glow with a sort of strange light?"

Athora was staring at him, mingled astonishment, hope, and fear in her eyes. "Yes, yes! But how did you—"

"And," continued McGurn, smiling now, "is it shaped in the form of a man, arms folded across his chest?"

Panting, the girl sprang to her feet. "How could you know that? You are not of my country and yet—"

McGurn rose leisurely from where he sat beside the fire. "Wait here," he said and climbed up the cliffside to his cave. The others were standing now, watching him, but it was only Lua whose expression did not contain wonder.

A moment later, McGurn, an object wrapped in white cloth under one arm, slid slightly to the ground and handed Athora the parcel. "Try that for size," he suggested, his grin evident in the dancing light of the fire.

With rapid movements of unsteady fingers Athora tore away the wrappings, then cried out in awed tones as the gleaming statue was exposed. Even in the darkness it glowed with that strange pulsating brilliance McGurn had observed earlier, and giving it an unearthly beauty almost frightening to behold.

"The Golden God," whispered Athora breathlessly; and both Rhodia and Fargolt echoed the words.

The princess whirled on McGurn. "Where did you get this? Do you know that to touch the Golden God, unless you be the high priest himself, is a crime punishable by death? Do you—"

"In that case," the young American said soberly, "where does it leave you?"

"What do you mean?"

"It's in your hands right now…"

"B-b-but," she stammered. "I had to touch…" She stopped there, thinking intently for a moment, then raised her eyes and smiled at him. "What a foolish thing for me to say. I am sure there could be no punishment for recovering the Golden God and restoring it to its rightful place… How did it come into your possession, Reed McGurn?"

The American threw more branches on the fire and sat down again with Athora and the others. Briefly he recounted the adventures of the afternoon before the visitors from Atland had arrived. He made no mention of the strange weapon by which Avar-Ak had eliminated Kraga, the lion; for he remembered what Athora had said about the "xorth" as she called it. Since the ray gun was so rare, owning one might someday mean the difference between life and death for him. He knew that Fargolt hated him utterly; too, he had noticed the glances the pantar kept shooting at Lua. Although he told himself Lua meant nothing personal to him, he regarded her too highly to allow someone like the Atlandian warrior to win her.

When he was finished, Athora rewrapped the Golden God in its cloth, her fingers gentle with reverence, and rose to her feet. "It is late," she said, "and tomorrow we must be up early and on our way to Atland. Because the Golden God will be restored to its rightful place I need not be afraid to return." She smiled tenderly at McGurn. "And you shall come with us, my friend. Atland and my father will honor you for your part in recovering the holiest object in all the world. You shall become a noble of the court, the wealth of Atland will be placed at your feet, and her fairest daughters will vie for the honor of becoming your mate."

THERE was an unmistakable message in that last sentence—a meaning that set McGurn's heart to pumping even as doubt divided his mind. She was perhaps the most beautiful woman he had ever seen, her position in this strange world was the highest, with her life could go on filled with pleasure and luxury…but doubt assailed him. It was a man's prerogative to choose his own woman; and while Atland's princess might easily have been his choice were the decision left up to him, he was not ready to make that choice.

"I can hardly wait," he said lightly, and let it go at that…

An hour later the little group retired to caves in the cliffside. Athora and Rhodia shared one well above the ground; immediately below that Fargolt spread his sleeping furs for the night, while Reed McGurn and Lua took caves close by.

Slowly the night wore on, Mua, the moon, rose to flood jungle and plains with silver radiance. The great cats roamed the land, filling the night with their hideous cries.

There was a movement among the branches of a jungle giant bordering the clearing in front of the caves and the half-naked figure of a giant Cro-Magnon warrior dropped lightly to earth. His keen eyes scanned the rugged face of the escarpment, picking out those caves where the five people lay sleeping.

Bitog, fighting man of the tribe of Mosat, had come in search of his woman.

Satisfied finally that those within the caves had posted no sentry, Bitog slunk like a disembodied spirit across the moon-flooded clearing. Pausing at the cliff's base to listen again, he drew his flint knife and placed it crosswise between his teeth, then swarmed silently upward toward the mouth of the cave he had selected. He knew exactly where each member of that group was sleeping, for he had watched them enter several hours before.

With infinite stealth Bitog drew himself onto the narrow ledge outside the cave he meant to enter. For several moments he crouched there, his keen ears picking up the sound of even breathing from within—sounds that told him exactly where the girl lay sleeping. Then, lips curled in a grimace of anticipation, Bitog faded into the shadowy interior…

"Aieeeee!"

Reed McGurn woke as the shrill, high-pitched scream cut through the night. For a brief moment he lay there while his sleep-drugged mind struggled back to full consciousness.

"Aieeeeee!"

With a startled oath the American leaped to his feet and raced to the stone lip of his cave. He was just in time to see the burly figure of a cave man slip to the clearing and go bounding toward the forest, a struggling figure across one broad shoulder. His hand shot to his hip, only to come away empty. The Webley lay beside his couch of branches where he had left it; and even as he cursed his thoughtlessness he knew he would not have dared fire for fear of hitting the cave man's victim.

Already the others were swarming from their caves, but before any of them could do more than cry out in alarm, Bitog was gone, the jungle having swallowed him up like a pebble tossed into an angry sea.

It was a sober and silent group who stood at the foot of the cliff, staring into each other's anguished faces…a group made up of McGurn, Fargolt, Rhodia, and Lua. Somewhere in the jungle darkness was Athora, daughter of Ashtoth, in the brutal hands of a cave man.

Only Lua could furnish a clue to the kidnaper's identity. "It must have been Bitog," she told them. "He must have been stalking Reedmcgurn and me since the night I escaped him. Because of the darkness he took Athora believing her to be me."

Rhodia, tears streaming down her cheeks, caught Fargolt by the arm. "Go after her, Fargolt! Find her before it is too late…"

THE pantar pulled away roughly. "How would you expect me to find her? Have I the eyes of Kraga, to follow that wild man at night? We can do nothing. Athora is as good as dead right now as far as we're concerned."

McGurn gave him a contemptuous glance. "Atland must have a great army if it's made up of warriors like you."

"What would you suggest?" Fargolt said hotly. "Maybe you'd like to go tramping around in that jungle, trying to find her."

"Like it or not," McGurn said, "that's exactly what I'm going to do..."

Turning, he clambered quickly up to his cave, returning a moment later with his Webley and the huar in his belt and the xorth in one hand. At sight of that latter weapon Fargolt's eyes widened.

"A xorth!" he exclaimed. "Where did you get it?"

"What difference does it make? Listen, here's what I want you to do. Stay here with the women until dawn. Then take that airship of yours and cruise above the trail over there until you spot me. This Klysan, as you call him, who took Athora, will have to follow it. I may be able to pick up his trail. If I find him I'll keep him in sight until you show up or until I get a chance to take a shot at him without hitting the princess. If I can't find him, you pick me up and we'll go to Atland and bring back an army."

"By that time," Fargolt said gloomily. "Athora will be dead—or worse."

"There's nothing worse than dead. Forget this 'a fate worse than death' stuff and do as I tell you. Understand?"

"Yes," said Fargolt sullenly.

"All right." Without further word McGurn turned and started across the moonlit clearing, his goal the mouth of the elephant path.

"Wait! Wait for me, Reedmcgurn!"

The American wheeled about just as Lua came racing to join him. "I am going with you," she declared.

"You'll do nothing of the sort," he snapped. Then, his voice suddenly gentle: "Listen to me, Lua. To take you along would slow me down. I know you are more at home in the jungle than I, but you're still a girl and I would have to take care of you. Go on back to Fargolt and make sure he carries out the orders I gave him. Here—" He handed her the huar from his belt. "Take this and don't let go of it. I don't trust that pantar any farther than I could throw Pakar, the elephant, but I have no choice. If he tries any funny stuff, drill him."

Much of the mixture of two languages was lost on Lua, but enough came through for adequate comprehension. She took the huar without another word and was turning to retrace her steps when Reed McGurn reached out, caught her about the waist, and planted a light kiss on her full lips.

"That's for luck," he said, releasing her. An instant later he was gone.

CHAPTER ELEVEN
Kidnapped to Clyrus

FARGOLT and Rhodia were standing at the foot of the cliff as Lua came slowly back to join them. At sight of the huar she was holding, Fargolt put out his hand to take it, saying:

"You won't need that, Lua. Let me have it. I shall stay on guard the balance of the night."

The cave girl gave a curt shake of her head. "No, Reedmcgurn told me to use it for my own protection."

Fargolt blinked. "But I am here to protect you…"

Lua had never been one to practice diplomacy. "Reedmcgurn says I may need protection against you…"

The pantar's outstretched hand fell to his side. "Why, that's not true. I would not harm you for anything in the world. In fact I—I—"

A glimpse of Rhodia's blazing eyes and set jaw stopped him there. It had been only a short while ago that he was saying such a thing to Athora's handmaiden. That had been different however. Then he said such things for a purpose: to win the trust and confidence of some member of the royal family in hopes of obtaining information of value to Clyrus.

"You had best retire, Rhodia," he said smoothly. "We must leave early and there will be little time for sleep before dawn."

The woman ignored him. "Come, Lua," she said kindly. "Let us spend the balance of the night together."

"Wait…" Fargolt, his conciliatory attitude forgotten, stepped between them. "Lua remains here with me. I have something to say to her—alone."

In answer, Lua brought up the huar's muzzle and pointed it at the Atlandian's chest. "Get out of my way or I will kill you…"

"But, Lua, I—"

The girl's finger came down lightly on the weapon's firing button, and in that action and the sudden tightening of her lips Fargolt knew another second's delay on his part would result in his death.

And so he stepped hastily aside and in another moment he was alone, Rhodia and Lua having entered the former's cave.

For more than an hour Fargolt remained at the foot of the cliff, his active brain sorting over one plan after another. He thought of the lovely cave girl asleep on her bed of skins and of how he wanted her. He thought, too, of that golden image somewhere in that same cave, and of the power possession of it would give him. And as he squatted there, thinking, eyes fixed unseeingly on the dark depths of jungle a short distance away, a plan began to form in his mind—a dangerous plan but one well worth a great deal of danger…

With the final shaping of that plan came an impatience to put it into action; but he fought down the impulse, realizing haste would cost him success—even his life. And so he permitted another hour to drag by while he sat unmoving, and Mua, the moon, sank lower in the heavens, leaving the face of the cliff in heavy shadow.

Finally Fargolt got stiffly to his feet, shivering a little in the cool damp air, and made his way to the dyark's cabin. From a locker in one wall he took a brace of huars and thrust them into his belt. Turning, he descended to the ground and returned to the cliff. With great care he picked his way up the almost vertical incline, pausing at last on the narrow ledge outside the cave where Lua and Rhodia lay sleeping. At least he hoped they were sleeping; had they decided to spell each other as sentries during the remainder of the night, he was doomed. Neither would hesitate for a moment in killing him the moment he put a foot within their cave.

For a little while he stood there flattened against the cliffside while his ears strained to catch the sound of even breathing from within. Satisfied at last that both were sleeping, he lowered himself to hands and knees and slowly, with many pauses, inched his way into the cave. Gradually his eyes grew accustomed to the dim light enabling him to make out two low mounds of furs at the cave's extreme rear, and it was toward those mounds that he worked his way.

Twice he flattened himself convulsively against the bare rock floor as one of the sleepers stirred, only to go on again as quiet returned. Finally he had reached a position directly between the two of them, and now he came lightly to his feet, a huar in his right hand.

STRAINING his eyes to their utmost he was able to make out the tousled blonde hair and a bare shoulder that identified the girl on his left as Lua, daughter of Yortak. A cruel smile twisting at the corners of his thin lips, Fargolt leveled the muzzle of his huar at the covering of furs outlining Rhodia's slender form. His finger was already on its way down to the firing button when sudden doubt assailed him.

Might not the flash of fire from the huar's muzzle awaken Lua? He knew these Klysans could move with incredible speed when once aroused. There was a better way…

A single silent step brought Rhodia's dark hair within reach. Reversing his hold on the huar, he swung its metal butt up and back, then brought it down with controlled force against the exposed temple.

There was a barely audible thump, a slight involuntary twitching of muscles, and the utter limpness of unconsciousness.

Even as the blow went home Fargolt's eyes swung to the other sleeper. She did not stir and her even breathing never faltered. The pantar released his breath in a relieved sigh and, extending one of his sandaled feet, prodded the sleeping girl.

Lua awoke with a start. Blinking her eyes against the darkness she made out the man's figure standing above her, a huar's muzzle pointed at her head.

"Get up," growled a deep voice she recognized immediately as that of Fargolt. "And don't try any tricks if you want to stay alive."

More angry than frightened, Lua obeyed.

"Turn around…"

Without a word Lua did as directed. Fargolt, one eye on the cave girl's lovely back, bent and roughly pulled away the furs covering Rhodia's limp form. With a savage jerk he tore away her cloth belt, then ordering Lua to place her hands at her back, wrists crossed, he drew several folds of the material around them and tied them tightly.

Lua, helpless, felt a strong hand fasten on her bare shoulder and she was whirled around to face her captor. An evil smile lighted the pantar's thin face as he pulled the bound girl roughly to him. "You are mine now," he whispered hoarsely and bent his head to press his lips tightly to her mouth.

Suddenly he uttered a sharp cry of pain and staggered back, one hand pressed to his bleeding lip where the untamed daughter of Yortak had bitten him. "Klysan," he snarled. "Daughter of a beast! I'll teach you manners before I've finished with you." And lifting his hand he dealt her a savage blow across the face, sending her sprawling to the floor.

Half-dazed, Lua felt powerful fingers fasten in her hair and she was dragged back to her feet. She stood there, swaying a little, her lips locked to prevent giving this man the satisfaction of hearing her cry out.

Fargolt thrust his face close to hers. "Where is the Golden God?" he demanded.

In reply Lua spat full in his face. With an oath he dug his nails into her shoulder. "Where is it?" he snarled. "Answer me, Klysan!"

When he saw that nothing would wring an answer from her, he shoved her aside and set out to ransack the cave for the object he desired. A moment later he uttered a soft sound of satisfaction as he drew a cloth-wrapped piece of metal from Rhodia's bed of furs. After drawing aside the wrappings sufficiently to make sure they contained the Golden God, he turned back to the silent Lua.

"Come," he said, jerking his head toward the open air. "We are going to Clyrus."

LUA neither spoke nor made an effort toward obeying the command. With an obvious effort Fargolt kept control of his temper.

"Listen," he said sharply. "You are coming with me. You can either do so willingly or be dragged. I leave the decision to you."

Lua felt a wave of hopelessness sweep over her. She was realist enough to know that pride would avail nothing but bruises. If only Reedmcgurn were here! But he was somewhere in the jungle, blundering through darkness in search of the girl he loved...

The realization came to her that she would never see him again. Nothing mattered any longer. Stubbornly she set her softly rounded chin and without a word she turned and walked to the cave entrance, her shoulders squared, her head unbowed. Fargolt, a triumphant smile on his lips, followed her out.

Getting his prisoner down that rocky scarp without giving her the freedom of her hands presented the Atlandian with a problem. After a moment of head scratching he came up with a solution. Returning to the cave, he dug through the mound of supplies stored there earlier in the day and came up with a coil of rope, one end of which he used to fasten a loop under Lua's arms. By this means he lowered her slowly to level ground, then slid quickly down to join her.

In the dyark's cabin, Fargolt tied his captive firmly in one of the seats and placed the cloth-wrapped figure of the Golden God beside him in the pilot's chair. Now nothing was left to do but to close and lock the open cargo hatch, and the opening to the cabin itself and he would be ready to take off for Clyrus...Clyrus, where wealth and high position awaited him as a reward for placing in the hands of Mentanek the power to become ruler of both Clyrus and Atland. He put out a hand to fondle the cloth-swathed idol. Here at his fingertips was power beyond expression. A random thought made him hesitate. Might it not be wiser to return to Atland and win even greater wealth and position from a grateful Ashtoth? But even as the thought crossed his mind he dismissed it. He had snatched Athora from under the very nose of her father; and now that she was gone never to return, he was certain to be blamed for her disappearance. Then, too, Sar-Gath, Clyrus's high priest, would still expect him to serve as a spy, forcing him to continue in that capacity by threatening to expose his past record.

No. Clyrus was his best market.

Rising, Fargolt went forward to the open door of the cabin, dropped lightly to the ground, and swung shut the cargo hatch.

He was in the act of setting its catches when something hard was suddenly thrust into his back and a harsh voice said. "Put up your hands."

AS REED McGURN entered the mouth of the game trail, it was with the complete certainty that he was on a fool's errand. None knew better than he his complete lack of ability in tracking down an elephant in broad daylight, let alone following what at best would be the almost invisible spoor of a native of these parts.

Still, he reasoned, he would be less a man if he failed to make the effort. Reason told him, too, that there was a chance for success; Athora's kidnaper must have taken this same trail since there was no other leading from the clearing. If McGurn could overtake him before the trail forked, the princess might well be rescued almost at once; if not it was up to him to determine which fork the cave man had taken.

And so the young American moved resolutely ahead, huar ready in one hand, his flashlight burning in the other. On either side of him loomed an impenetrable blackness cast by the walls of foliage; while to his ears came eerie rustlings to pluck at his nerves. Now and then he caught the distant challenge of some giant cat, its fearsome voice sending little shivers along his spine. From time to time he stopped there in the trail, his ears straining to catch some indication that Athora and her captor were nearby. But on each occasion he heard nothing other than the now familiar noises of a nocturnal jungle.

Perhaps an hour after leaving the caves McGurn reached the place where the trail forked. Dropping to his knees in the dust and powdered vegetation he swept the rays of his flash over the surface. At first he found no more than a confusion of indecipherable marks, but gradually he began to recognize many of them for what they were. Here a giant cat had paused to sharpen its claws against a tree bole; he could see the marks of its paws both in the trail itself and on the ripped bark of the tree itself. Overlapping those marks in the dust were what appeared to be prints from a dog's paws; probably, he thought, the spoor of a jackal or hyena. And here—here was a print left by what could only be a man's naked foot…

It was well along the left and pointed in the same direction McGurn was heading. Its size ruled out the possibility that Lua had left it there the day before, and its depth indicated the man who made it was either very heavy or had been carrying a weight. A weight!

With renewed hope and increased misgivings Reed McGurn started out again, moving at a slow trot along the trail's left fork.

Not long thereafter he came into a wide clearing, which he recognized at once as the place where Avar-Ak had died beneath the fangs of Conta, the lioness. He was well across it when a sudden thought stopped him in his tracks.

What if Athora's captor had decided he was far enough from the caves to be safe, for the night at least, of possible pursuit and discovery? In that case would he not lay up for the balance of the night, intending to resume his flight with the coming of dawn?

It was a sobering possibility and McGurn spent a long moment weighing it. He dared not risk passing his quarry under cover of darkness, nor did he want to give the cave man an opportunity to hopelessly outdistance him.

Finally the American decided the better course would be to wait until dawn before resuming the chase. Continuing to the opposite mouth of the trail, he swung himself lightly into the branches of a jungle giant and climbed upward until he found a comfortable crotch where he might rest during the remaining hours of darkness.

Seconds later he was sound asleep, while a giant python a few feet away uncoiled slowly from its branch and slithered deeper into the forest, its belly filled an hour before.

IN THOSE first few seconds after being snatched from her bed by invisible arms, Athora, princess of Atland, went through an agony of fear heightened by ignorance of who—or what—had thus rudely seized her. It was not until she was borne into the open and saw, in the moonlight, that she was locked in the grasp of a naked

Klysan that complete understanding of her plight struck her with stunning force.

She must have fainted then, for when she came back to awareness of her surroundings it was to find herself hemmed in by walls of foliage that moved past her in a bobbing rhythm. Beneath her was a broad bare shoulder, its animal heat penetrating the thin material of her tunic.

Aroused now to full consciousness she opened her mouth to scream—a scream never uttered as the realization swept over her of how futile any cry for help would be. Strangely, this feeling of utter despair cleared her brain of its paralysis and she began to think quickly and with amazing lucidity.

For the moment, at least, there was nothing she could do. To attempt to wriggle free of this cave man's iron embrace would be worse than useless; it could only result in arousing his anger. The thing to do was wait—wait until his muscles tired and he was forced to rest; only then might she hope to accomplish an escape.

But it began to appear those rippling muscles were immune to weariness. Still moving at a brisk trot her captor reached a fork in the trail, swung left, went on with no sign of slackening his pace. With what amounted to almost a physical effort Athora beat down the panic within her and willed her mind to a state bordering on composure.

Sometime later the cave man came to a good-sized circular clearing, across which he trotted with loose, swinging strides. On the opposite side, where the elephant path appeared again, the princess caught a brief glimpse of a pile of gnawed human bones among tall grasses—evidence of a recent jungle tragedy. Then darkness closed in again as the forest swallowed up the cave man and his burden.

A few minutes later, just when Athora had given up hope that her captor intended to rest short of his unknown goal, he turned at right angles to the path and leaped lightly into the branches of a tree, the girl's weight seeming to handicap him not at all. With easy celerity he swarmed upward, pausing at last at a point where two sturdy branches extended outward side by side. Here the cave man deposited Athora ungently; and as she clung tightly to her softly swaying perch high above the ground, her captor turned and without a word dropped lightly into the darkness below.

Bewildered by this sudden desertion, shivering under the bite of chill, damp air, the daughter of Ashtoth looked quickly about for some avenue of escape. She was at a loss to explain the man's abrupt departure, but she realized this moment might be her last chance to regain her freedom.

Carefully she rose to her feet on one of the swaying branches, but a single glance at those horrid depths beneath sent her into a paroxysm of shivering so intense she was unable to remain standing. And so it was that when the cave man returned a few moments later, a length of stout vine looped about one shoulder, he found his captive crouched in a pitiful heap against the tree bole and sobbing uncontrollably.

When he saw she was oblivious of him standing there be put out a hand and prodded her sharply, causing her to shrink back so convulsively that only a quick movement on his part kept her from tumbling into those Cimmerian depths.

After a moment she was able to gain some semblance of control over palsied muscles and her heart ceased trying to pound its way through her ribs. She looked at him standing easily on one of the two boughs. She saw the evil in his wide face, the heavy lips curled back in a smirk of anticipation, the narrow eyes that seemed to gleam redly in the faint light. And seeing these all hope left her and her head came up proudly.

"Who are you?" she demanded, her voice perfectly steady, "and what do you want of me?"

"I am Bitog," growled the cave man. "I am a great hunter and a mighty fighter. I am taking you to the caves of my people. He took my mate; now I have taken his."

"'He'?" repeated Athora, bewildered. "Who is 'he'? Who took your mate?"

BITOG shook his head angrily. "You know who I mean. He is one of you. He took Lua from me. I followed him. I saw him meet you and the other she. I saw how he looked at you and how you looked at him. Then I knew he wanted you instead of Lua. That is why I took you instead of her."

Despite the hopelessness of her present position Athora's heart bounded with sudden joy. It was true—she was in love with Reed McGurn! That was why she hated his cave girl companion from the first—why she was content to be with him. And he loved her! It must be so when even a wild man from the caves could tell from watching at a distance.

If only she could win her way back to the man she loved… Her quick mind began to examine what this—this Bitog had said. Perhaps in his words was the key to escape…

"You are wrong, Bitog," she said with a calmness that amazed her. "He does not love me. It is Lua he wants; I am nothing to him. He boasted how he had taken her from you, said you were no warrior at all to give her up so easily."

Bitog's small eyes began to blaze and a low growl rumbled in his throat. Athora hurried on, seeking to follow up her advantage.

"I am the only one who can get Lua for you. Return me to the cave and wait in the jungle next to the clearing there. I will drive her away and when she enters the jungle you can take her. Thus can you punish this man for boasting how he took Lua from you."

Bitog wet his thick lips. "You want him. I saw you looking at him."

Athora hesitated. "Yes," she said quietly. "I want him, but he has eyes only for this Kly—, for Lua. That is why I want to get rid of her."

In the silence that followed, Bitog scratched his head and wrinkled his brow in thought. Athora held her breath, her heart pounding with swelling hope.

"No," he growled suddenly; and with the guttural sound Athora's soaring spirits dived to the utter depths of despair. "No, I do not need you. I am a mighty fighter. With only my hands I slew Shanda, the leopard. Since he wants Lua instead of you, I will go and take her from him. I do not need a she to help me…"

"But—but what will you do with me?" cried Athora.

He scowled at her. "I do not know—yet. Maybe I will kill you. Now I am going to sleep."

Ignoring her protests he uncoiled the vine from its place on his shoulder and with deft movements of his giant hands bound her tightly to the tree bole, fastening the knots at the far side where she could not reach them. This left her in a sitting position, legs extended along both branches, and despite the vine about her body not an uncomfortable one.

The frightened girl made several attempts to renew the conversation but Bitog ignored them. Satisfied finally that she would not be able to get away, he leaped lightly to the limb directly above her, settled his mighty frame into a nearby fork, and fell instantly asleep.

The hours that followed were the longest in Athora's experience. Several times she dozed, only to be awakened with a start by a savage roar or scream from the throat of a hunting animal moving along the trail below. The chill, dank air seemed to penetrate her entire body, and to increase her trembling came small sounds from the leafy fastness hemming her in on all sides.

Near dawn she was able to sink into a sleep so deep no sound was able to penetrate it…

A ROUGH hand shook her awake and she opened her eyes to find Bitog's forbidding countenance hovering above her. While the cave man loosened her bonds she gazed about, drinking in the already warm air rising from the steaming earth below. From the direction of the sun's rays she concluded it was already an hour above the eastern horizon.

Bitog bent now to lift her to his back. Again she pleaded to know what he meant to do with her, but he only shook his head and growled impatiently. Swinging her lightly across one shoulder, Bitog slid rapidly to the ground and stepped into the path.

For a moment he stood there indecisively, as though in doubt as to whether he should turn back in quest of Lua or go on to his caves. Athora, sensing what was passing through that savage brain, made one last effort.

"Go back," she said sharply. "Before noon he intends to take Lua away in the flying bird which brought him here. If you wait longer he—and she—will be gone where you never can find them."

With a single motion he tore her from his back and tossed her to the ground at his feet.

"Yes," he snarled. "I will go back for her now. But you will be in the way. I am going to kill you…"

"No, Bitog! No!" With desperation born of fear she sought to scramble from beneath his reaching hands, but in vain. The clutching fingers shot out to grasp her about the throat, putting a sharp end to her shrill scream.

A haze began to form before her eyes. Wildly she clawed at his wrists while her taut body arched and threshed from side to side. But the mighty hands only increased their awful pressure. There followed a rushing, falling sensation as though she were plunging from a great height, dimly she was aware of a heavy, evenly-spaced thudding sound like a giant drum being beaten far away.

"It is my heart pounding," she thought wonderingly, and then darkness closed in and she knew no more.

AS FARGOLT, pantar of Atland's Air Fleet, felt the unseen object press into the small of his back, he uttered an involuntary gasp of alarm and his arms shot up in token of surrender even before he heard the command to do so. He felt a hand slip lightly along his belt and remove his huar, then the voice said:

"All right. You may turn around. Slowly…"

Fargolt obeyed, gradually lowering his hands. Facing him was a short, slender, dark-faced man clad in a tunic similar to his own. There was a huar in his hand, its muzzle trained on the pantar.

For an instant the two men stood staring into each other's eyes. Then the stranger said in a flat, inflectionless voice:

"There are seven hills."

Fargolt's heart soared with relief. "By the Golden God," he gasped. "Then you are from Sar-Gath!" He passed a hand shakily across his forehead. "What a start you gave me! Is Sar-Gath here?"

The stranger's expression remained stern and unyielding. "There are seven hills," he said again.

The Atlandian made a gesture of impatience. "Of course. Do the hills have names?"

"The first is called Men," intoned the stranger.

"And the second?"

"Tan."

"The third?"

"It has no name."

"The fourth?"

"Ek."

The stranger drew back a step and held Fargolt's huar out to him, butt first. "Here is your huar," he said. Fargolt made no effort to take the weapon and for the space of a full yad neither man moved. Then Fargolt said, "Mentanek," the stranger returned his own huar to his belt and Fargolt reached out and recovered the huar that belonged to him.

"How were you able to find me?"

Fargolt asked, now that the air of tension between the two men was gone.

"Your dyark was followed from the moment you left the palace roof," explained the other. "Thanks to your note to Sar-Gath he was able to dispatch a dyark in time."

"Did the high priest accompany you here?"

"No, Atim-Lek, an under-priest, is in charge."

"Where are you camped?"

"In a clearing not far from here."

"Does Atim-Lek wish to speak with me?"

"Not at this time. His orders are to remain here with the princess. On the morrow a searching party will succeed in 'locating' you. It will be made up of three Clyrusian dyarks pressed into service by Sar-Gath, who made haste to offer their services to Ashtoth the moment he heard Athora had fled from Atlantis."

Sadly Fargolt shook his head. "You have arrived too late," he said solemnly.

"Too late?" exclaimed the other sharply. "What do you mean?"

In short, rapid sentences the pantar recounted the events of the past few hours, omitting however any reference to the Golden God and the fact it was now in his possession. When he was finished, his listener stood lost in thought for several minutes.

"You were about to take off in your dyark when I arrived," he said finally, and Fargolt was aware the man's suspicions were now aroused. "Where were you intending to go?"

"To Clyrus," the pantar replied quickly. "I felt it my duty to report directly to Mentanek that Ashtoth's daughter was dead."

"Dead?" snapped the other. "I thought you said a Klysan had taken her."

Fargolt shrugged. "Is there a difference? She will be dead before we, or anyone else, can find her."

"I see. And this cave woman—why were you taking her with you?"

Fargolt's expression twisted into a frank leer. "She is very beautiful. Besides, she could serve to bear out my story of Athora's fate."

"I see," said the Clyrusian a second time, and in his voice was a sudden chill. "Wait here," he continued, starting to turn away. "I must return and inform Atim-Lek of what—"

ABRUPTLY he whirled back, huar in hand to cover the surprised pantar. "Put up your hands," he snarled; then, as Fargolt, his amazement clearly evident, obeyed, he added:

"I think you are lying. You are a spy, and spies are notorious for double-dealing. You are coming with me to tell your story to Atim-Lek. Turn around."

"But I assure you—"

"Shut up. And turn around while I take your huar."

Fargolt, his mind racing, slowly turned his back to the Clyrusian. He knew Atim-Lek would be certain to come back here to conduct an investigation. Discovery of the Golden God would result, and even without knowing the under-priest there was little likelihood he would be willing to permit Fargolt to be the one to hand it to Mentanek. No, once that Golden idol was in Atim-Lek's hands, he would find some means of disposing of the Atlandian pantar and thus take over the rewards Fargolt had figured were to be his own.

He was aware of a hand closing about the grip of his huar and the weapon was carefully withdrawn. "All right, you may turn back. We go now to speak with Atim-Lek."

Fargolt, obeying, lowered his hands slowly, his quick mind seeking frantically for some ruse to turn the tables. Then:

"Wait," Fargolt said. "Must I leave the cave girl alone in the dyark while we are gone?"

"What does it matter?" the Clyrusian said indifferently. "She can run away for all I care. I am not interested in your woman."

"Not that she will escape," Fargolt pointed out. "She is securely bound. But the cabin door is open and one of the big cats may be drawn there by her scent. If that happens we might have difficulty in routing him out again."

The Clyrusian shrugged. "Very simple. Close the cabin door; then nothing can get in."

The pantar kept back a satisfied smile with difficulty. "A good idea. Wait here; it will take me only a moment."

"Do you think I'm a fool?" snapped the other. "If I stayed here what would prevent you from seizing the controls and taking off. No, you shall close the cabin door but I will be right behind you, my huar aimed at your back."

"As you wish."

The two men, one behind the other, moved along the dyark's side until they came to the cabin entrance. Fargolt mounted the three steps leading up to it and swung the heavy door closed. While fumbling with its catch, he glanced quickly over his shoulder, noting the Clyrusian was standing at the foot of the steps, huar ready in his hand.

Finishing, Fargolt turned to descend, his feet level with the man's head.

Suddenly the pantar kicked out one foot with savage fury, catching the Clyrusian under the chin and sending him sprawling. Before he was able to recover and bring his huar into action Fargolt was upon him, one hand on his right wrist, the other searching frantically for his throat. Before the dazed Clyrusian could put up an adequate fight, the huar was torn from his hand and Fargolt had leaped clear.

The man from Clyrus read his fate in the cruel eyes sighting along the huar's barrel. "No," he cried, flinging up one hand as a futile shield. "No. Don't kill me! I'll—"

Flame lanced from the huar's muzzle, putting a grisly period to his words and a small scorched hole in the center of his forehead.

A grim smile touching his lips, Fargolt turned from the dead man and went back to the dyark. Entering, he made fast the door's inner catch and took his place at the controls, ignoring Lua's hate-filled eyes as he passed the seat to which she was bound. He dropped a caressing hand to the cloth-wrapped idol for one ecstatic moment, then reached for the controls.

An instant later the dyark streaked silently skyward, swung its nose toward the southwest and faded into the night.

CHAPTER TWELVE
Captured

SUNLIGHT lancing through a break in the ocean of foliage above him awakened Reed McGurn. For a few moments he sat unmoving while his sleep-fogged mind brought him up to date. Then memory of the previous night's events came back to him and he pulled himself upright on a swaying branch and prepared to descend to the trail below and once more take up pursuit of Athora's abductor.

Cramped muscles complained sharply as he stood erect and he spent a minute or two flexing, them back to normal. Slowly he let himself down from branch to branch, pausing among those directly above the trail until he could make certain no enemy, human or animal, lurked nearby.

Huar in hand he dropped lightly to earth, his eyes and ears alerted to his surroundings. Multi-colored butterflies, large as birds, hovered about giant jungle blossoms, insects filled the morning air with a drowsy hum, a small, rabbit-like creature darted suddenly into the open trail, skidded to an abrupt halt at sight of McGurn, then sprang for cover.

McGurn rubbed a hand across his unshaven cheeks, yawned, scratched his naked sides, yawned again, then turned and started along the trail. As he moved ahead he scanned the dusty surface, puzzling over the marks he found there. Almost immediately he caught sight of shallow prints of naked feet identical to the one he had found the night before. Cheered by this evidence that his quarry was still ahead of him, he pressed resolutely on.

He was moving briskly along, ten minutes later, when the sound of a sharp cry of protest came to his ears from around a bend in the trail perhaps a hundred yards ahead.

Even as the cry reached him he knew Athora had voiced it. The weapons in his belt forgotten he raced ahead with every ounce of speed he could muster. Thus it was that as he rounded that bend he was unable to stop before crashing heavily into the body of a half-naked man crouched above Athora's motionless form.

The impact sent both men sprawling. Bitog was up in a flash, springing at McGurn while the latter was still on his hands and knees. Mighty hands closed about the American's neck, jerking him up and forcing him back in the same smoothly flowing motion.

Off balance, arms flailing helplessly, McGurn was face to face with death within seconds of the moment he had floundered into Bitog. Already he could feel his senses reeling as iron fingers closed tighter about his neck, shutting off all air to his laboring lungs.

Through a red mist he saw the exultant expression inches from his face, McGurn drew back one leg to brace himself, then brought up his other knee in a savage thrust that buried it in Bitog's groin.

A scream of agony burst from the cave man's lips and he released his hold on McGurn, falling back and doubling over in pain. The American might well have ended the battle in that moment, for Bitog was temporarily helpless and McGurn could have finished him off with the Webley.

But blind unreasoning fury drove everything from his mind except the overpowering urge to batter his enemy to lifeless pulp. Uttering a maddened scream more bestial than any beast's, he leaped forward to close with the mightily muscled cave man. It was his fingers now that sought an exposed throat, and as they thudded home he cried out again, this time with insane exultation.

Bitog, strength sapped by the horrible pain in his groin, toppled backwards and crashed heavily to earth. McGurn followed him down, knees pressing now against those broad shoulders, and he began to strike short vicious blows against the Cro-Magnon's exposed face. The first two flattened the nose, splattering blood against McGurn's naked chest; the next three splintered several teeth and cracked the jawbone.

It was then that Bitog lost his temper.

Bringing one arm around in a mighty sweep he catapulted the American flyer completely across the trail and through the wall of foliage. Bellowing like a wounded buffalo, he leaped after him, his flint knife torn from its sheath and raised for the kill.

MCGURN, shaken though he was by the awful blow, drew his Webley with a single swift movement and sent three bullets into Bitog's broad chest.

For a little while there was no sound within the trail but that of McGurn's labored breathing. Bitog, stone-dead, lay in a sprawling heap, his naked feet protruding from the wall of undergrowth. A few birds, disturbed by the sound of shots, circled overhead.

At last McGurn felt sufficiently strong to regain his feet. He stood there swaying a little, shaking his head to clear his fogged sight. Finally he staggered into the trail and approached the motionless body of the princess Athora.

A brief examination showed him she still lived, nor was there any sign of a wound. He noticed purple bruises on the soft throat where Bitog's fingers had pressed, and only then did he understand how near she was to death when he arrived.

Gently he swung her up into his arms and turned toward the caves. He moved slowly, staggering now and then under her weight, for he was very near to complete exhaustion.

Athora was first aware of a rhythmic swaying sensation. She lay with eyes closed, fearing to open them lest this be the final delirium before death. But as the sensation endured she took courage and finally looked up into the handsome face of Reed McGurn.

"You," she murmured. "How can that be?"

McGurn smiled down into the lovely face so near his own. "How do you fee?"

"Wonderful!" She smiled too—a smile of relief and thanksgiving—a smile that fled suddenly as realization came. "The Klysan… Where is he?"

"Dead."

"You killed him! You came after me—came to save me from him! Why did you do it, Reed McGurn?"

He stopped and put her lightly down on her feet. "Think you can make it under your own power?"

"Why did you do it, Reed McGurn?" she insisted, placing a hand on one of his arms.

His shoulders lifted and fell in a faint shrug. "The hero in me, I guess," he said in English; then, as she frowned in puzzlement, "I could not let the wild man take you without making some effort to stop him, Athora."

Her hand crept slowly up along his arm and she smiled deep into his eyes. "Was that the only reason? Tell me in words what I see in your eyes. Tell me, Reed McGurn..."

There was only one proper answer—and McGurn was human enough to make it. Without a word his arms came up and drew her close, he bent his head and pressed his lips to hers in a long kiss...

And then, unbidden, there came before his mind's eye the vision of another girl—a girl with an oval suntanned face with soft tendrils of blonde hair falling about smoothly rounded shoulders and whose sparkling blue eyes were strangely alight as she lifted her red lips to his kisses...

He drew away from Athora almost rudely, but the girl was too happy, too breathless with the realization of love, to notice.

"Come," said McGurn hoarsely, "the others are worrying at our absence. We must hurry back to them."

She laughed aloud, for no reason than a supreme happiness bubbling within her. With a possessive little motion she locked an arm through one of his and together they walked back toward the caves.

"My father will welcome you, Reed McGurn—welcome you because you are good and noble and worthy of fathering future rulers of Atland. And my people will love you, too, and hail you as the savior of their princess. Even more, it is because of you that the Golden God will be restored to Atland—an act alone to make you their hero. And when we stand before the Golden God, in the temple of Ammon-Re, and hear the solemn words from Clat-Ron—words that will make us as one for the rest of our lives—then will my happiness be complete."

MCGURN allowed her to babble on without interruption, his own thoughts as deeply troubled as his companion's were gay. Why had the image of Lua intruded at the moment he was holding another woman in his arms? Certainly he was not in love with a wild savage who lived in caves and consorted with such animal-men as the one he had just slain. Now that he was forever doomed to spend his life in an age 20,000 years before he was born (*that doesn't make sense!* he thought wildly), he would be a fool indeed not to make the best of them in surroundings such as Athora had described.

But what of Lua? Well, what about her? A pretty face and a shapely body—he'd passed up plenty of those in his day. No sir—he'd marry this girl beside him and maybe someday be king of Atland and have a harem of girls like Lua! But a man who's planning on getting married shouldn't be thinking about having a harem—not if he was in love with the girl he was going to marry…

They rounded the last bend of the trail and stepped into the familiar clearing. McGurn, picturing the others grouped about the base of the cliff impatiently awaiting word of Athora's fate, came to an abrupt halt at sight of the empty expanse of open ground.

No one was in sight. The clearing was completely deserted of life. And of something else, too—although it was Athora who first put the realization into words.

"The dyark!" she cried in horror. "The dyark is gone. They have deserted us—left us here in the jungle!"

"Come on!" shouted McGurn, and side by side they raced across the field of grasses.

A few yards short of the scarp McGurn came to a sharp halt at sight of something lying among the long grasses. Athora, attracted by his sudden cry, stopped and came back to join him.

"What is it?" she asked, catching a glimpse of the partially concealed object.

The American pressed forward and pushed aside the matted vegetation. "A dead man—someone I've never seen before. Looks as though a huar got him; there's a hole burned into his skull. Ever see him before, Athora?"

She stared at the limp figure and turned away, shuddering a little. She had seen the horde of ants. "No, Reed McGurn. He is a Clyrusian."

"Clyrusian? That's the country whose king you were supposed to marry?"

"Yes. What do you think this means, my prince?"

McGurn's jaw set in harsh lines. "Probably some Clyrusian dyarks were out scouting around, maybe looking for you, and saw our ship down here. They must have come down and tried to take over and Fargolt shot one of them. After that they must have grabbed our three friends and took off with them."

"Unless—" Athora's voice faltered. "Unless they lie dead in the caves."

With those words came full awareness to Reed McGurn of what Lua's loss meant to him. Forgotten instantly was the dream of someday ruling Atland at the side of Ashtoth's daughter. Suddenly he knew that without Lua life was no longer worth living, that his sole purpose in life from this moment on was either rescuing her or, if she were dead, avenging her death.

Without a word he turned and raced with long strides toward the towering cliff, scaled those heights with an agility he had not known he possessed and disappeared into Lua's cave. An instant later, as Athora watched wide-eyed, he reappeared again, going directly to the cave where the princess and Rhodia had spent the previous night.

SEVERAL minutes passed before he came out, and then he slid lightly to earth and rejoined Athora, his face set in an expression of mingled anger and horror.

Alarmed, Athora caught him by the arm. "What is it, my prince? What did you find that makes you look so—so—"

"Rhodia," McGurn said woodenly. "A blow on the head…killed her."

"Oh *no!*" Athora, color draining from her cheeks, fell back, a hand pressed to her lips. "Not Rhodia! She was like my own sister. Why did she have to die? Why could it not have been that Klysan? She was of no use—"

McGurn's expression stopped the flow of grief-stricken words like a slap across the mouth. "I—I'm sorry, Reed McGurn. I did not mean that, of course. I forgot that she was your friend…"

The words. "More than a friend; I love her!" trembled on the man's lips but he bit them back. "It's all right, Athora," he said tonelessly. "Right now I've got to figure out a way to reach Clyrus—if that's where she was taken—and get her away from the men who took her."

The girl from Atland shook her head. "It is not possible, my prince. Even were you able to reach Clyrus's shores you could never hope to find your way to her—let alone take her to Atland."

She came close to him and slipped her arms about his neck, bringing his face near her own. "Forget her, Reed McGurn," she whispered hotly. "I will make you forget her. Am I not beautiful enough—desirable enough—to make you forget other women?"

But the American's expression did not soften and with firm gentleness he disengaged her hold. "You've forgotten something, Athora," he said. "What about the Golden God? The Clyrusians took that, too."

Horror flooded her face. "With the Golden God in their hands," she cried. "Atland is doomed. Once our people discover the truth, they will rise against my father, the nobles, and our priests. Civil war will result and leave Atland prone and bleeding—easy prey for the warriors of Clyrus. What can we do, Reed McGurn?"

"I've got to get to Clyrus," he said harshly. "And I've got to go alone. Where many men would fail, one might win through. I figure I'm the one, since I have even a bigger stake than a hunk of gold."

Athora, her shoulders sagging hopelessly, turned away. "There is nothing you can do, my prince. Within a few days word will reach Atland that the Golden God is in Clyrusian hands—they will see to that. Meanwhile you and I are stranded here in the heart of Afrota. It may be days—months before we are found. Maybe never."

"I'm not going to stand here waiting for somebody to find us," the man declared. "In what direction does Clyrus lie?"

"What you are thinking is madness," Athora said. "It would take two days to reach the great water alone; and even if you got that far, you could not cross the water to Clyrus without a dyark or petrix."

"We'll cross that water when we get to it," McGurn said grimly. "Right now I'm going to get some of the supplies together you brought here. We'll rest until mid-afternoon, then start for the coast."

"Where you go, I go," Athora said with a simple dignity that brought a sharp lump into McGurn's throat.

McGurn started a fire near the spring and they made a hasty meal from provisions taken from Athora's dyark the day before. Afterwards he made up a bundle of supplies large enough to last the two of them for several days and, at Athora's tearful request, dug a grave at the base of the cliff and buried the mortal remains of the faithful Rhodia. It was a solemn moment as McGurn placed the cloth-shrouded body therein and spoke the brief burial service Athora taught him. He sent the princess to one of the caves before filling the grave and over it he placed several large rocks from those lying about the foot of the escarpment.

Afterwards, he went to one of the caves and slept until mid-afternoon, then rose and entered Athora's cave to awaken her. Gently he stooped above her sleeping form and shook her lightly by the shoulder.

"Time to start, Athora."

She smiled sleepily up at him, stretched like a cat, and got to her feet. "This is madness, Reed McGurn—but a girl must obey the man she loves. Come."

They descended to the clearing and the princess helped him to adjust the pack across his shoulders. With his Webley, plus the two strange weapons he had taken from Avar-Ak's dead body, thrust on his belt, McGurn took on a war-like appearance as he crossed the expanse of grasses, Atland's princess at his side.

At the trail's mouth they hesitated as though reluctant to plunge into that wilderness of growing things.

"Are you sure this leads to the great water?" McGurn asked.

"I am sure of nothing in this awful place," the girl replied, "all I do know is that Clyrus lies to the west and this trail points in that direction."

McGurn shrugged. "That's enough to start on, anyway. Let's go."

A dozen strides they took—then the walls of foliage on either side of the trail parted and four tunic-clad men rose to confront them, huars trained on their hearts.

CHAPTER THIRTEEN
Losers Weepers

LUA, awakening with a start from fitful slumber, opened her eyes to find sunlight pouring in the dyark's windows. For a little while she gazed at the waste of empty water far below, then turned her head to meet the mocking light in Fargolt's eyes.

"We have only a little way to go," he said lightly.

"Where are we going?" Lua asked perfunctorily.

"To Clyrus! To civilization—where there are people and broad streets and luxurious homes instead of animals and elephant paths and holes in a cliff! You'll see things to open your eyes, my dear—see them and, as my woman—own them too. Oh, I have great plans for you. When you get rid of that piece of panther hide and into a tunic, and when a slave woman dresses your hair into something different from a bird's nest—then every man in Clyrus will be at your feet. But they'll be there too late—now you belong to me..."

Hatred began to swell within the girl—hatred to mix with the fear this man had aroused in her the night before. She thought of Reed McGurn and the realization that she would never see him again added to her hatred for this grinning man who had taken her. She twisted suddenly in her seat; only then did she discover that her bonds had been removed while she slept. She was free to move now—now that freedom was worthless.

Far below the white metal sides of the dyark a thin edge of land came into view at the southern horizon. Low clouds above that land changed into mountains as the dyark sped onward. Then they were above land, and far below Lua made out her first city—a series of straight lines crossing other lines in geometric designs. Encircling them all was a great wall; and as the dyark dipped lower she was able to make out buildings and gardens and even tiny dots along the streets and avenues—dots she realized were people.

"The city of Clya—the largest in Clyrus," explained Fargolt, seeing the wonder in her face. "That huge white stone building surrounded by gardens is the palace of Mentanek, king of Clyrus—the man we have come to see."

Suddenly a shadow seemed to pass across the sun, moving quickly, and Lua looked up, startled, to see three gleaming dyarks slanting down toward their own ship. At the windows of the other craft she made out many men with huars in their hands.

"They recognize our dyark as one belonging to Atland," Fargolt told her, his hands moving lightly over the controls. "Atland's dyark's are subject to suspicion."

A moment later Fargolt stopped the forward motion of the ship and it began to settle slowly down like a descending elevator. Directly below was the palace landing stage covering its entire roof, with a score or more dyarks visible about the edge.

With a faintly grating jar the great sky ship came to rest in the exact center of the field. A squad of Clyrusian guards, huars drawn, raced toward it, and as Fargolt left the controls and went forward to swing open the heavy door, a pantar stepped forward to meet him.

"Greetings, Atlandian," he said with unsmiling politeness. "How may I serve you?"

"Greetings," responded Fargolt. "I wish an immediate audience with Mentanek, king of Clyrus."

The lieutenant of guards blinked. "Mentanek is not so easily reached," he said shortly. "What is your reason for requesting an audience with him?"

"A reason," replied Fargolt stiffly, "of sufficient importance that I need not give details to a common pantar. Inform him at once that Fargolt, a noble of Ashtoth's court, wishes to see him without delay; that I have with me the most coveted object in all the world—an object which I am willing to turn over to him for certain considerations which I will name only to him."

A wave of red crept into the other's cheeks at the reference to a "common pantar." He said, "If the noble Fargolt will accompany me, I shall inform my immediate superior of your wish to see Mentanek."

"Very well," agreed Fargolt. Turning his head, he called for Lua to join him, and she came forward reluctantly.

At sight of the half-naked girl, the Clyrusian's eyes went wide. "A Klysan!" he exclaimed. "Is this the 'coveted object' you mentioned?"

"I would regret," Fargolt said smoothly, "being forced to inform Mentanek that one of his pantars has been guilty of insolence to a guest. I am waiting to speak with your immediate superior."

Muscles tightened the guard's lower jaw. "Follow me."

FARGOLT, the cloth-wrapped object under one arm and Lua at his side, followed the guide to an opening in the roof and down a flight of steps into the palace interior. The cave girl's eyes almost bulged with fascinated wonder as she crossed one beautifully appointed room after another. All this was something far beyond her most vivid imaginings: the thick-piled rugs, the chairs and sofas and polished, inlaid woods—all were things from another world of beauty and soft living, of shelter and comfort.

Their guide stopped finally before a closed door of gleaming wood and rapped lightly on its panel. A deep voice from within bade them enter, and a moment later they were standing before a tall, broad-shouldered man seated behind a large table, its surface inlaid with bits of ivory and gold.

"I bring," said the guide stiffly, "the noble Fargolt of Atland, a member of Ashtoth's court, and his companion, a Klysan woman. The noble Fargolt seeks an immediate audience with Mentanek."

The man behind the table swung his leonine head from Fargolt to the girl and back to Fargolt again. "I bid the noble Fargolt welcome," he said in a rumbling voice. "Will you and your—ah—companion be seated, please?"

While they were following the suggestion, the seated man dismissed the guard who went out, closing the door behind him.

"I am Rythark, commander of the palace troops," said the man behind the table, leaning back to fix piercing eyes on the visitor. He laid the tips of his fingers together and smiled at Fargolt and Lua above them. "As you can readily understand, Mentanek's time is limited and he is unable, unfortunately, to grant audiences to the many who seek him out. If you would care to tell me something of the reason behind your request, I shall do what I can to help you."

Fargolt closed his hands tighter about the object he carried. Nothing could compel him to tell anyone other than Mentanek himself what lay inside that cloth covering. Nor was it necessary that he do so. There was another way to win the audience he desired…

"I am more than a member of Ashtoth's court," he said warily. "From time to time I have been of service to Clyrus through Sar-Gath, her high priest. I tell you that so you may know my sympathies lie with Clyrus."

Rythark inclined his head slightly but did not speak, his face remaining impassive.

"Recently the princess Athora of Atland disappeared from Atlantis. I know where she has gone and what has since happened to her. That information I wish to give to Mentanek in person, for I am quite aware of his interest in her."

"I understand fully," the commander said gravely. "Remain here, if you will. "I shall acquaint the noble Mentanek of your wish to give this information to him."

Rising, he crossed to the door and went out, the heavy portal swinging shut behind him.

Minutes, passed on leaden feet. Lua sat slumped a little on the chair's soft upholstery, listening to the far away sounds of city life floating in through the window. She was cut off from all things familiar—alone in an awe-inspiring world, faced with a dark future beside a man she had met only a day before—a man she had hated from the first. A growing despondency sapped her characteristic animation and sparkle, leaving her but a spiritless shell of her former self; but deep within her was growing the determination to someday escape this bewildering world and return to her own kind. It might be many moons before an opportunity presented itself, but an untiring patience was part of her heritage and she could wait. Somewhere in her vast land Reedmcgurn still lived and perhaps the time would come when she could find him again. It would be that hope which would enable her to bear up during the long months that might pass before she could escape from Clyrus.

She stole a side glance at the man who had taken her from the land of her people. How confidently he sat there, an expression of smug certainty on his dark face. From what the princess Athora had said that night by the fire, she knew Fargolt was depending on the Golden God he carried to win him a high place in Clyrus. Well, let him have his high place. He would find that the girl with whom he meant to share that position would give him little happiness.

The opening door ended her thoughts, and Rythark, commander of the palace guards, came in.

FARGOLT rose to face him. A subtle change had come over the commander during his absence; his manner was a shade more cordial, his former faint air of condescension was no longer evident.

"The august Mentanek awaits you and your companion, noble Fargolt," he said almost cordially. "Be kind enough to come with me."

Once again the way led through luxuriously appointed rooms, many of them containing members, both men and women, of the court who stared in frank wonder at the lovely blonde girl in her scanty covering of panther skin. Up a broad flight of carpeted steps rising from the center of a mammoth hall lined with a full two score of palace guards, along a wide hall with richly colored tapestries lining its walls, and finally into a huge square chamber.

Other than half a dozen fully armed warriors against the far wall and a man seated in an oversized chair of ornately carved black wood atop a raised platform, the vast room was empty of life. But neither Fargolt nor Lua was aware of the surroundings, so completely did the man on the platform rivet their eyes.

Standing, he would have passed the six-foot mark by at least seven or eight inches. Yet so immensely gross was his body that the man seemed stunted in height. His weight must have bordered a quarter of a ton, his legs would have better graced a full grown elephant, his arms were great pendulous lengths of flabby flesh tipped fingers the size of an average man's wrist. Beneath a tent-sized tunic of purple and gold a monstrous mound of swelling flesh marked a gargantuan belly supported by the immense thighs. Sparse reddish locks topped a head like a huge round boulder, against the surface of which were stuck, like berries in a mass of uncooked dough, a pair of unblinking button eyes, a small round knob of nose and a small, almost womanish mouth. There must have been a neck for that impossible head to rest upon; if so it was completely obscured by incredible jowls hanging in multi-wrinkled folds almost to the sagging breasts.

Fargolt, in the past, had heard descriptions of Mentanek of Clyrus and was, in part, forewarned of what to expect. But as for Lua, daughter of a race that contained only lean hardened men fit to face the rigors of jungle life, she could only stand and stare in open-mouthed amazement at this utterly incredible travesty of a human being.

A sharp nudge from Fargolt's elbow snapped the spell and she moved ahead beside him to the feet of the elevated chair.

Rythark bowed low before the porcine monarch of Clyrus. "The noble Fargolt of Atland and his companion," he said in introduction.

"We bid you and your lovely companion welcome, noble Fargolt." The words were like distant thunder and seemed to rise from subterranean depths within that mountain of flesh, while the black eyes peered at them over folds of the protruding cheeks. "My faithful Rythark informs me you have information concerning Atland's loveliest creature—Athora, daughter of Ashtoth, who has been reported missing from her country; kidnapped, I understand, by some treacherous pantar by the name of—now let me think…ah, yes…by the name of Fargolt. Now there's a strange coincidence indeed. To think that the infamous abductor of my good friend's daughter should bear the same name as you, a nobleman of his court!"

A cold finger seemed to move lightly along Fargolt's spine. But when he spoke there was nothing in his tone or demeanor to so much as hint of his sudden fear.

"The story you have heard, noble Mentanek," he said, "has evidently been somewhat garbled. "The princess Athora was not taken by force from Ashtoth's palace. Instead she fled from there because she did not wish to marry you. A regrettable lack of judgment on her part, of course," Fargolt made haste to add as he noticed the look of black fury forming on Mentanek's wide countenance. "But the gracious Mentanek, from his vast store of knowledge of people and their ways, will understand that Athora was—is young and has never had an opportunity to learn firsthand of your personal charm and desirability."

At those last few words Mentanek's expression cleared, whereupon Fargolt went on, describing in detail the flight from Atlantis and the adventures amid Afrota's jungles. Mentanek listened without interruption, the fingers of one massive hand toying with the butt of an oversized huar thrust within the folds of his golden sash.

There were two things Fargolt failed to include in his recital: the fact that the stranger from another world had gained possession of the Golden God, and the killing of a Clyrusian priest shortly before he—Fargolt—had taken off for Clyrus itself. The first item he was saving as a fitting climax to this audience with Mentanek; the second was something he feared Clyrus's monarch might view with a fatal—to Fargolt—disapproval.

FOR some little time after Fargolt concluded his story Mentanek sat lost in thought. At last he stirred slightly on his mammoth throne, small ripples of disturbed fat flowing smoothly under his tunic.

"And so, noble Fargolt, it would appear Atland's most beautiful woman is dead."

"Either dead," replied the pantar, "or hopelessly lost as the victim of a Klysan."

"How regrettable…" Mentanek's sigh rustled in his nose like wind in a cave. He spread his hands in a gesture of finality. "Well, on to other things. I understand you made some mention to one of my palace guards that you have with you the…uh…'the most coveted object in the world.' I believe that was the phrase you used." He pointed one of the saplings he called fingers at the package under Fargolt's arm. "Is it that which you carry there?"

Fargolt inclined his head. "It is, noble Mentanek."

"Well," mumbled the king impatiently, "open it up. Let's see what you describe in such glowing language." He held up an enormous palm as Fargolt was about to speak. "Allow me to point out, my friend, that as you strip away those coverings a number of huars will be trained on you by my faithful guards. Merely a precaution, of course, unfortunate when dealing with so noble a guest as you… You were about to say…?"

"Only this," Fargolt said equably.

"I am about to lay in your hands the world's greatest treasure as a token of my unswerving loyalty to Clyrus and her great king. By doing so I shall forfeit my position and all my holdings in Atland. For this reason I make so bold as to request a position as nobleman of your court and with all the wealth that goes with such a position. It is understood, of course, that my gift must be of such importance as to merit so magnificent an award. Does this have your majesty's approval?"

"Reveal your treasure!" boomed Mentanek. "Who knows—it may be worth a kingship," and his sudden roar of laughter beat through the huge room like breakers on a distant shore.

With steady fingers Fargolt loosened the wrappings of cloth, doing this in such a way that he might strip them completely away in a single motion thus making its revealment more highly dramatic. Then:

"Behold, mighty Mentanek—the Golden God!"

With one sweep of his hand in unison with the cry he tore apart the cloth, and held high the gleaming, pulsating length of the golden image of Ammon-Re!

A swelling gasp of amazement, awe, and superstitious fear welled from the throats of the Clyrusians as each man instinctively made the sign of the holy triangle with a trembling forefinger. Mentanek braced his massive forearms against the armrest of his throne in a spasmodic effort to rise, then sank back, defeated by his own bulk.

"Place it in my hands," he panted, and Fargolt, face reflecting supreme satisfaction over the sensational response he had gained, stepped forward and laid the statue in the center of Mentanek's hands.

For a long moment the king sat there and stared down at the image, his vast face stained with the emanation of pulsating light from the Golden God. At last he lifted his eyes to Fargolt standing before him. "Then the rumors we heard here in Clyrus were true," he whispered harshly. "It was you, instead of an underpriest, who stole the Golden God..."

"I did not steal it," Fargolt replied. And in a few words he explained how the fabulous image had come into his possession.

Mentanek cut short his explanation. "Rythark!" he bellowed.

The commander of the palace guard stepped forward hastily. "Yes, noble Mentanek?"

"These guards—" The king's small glittering eyes swept over the six armed attendants. "They are to be trusted?"

"Completely, your majesty."

"Would you stake your life on their faithfulness?"

"I...ah... Few humans are worthy of complete trust, noble Mentanek."

"Exactly." A grim smile touched the king's tiny mouth. "Order them to turn their backs, facing the wall."

Rythark barked out a command and as one the six guards wheeled, presenting an evenly spaced row of backs to the king.

WITH a calm, almost casual air, Mentanek pulled the giant huar from his belt, leveled its muzzle, and holding the button in firing position, mowed down all six of the guards!

Lua uttered a sharp scream of horror and shrank back and Fargolt blanched visibly and he felt his knees tremble. Even the iron-faced reserve of the commander faltered slightly and tiny muscles rippled along his stiffly set jaws.

Mentanek, still holding his huar, turned his attention back to the others. "I regret the loss of six men, Rythark," he said easily, "but there must be not the slightest chance that word of our having the Golden God gets out."

He hesitated, while his thick tongue came out slightly and wetted his lips. "Get word immediately to Sar-Gath to return from Atlantis. Within a lat I want the commanders of my armies here for a council of war."

"War, noble Mentanek?" repeated Rythark, his expression startled.

"War was what I said. Within three days we move against Atland. Oh, there will be no fight worthy of the name. Once the rulers and people of Atland know we hold the Golden God, Atland will lie prostrate before us. Then it will be simply a matter of marching in and taking over."

Rythark jerked his head toward Fargolt and Lua who had been listening open-mouthed.

"And your guests?" he asked. "Shall I show them to their quarters?"

"Ah, yes. My guests." Mentanek beamed at Fargolt's wan expression. "I have given my word that our friend shall be rewarded for his services to Clyrus and to me. Noble Fargolt, you are indeed worthy of being a nobleman of my court—and a nobleman you shall be from this moment. Great wealth is yours and a residence worthy of your station."

Fargolt was smiling now—a smile of mingled relief and satisfaction.

"However," Mentanek went on, still speaking in a friendly rumble, "it seems you have broken two edicts handed down through the ages from the days when Clyrus and Atland were one great nation. You understand, of course, that I did not make these edicts—in fact I do not wholly believe they are just. But as king of Clyrus I am bound to enforce them."

The smile was gone now from Fargolt's lips and fear was in his eyes. "Wh-what laws are these, noble Mentanek?" he faltered.

"Surely," Mentanek said warmly, "you are aware of the law that states any person other than a high priest, king or nobleman who lays a hand on the Golden God must pay by losing his life?"

"But I am a noble. Your own words confirm that."

"True-true," admitted Mentanek soothingly. "Because you are a noble, your crime is no crime at all and the charge is dismissed."

Relieved color seeped back into Fargolt's cheeks. "I am grateful to your majesty for being so lenient."

"The other edict you have violated," the king went on placidly, "has to do with any nobleman of either Clyrus or Atland mating with a Klysan. This law, as you may know, was evolved to keep pure the blood of both countries' ruling classes. Now it is easily apparent that you have taken this young Klysan as a mate, the penalty for which is death."

"But she is not my mate!" cried Fargolt, plunged again into the depths of fear. "While I admit I brought her here for that purpose, being unaware of the edict against it, I have not taken her as my mate. From this moment I reject her; do with her as you wish…"

"As to that," Mentanek said easily. "I believe you wholeheartedly. However, we have no complete proof, and since you are a nobleman who has taken a Klysan as a mate, I must order your death…"

"But I am not a nobleman!" cried Fargolt, seeing an avenue of escape. "I am but a simple pantar of Atland! Oh, I admit I called myself a nobleman that I might more readily gain an audience with you. But I lied; I am no nobleman."

"Not a nobleman?" Mentanek stared at him in mock surprise. "Ah, but you are, noble Fargolt. Did I not, only a few yads ago, name you a nobleman of my court? Are you refusing the honor I bestowed upon you—the honor you yourself won from me?"

"Yes, yes!" wailed the fear-stricken pantar. "I decline the honor. I am no nobleman nor do I wish to be…"

"Wait!" Mentanek said, horrified. "If you refuse to accept nobility, then you must die for having laid hands on the Golden God. For only a high priest or king or a nobleman may touch the image Of Ammon-Re and continue to live…"

"I—I—" The full hopelessness of his position came home to Fargolt in that moment and he bowed his head and sought wildly for some way out. Suddenly the awareness came to him that the mammoth monarch was toying with him, sadistically enjoying this torturing with words, that he had been doomed to die from the moment he unveiled the Golden God. And with the realization came the calm of utter despair and he lifted his eyes—to stare full into the muzzle of Mentanek's huge huar.

An instant later Fargolt, pantar and traitor, crumpled into a lifeless heap, a small scorched hole showing in his forehead.

Lua, daughter of Yortak, watched him die and grim satisfaction filled her untamed heart. Another moment might find her still in death beside him, but first he had paid for bringing her to this horrible place.

"Thus ends the career of our latest nobleman," said Mentanek dolefully. "What a loss to Clyrus and her king. Have his body disposed of, Rythark," he said, turning to the commander, "and get word to Sar-Gath and the officers of Clyrus's forces."

"What of this Klysan?" the other asked, indicating Lua.

Mentanek fixed his beady eyes on the cave girl, carefully noting her obvious beauty and the proud lines of her carriage and the lilt of her head. "A lovely specimen, Rythark—too lovely by far to waste as a mere gift to my guards. Confine her to one of the special rooms in my apartment. Perhaps I shall permit the guards to have her…later."

CHAPTER FOURTEEN
All Hope is Lost

AT SIGHT of the strangers, McGurn's hand darted for his Webley, only to stop short as he realized there was no chance of success against the four huars trained on him.

"Raise your hands above your head," ordered one of the four. As McGurn complied he noticed that this man differed from the others in that the belt of his tunic bore a design of golden triangles worked into the material. His skin too seemed darker than that of his companions and there was an imperious cast to his strong-nosed countenance that bespoke the leader of men.

The man's eyes shifted to the princess Athora and for a long moment he stared at her without speaking, his impassive face betraying nothing of his thoughts.

"You are Athora, daughter of Ashtoth of Atland." It was a statement of fact, not a question. "I am Atim-Lek, priest of the temple of Ammon-Re in Clyrus. "Where is Clentark?"

"I know of no one by that name," Athora replied stiffly. "Why do you ask me?"

"Clentark is one of the temple guards who accompanied me here," Atim-Lek replied. "It was his duty to keep an eye on you and your party during last night. When another of the guards came to relieve him at dawn Clentark disappeared."

Athora shrugged disinterestedly. "I have not seen him. Also, I demand to know by what right you post guards to spy upon us. Unless your explanation is satisfactory to me I shall report the matter to my father. You may be certain he will get an answer—direct from your king!"

Atim-Lek heard her out with chill and distant politeness, then shifted his attention to Reed McGurn. He took in the American's strange garb without comment, then said to him:

"Where is Clentark? Where are the other members of your party? Why is your dyark no longer within the clearing?"

McGurn's eyes narrowed. "Look, friend, the lady asked for an explanation. If I were you—"

"Answer me!" Atim-Lek snapped.

McGurn's lips curled in a one-sided smile. "You," he said softly, "can go to Oruzal."

There was a collective gasp from the guards and Atim-Lek's dark face turned suddenly livid. Without warning his hand darted out and dealt McGurn a savage blow across the mouth. The young American staggered slightly under the impact, then he recovered and would have leaped upon the other had not he caught a glimpse of the four huars trained on him.

Athora caught him by the arm. "Do not anger them into killing you, my prince," she said softly. "My father will exact payment for every indignity you and I suffer at the hands of these Clyrusian animals."

Atim-Lek, face impassive once more, stepped back and motioned to one of the guards. "Search him," he ordered. "Remove his weapons."

The man came forward cautiously and snaked the Webley, the huar and the xorth from McGurn's belt and handed them to Atim-Lek. At sight of this last weapon the priest uttered a brief exclamation of surprise and satisfaction and slipped its barrel under his belt.

McGurn, unarmed now, let his lifted hands slowly to his sides without drawing comment from the priest. To Athora Atim-Lek said: "There is nothing you can hope to gain by refusing answers to my questions. Where is the dyark in which you came to Afrota and where are the other members of your party?"

"Who should know those answers better than you?" retorted the princess.

Atim-Lek frowned. "What do you mean?"

"I mean," Athora said hotly, "that you or some other Clyrusians came here while Reed McGurn and I were away, killed my handmaiden, and took the others away in the dyark. I suppose they are in Clyrus now—and the moment I return to Atland I shall see to it that Fargolt and—and Lua are taken from there and brought to my own country and that those who took them are punished."

THE PRIEST was shaking his head. "Had anyone from Clyrus taken them, I would have known. For some reason you are lying. If your dyark was taken without your knowledge some member of your own group must have done so."

"Attempting to put the blame on my people will avail you nothing," replied Athora coldly. "You shall answer to Ashtoth, my father, for—"

"Wait…" exclaimed McGurn. "What about Fargolt, Athora? He may have killed that Clyrusian we found near the caves and, fearing there were others about, taken Lua and flown back to Atland."

"And deserted us? Fargolt would never have done that."

"Why not? He must have given you up for dead, believing I would never be able to rescue you from that Klysan. And feeling about me the way he did, he would have no reason to wait for me to return."

"You've forgotten that somebody slew Rhodia. Fargolt would have no reason to do that; he was in love with her."

McGurn stared at her incredulously. "Like so much he was in love with her! Not the way he was eyeing Lua!" A startled expression abruptly swept across his square face. "I'll bet I know what happened. He figured you and I were gone forever. He saw a way to make himself a hero by bringing the Golden God back to Atland and telling your father a Klysan had murdered you and Rhodia. Because he was smitten by Lua he took her along instead of killing her as well."

"I can't believe it," murmured Athora. "And yet—it would explain everything that's happened."

"You have answered my questions," said a quiet voice, and McGurn and Athora, suddenly remembering that they were not alone, turned back to find Atim-Lek smiling with complete satisfaction.

"So it was you," continued the priest, "who made off with the Golden God. Rumors had reached Clyrus that Ammon-Re's image had been stolen. And you say that a pantar named Fargolt has taken it back to Atland?"

Athora was aware of a strange sinking sensation. "I do not recall naming his rank."

"Nor did you." Atim-Lek's smile broadened. "You see Fargolt is a spy, in the service of Mentanek of Clyrus. When you selected him to bring you to Afrota, my princess, he sent a note to Sar-Gath, high priest of Clyrus, informing him of your intentions. As a result I was ordered to follow your dyark here that we of Clyrus might keep informed of your exact position.

"And now that Fargolt has fled carrying the Golden God, there is little doubt but that he took it directly to Clyrus and has placed it by this time in the hands of Mentanek..."

"No..." gasped Athora, aghast. "I do not believe you! No man of Atland could be capable of delivering his country to Clyrus!"

Atim-Lek shrugged. "Perhaps you are right. But the possibility that you are wrong is strong enough to force a change in my plans. Instead of returning you directly to Atland, my princess, I shall stop first at Clya to speak with Mentanek. Should the Golden God now be in his possession his plans will doubtless be changed."

Ignoring Athora's protests and threats, he ordered his guards to escort the prisoners through the jungle to his own camp. Arriving there, Athora and McGurn were hustled aboard the gleaming dyark and minutes later the ship was aloft and on its way to Clya.

Under the watchful eyes of the guards Reed McGurn and Athora sat side by side watching the steaming jungles and grassy plains below give way finally to the ocean's empty wastes. To the American flyer the flight was of keen interest and he longed to be given an opportunity of examining the mechanism that powered so swiftly and in utter silence this streamlined craft. But any request along those lines would unquestionably be denied and he remained silent.

SOME time later he became aware that the soft shoulder against his own was shaking spasmodically and he turned his head to find Athora was crying silently into her hands.

He placed a tender hand on one of her arms. "Courage, my princess," he whispered.

She lifted a stricken face. "What shall we do, Reed McGurn? If what this priest says is true, then Atland is doomed—and with it my father and all his friends and mine."

"Wait until you know before giving up. And even if they do have the Golden God, keeping it may be difficult. From what you've said of Ashtoth, I can't see him giving up without a fight."

"When the armies of Mentanek march against Atland," she said brokenly, "bearing at their head the image of Ammon-Re, the soldiers of Atland will lay down their arms in defeat and the people will turn on my father and tear him to pieces. You are a stranger among us, Reed McGurn; you do not understand."

"But it will take a few days to get that far," McGurn pointed out. "And in the meantime Mentanek may find someone has pulled that idol right out from under his nose. If Clyrus has planted spies in Atland, it sounds reasonable to suppose Atland has spies in Clyrus—and all of them will be doing their best to regain possession of the image."

Athora appeared to brighten a little, but McGurn felt it was more in gratitude for his efforts than any actual revival of hope.

Darkness came while they were still aloft and soon thereafter Athora sank into troubled sleep, exhausted by the day's events, her head pillowed on McGurn's shoulder. The American aviator sat very still, his thoughts on another girl—a girl who meant more to him than all the countries and peoples and golden images in this forgotten world. He pictured her suntanned body beneath the scanty covering of panther skin, her clear blue eyes and wealth of blonde hair and the proud and clear-cut beauty of her features. The thought of her in the arms of the perfidious Fargolt closed a cold hand about his heart, even as it fired the resolution within him to rescue her—or avenge her—though an entire city stood between them. All he asked was an opportunity—no matter how slender—for escape from his present captors; and if Lua was anywhere within Clyrus he would find her…

He was suddenly aware that the dyark was slowing its speed, and he looked quickly out the opening next to him. Far below he saw twinkling lights in great numbers arranged in a circular pattern; and as the dyark sank lower he began to make out shadowy shapes that became two and three-story buildings lining broad avenues and narrow streets.

In the exact center of the circle was a great edifice of white walls surrounded by a park-like enclosure. The roof of this sprawling structure seemed to drift slowly up to meet the dyark and McGurn could see many lights marking its edges.

There followed a slight grating sound as the monster ship came to rest. Rythark left the controls and went to open the passenger hatch, then turned and motioned for his guards to fetch the prisoners.

McGurn descended the three metal steps to the roof and turned to help Athora. She dropped lightly beside him and slipped an arm through his, her attempt at a brave smile proving largely tremulous. A group of palace guards had pressed forward as the dyark landed and Atim-Lek was in the act of properly identifying himself and the members of his party.

At this point on the roof, midway between its lighted edges, the gloom of night was fairly heavy. The priest and his personal entourage were answering questions put to them by a pantar of the roof guards and, for the moment, Athora and McGurn were free of surveillance.

It was an opportunity not likely to be repeated. McGurn caught the princess' attention, motioned for her to remain where she was, then turned and leaped lightly aboard the same dyark that had brought them to Clyrus…

Bracing himself for the sound of immediate alarm, the young American raced on tiptoes along the flooring to one of the several wall cabinets near the craft's stern. Through the hull openings he could hear the continuing murmur of conversation and an occasional scuff of feet against gravel. Evidently his absence had not yet been noticed, although an alarm was bound to come within seconds.

WITH lightning movements of his fingers, he opened the nearest cabinet, jammed back its locking mechanism and crawled within, pulling its doors closed behind him and holding it shut with steady pressure of his fingers…

A voice outside said something loudly, stilling all conversation for a second or two; then there was a babble of many tongues all at once and feet raced along the roof. A girl's voice, which McGurn recognized as Athora's said something, only to break off in a muffled cry of pain.

McGurn gritted his teeth and waited. Suddenly the line of light outlining the cabinet door grew brighter as a switch was thrown in the dyark's cabin, and feet echoed along the metal flooring.

"He's not in here," growled a man's voice, so close that McGurn started a little despite himself.

"Of course not," replied another. "Only a fool would run no more than a few steps, and only a fool would suggest it."

"What else would you expect a priest to be?" observed the first and both men laughed shortly.

Palace guards, McGurn told himself. He listened to them move carelessly about the cabin before one of them said. "Well, he's not here, that's certain. We'd best find Xyban and tell him so."

"He won't get far," declared the other. "Xyban has posted men at every exit along the roof. Even in the dark he's bound to be spotted; you saw the strange garb he wore."

"Yes. One of Atim-Lek's men says he's neither Atlandian nor Klysan. A stranger from another world, I hear."

"Perhaps Set sent him here from Oruzal. That would explain his ability to disappear so easily."

Their laughter faded as they left the cabin. McGurn let go a muted sigh of relief and allowed tense muscles to relax even as full realization of the hopelessness of his position swept over him. With armed men guarding every avenue to the building and streets below he was faced with the alternative of remaining in this black hole or venturing out to certain capture. As far as being free to accomplish his self-appointed tasks of finding Lua and regaining possession of the Golden God—well, he was as near to success as if he were still in custody.

If only he could get hold of a tunic! His naked chest and the torn uniform trousers were unmistakable evidence of his true identity. Clothed like the Clyrusians and able as he was to speak their tongue he might manage to bluff his way past guards and get on with his search.

But finding a tunic to fit him appeared to be as difficult as finding the Golden God itself. Perhaps if he…

The sound of voices ended his reverie and brought him to sharp attention. They appeared to come from outside the dyark, and a moment later he caught the sound of sandals slithering across metal, apparently moving directly toward the cupboard he was in. McGurn cautiously drew his legs beneath him and made ready to spring into action the moment that door swung back.

But the door remained closed and the footsteps faded again as they passed him by and went on toward the dyark's stern. Metal clanged sharply on metal, then a grating noise, which McGurn immediately identified as door fasteners being secured. Even as he reached that conclusion he felt the floor beneath him lurch, then press up against the balls of his feet.

The dyark was taking off—for what goal only Ammon-Re might know. McGurn eased his strained position and concentrated on holding the cabinet door from swinging open against some motion of the craft.

FOR what seemed no more than a minute the airship moved in a horizontal direction, then once more McGurn felt the dyark begin to sink slowly to earth. There followed the familiar grating sound that meant the white metal hull was grounded on crushed rock, and again sandaled feet moved toward his hiding place…and past. The sound of metal catches being released was repeated, a door clanged open, the line of light outlining the closed entrance to McGurn's hiding place disappeared as an unseen switch was thrown—and then silence.

For what must have been the better part of half an hour McGurn remained crouched behind that cabinet door, his ears straining for some indication that the dyark was in truth deserted. On three separate occasions he caught the sound of human voices but always at what seemed a considerable distance. Satisfied at last that it would be reasonably safe for him at least to quit the narrow confines of his present hiding place, he slowly pushed open the door and stepped out into the cabin beyond.

The interior was in complete darkness. Through the openings in both sides he made out light-tipped poles lining the distant edges of a roof, and beyond them was the blackness of a star-dotted night. As he watched, a human figure moved slowly across the roof some twenty yards from the dyark and faded from sight—the figure of a man in a white tunic, light glinting on the barrel of a huar thrust into his belt.

After a moment's thought, McGurn squatted on the floor and removed his heavy-soled service shoes, tucked them from sight in one of the numerous cupboards and started a careful and systematic search of the dyark.

He spent nearly another half hour in that manner and the net result was—nothing. Evidently huars were not standard equipment so far as the plane was concerned; nor was he able to find a tunic or sandals in any of the numerous compartments.

His captors had removed his flashlight and pocketknife while searching him at the time he was captured, and his cigarettes were cached away in his cave back in Afrota. But his fingers closed on a pack of gum in one pocket and he stripped the wrappings from two sticks and ground them between his teeth. It had been a long time since he had eaten and he was very hungry and thirsty, and the gum did much toward relieving him.

Moving with great caution he came up to the frame of the open door and, peered around it. An empty expanse of graveled roof stretched all the way to the lights marking its edge. McGurn went down the steps and, crouching, circled the dyark at the stern. There, he halted sharply and drew back into the shadow of the craft.

Not more than thirty yards away a mound-like structure marked an opening into the roof leading to the building's interior. Lounging there was the figure of a man, his light-colored tunic gleaming faintly amid the darkness. Some fifty or sixty yards farther down the roof was a similar opening, this one guarded by two tunic-wearing soldiers who appeared to be carrying on a low-voiced conversation.

There was only one course open to Reed McGurn, and no matter how long he stood there telling himself of its danger it was the one he must follow. And so, with a fatalistic shrug of his broad shoulders, he set out across that open expanse of gravel, moving in a wide circle as a means of coming up on the nearest guard from the rear.

Ten minutes later he was crouched behind that protruding mound, near enough to its guardian to hear the sound of his even breathing and the occasional whisper of gravel under his feet.

Sooner or later that man must move and when he moved to the right, he would come within radius of Reed McGurn's hands.

Minutes dragged by. At any moment one of the other guards stationed there might saunter by and put an end to the American's hopes. McGurn turned his eyes skyward and saw that the stairwell covering he was crouched behind had a narrow ledge running about its top, evidently placed there as an ornamental trimming. By standing on his tiptoes, he was able to close his fingers about that ledge and what had been a half-formed idea became a full-fledged plan.

With an agility born of desperation he drew himself up to the top of the mound. Wriggling forward he was able to gain a position above the opening itself and less than two feet from the unsuspecting guard.

WITH great care McGurn measured the distance between him and that exposed throat. His fingers must close there before a cry could emerge. Had not the surface supporting him been curved there would be no difficulty in gaining that hold; as it was a reaching movement might send him headforemost to the roof.

A heavy sigh of utter boredom escaped the guard's lips and he yawned widely, throwing back his head as he stretched his arms high…and stared full into Reed McGurn's eyes…

For a barely appreciable instant the sentry seemed paralyzed with terrified surprise. Then his lips sagged apart and a scream formed in his throat—a scream never uttered as steel fingers darted out to close about his neck.

Even as his hands tightened on the Clyrusian's throat McGurn slipped head first from his elevated position, his descending body forcing his victim backwards to the roof. Frantically he fought to loosen that terrible grip, tearing futilely at those implacable fingers and striking heavy blows at the grim face above his own. But McGurn's hold only grew the tighter, waiting as the efforts to dislodge him grew steadily weaker. Suddenly the guard's body twisted in a convulsive shudder, then sank into stillness and moved no more.

McGurn snatched the huar from the dead man's belt and flattened himself in the open doorway while his ears and eyes sought for a sign that the faint sounds of recent combat had carried to any of the other sentries patrolling the roof. Off to the left the two men he had noticed earlier still were deep in conversation—the only visible signs of life.

Stooping, McGurn took hold of the corpse and dragged it deeper within the stairwell entrance. Working in complete darkness, he stripped the body, stepped out of his own trousers and donned the tunic, tucking the huar under its belt. The sandals were a bit loose but they would do.

His good judgment told him it was time he got out of there. Turning, he groped his way deeper into the hallway, his progress barred after a few steps by another door, this one tightly closed. His fingers found and solved the latch within seconds and carefully he drew the door wide.

A flight of winding steps going down was revealed in the strong light cast by a series of glowing rocks set in tiny depressions in the wall. His interest piqued, McGurn placed a hand near one of them, discovering to his surprise that there was no indication of heat in connection with the radiance. The source of that light could hardly be radioactive, else the entire stairwell would be a death trap.

This was hardly the time to get scientific he reminded himself sharply and continued on down the steps, the huar back in his hand and ready for instant use.

Around one bend he went, then stopped before another door, this one also closed. He pressed an ear against the polished wood, listening for a long moment, but hearing nothing except the pounding of his heart. Squaring his shoulders, he released the catch and pushed into a narrow hall, its floor heavily carpeted.

There was no sign of life along its length. Hangings of some rich red material closed off one end ten feet to his right; to his left were the naked panels of another door.

One direction was as good as another. The drape-covered opening seemed his best bet—easier to hear through than wood and no chance of squeaking hinges while passing through.

The hangings seemed to sway slightly as he drew near and he froze, huar leveled. When, after a full minute, nothing happened he reasoned a current of air was responsible and inched his way forward again.

Another half minute passed while he stood close to the velvet-like curtain…ears cocked for the slightest sound from beyond it. Nothing. He lifted his hand to sweep aside the material—

"What is the meaning of this?" said a quiet voice at his back.

CHAPTER FIFTEEN
Beyond That Door

FROM the south, moving at great speed, a small scout dyark shot over the coast of Atland and swung east toward the capitol city of Atlantis. Rays of the setting sun flooded into its cabin, picking out the grimly set features of the man at its controls.

Doltanar, a member of the palace guard, had come on duty only a few minutes before when he caught a glimpse of the small dyark as it streaked across the circular wall of stone about Atlantis. Sight of the craft interested him only a little, since the air above Atlantis was usually dotted with dyarks. This one, however, was moving much faster than was considered safe in a zone where air travel was usually heavy.

Suddenly the small craft turned sharply and shot straight for the palace roof where Doltanar was standing. It was then he saw the emblem on its bow and he voiced a startled shout of alarm.

"Pantar!" he bawled. "Pantar Santak! A dyark from Clyrus…"

Feet pounded across the roof as Santak, officer in charge, hurried up with several of his men. By this time the small dyark was dropping for a landing—dropping much faster than good flying required.

"Draw your huars," snapped the pantar.

An instant later the craft thudded heavily against the landing strip, sending up a shower of crushed rock from the impact. The door was flung violently back and a tall slender man stumbled drunkenly down the three metal steps.

The officer caught a startled glimpse of a spreading red stain high up on the man's tunic and he darted forward to support the reeling figure.

"Who are you?" he demanded. "What's happened?"

The man shook his head as if to clear a haze from before his eyes. His thin angular face drained of all color and there were lines of agony sharply etched in his cheeks.

"Ashtoth," he mumbled. "Must see—him. Take me to him. Tell him Tanbor—"

His eyes closed and he slumped forward unconscious, saved from falling only by Santak's support.

"Get him below!" cried the pantar to his men, "and find someone to bind up his wounds and restore him to consciousness."

The guards lifted the limp figure and carried it toward the nearest stairwell and Santak hurried below, racing through the palace corridors toward Ashtoth's apartment.

CLAT-RON, high priest to Ammon-Re was pacing the floor in the apartment of Atland's king, while Ashtoth sat slumped wearily on an upholstered ledge near the windows overlooking the grounds below. Both men appeared to have aged during the past two days, their faces drawn with worry and fatigue.

"I can't under*stand* it," the high priest was saying for the tenth time in as many hours. "She couldn't possibly have known of the theft of the Golden God or of Mentanek's request for her hand. Yet we know she left Atlantis of her own accord; the guards she meant to take with her told us that. Then why—*why* has she run away? And where? Where could she have gone?"

Ashtoth passed a tired hand across his face. "I have fifty dyarks out hunting for answers to those questions, Clat-Ron."

THE PRIEST seemed not to have heard him. "She can't be in Clyrus or one of my spies would have sent word to me. The same goes for the Golden God; it is not in their possession. Yet only two lats ago Sar-Gath, the Clyrusian high priest, and the two men who came to Atlantis with him took off for Clyrus without first taking formal leave of you…a serious breach of court etiquette. Something has happened in Clyrus to call him back that hastily—something that may very well be tied in with Athora's disappearance and the theft of the Golden God."

"Clyrus! Clyrus! All I hear is Clyrus!" shouted Ashtoth in sudden anger. He leaped to his feet and began to storm up and down the room. "By the God, I have a good mind to order Mathlane and his armies to attack without warning. Mentanek's corpse alone would feed every fish in the ocean for years."

"We dare not attack them now," Clat-Ron protested. "If they have the Golden God a war would be fatal to Atland. We must be patient, my king. It can't be long before some clue will turn up as to what has happened to Avar-Ak and the Golden God."

"I don't *care* about the Golden God," cried Ashtoth, his worry and fear and uncertainty finally boiling over into almost incoherent rage. "My daughter is gone and all you can talk about is the Golden God. Well, I'm through wait—"

Knuckles suddenly beat against the door—a hasty, impatient knock different from the usual timid rapping it usually received.

Clat-Ron crossed the carpet in three quick strides and flung open the door. A man in the tunic of a pantar of the palace guard was standing there, face flushed with some inner excitement.

"An important message for the noble Ashtoth," he said. "I must see him at once."

"Come in, Santak," called the king, recognizing the other. "What is wrong?"

The pantar advanced to the center of the room and stood there stiffly. "A scout dyark from Clyrus has just landed," he said. "It was flown here by a man who has been badly wounded. He managed to say he must see you immediately, then fainted."

"A Clyrusian? Did he tell you why he wanted to see me?"

"No, noble Ashtoth. He mumbled something that sounded like: 'Tell him Tanbor—' and fell unconscious into my arms."

Clat-Ron's hand shot out and seized the pantar by one shoulder in a suddenly savage grip. "Could it have been 'Tanborin'?"

"It might have been. His voice was very weak."

"Who is Tanborin, Clat-Ron?" asked the king.

"An Atlandian spy I managed to get into Clyrus over a year ago. He is one of the temple guards there and has been of great value to us."

The priest turned back to Santak. "Take me to him at once."

"I will go with you," said Ashtoth.

The three men hurried along the corridor outside the king's private apartment and on into an adjoining wing of the palace. Outside the door to one of the rooms there Santak caught sight of Doltanar, one of the men who had helped in bringing the stranger down from the roof.

Doltanar jerked his head toward the door behind him. "In there."

They filed into a small room, in the center of which stood a low couch on which lay the wounded man, his eyes closed and his face incredibly pale. Bending over him was a white-haired man who was in the act of tying a white bandage about the other's shoulder. He looked up as Clat-Ron and the king entered and made the sign of the triangle, in formal greeting.

A glance at the wounded man's face was all that Clat-Ron needed. "It is Tanborin, all right. Is he badly hurt?"

"He will live," said the white-haired one quietly. "He has lost a great deal of blood from a huar wound in the shoulder."

"Is he conscious? Will he be able to talk now?"

"Yes. Try not to tire him. He is very weak."

THEY approached the bed and Ashtoth, compassion strong in his handsome face, bent and placed a gentle hand on the man's head. "Tanborin," he whispered. "It is Ashtoth, your king. Is there something you want to tell me?"

The eyelids fluttered and came open, revealing a pair of gray eyes clouded with pain. At sight of the monarch the cloud disappeared and the eyes flashed. He struggled to sit up, but the effort was too much for his weakened condition and he sank back, groaning.

"You must lie still," Ashtoth said. "Are you strong enough to speak? Can you tell me why you wanted to see me?"

"Yes," The whispered word was barely audible. "Listen! This morning a dyark came to Clya. From Afrota. Man called…Fargolt. A Klysan girl with him, Fargolt had…the Golden God. Gave it to Mentanek."

Clat-Ron, his face ashen, stared into the eyes of the king. "We are too late," he groaned.

The whispering words went on, growing slowly weaker. "Princess...Athora. Dead. A...Klysan killed her. In Afrota, Fargolt told Mentanek that I was there when...he told him. Mentanek shot us down so...no one else...would know. He...only...wounded me, I got out...stole a dyar—"

The whispering words stopped abruptly and Tanborin's eyes closed. The white-haired man stepped forward quickly and made a hurried examination.

"He is sleeping," he announced, straightening. "It would be wise to postpone further questioning until tomorrow."

Ashtoth, face twisted with grief he was fighting to hide, shook his head. "That will not be necessary. We have heard enough. Come, Clat-Ron."

Not until he and Clat-Ron were back in his apartment did the king speak again. "Athora is dead," he said brokenly. "You heard him say it."

The priest went to the window and stood there staring unseeingly down into the gardens. "Yes, my king. I heard...I loved her, too."

Ashtoth crossed over beside him and dropped a hand on his shoulder in silent understanding. "I know. We share a mutual loss, my friend. But we are leaders of our people. It is our duty to put aside our personal grief to serve those who look to us for protection. We must regain possession of the Golden God before the fat beast Mentanek can use it against us."

Clat-Ron threw his clenched hands wide in a sudden gesture of desperation. "I know, I know! I have thought of nothing else. But how—how can we hope to take back something guarded as closely as Mentanek will be guarding the Golden God?"

The king's shoulders squared with sudden resolve. "First...by thinking... We are both students of war and battle, of campaigns and the elements of strategy and surprise. In this case the problem is clear. Now call on all the things you have learned in an effort to find a solution. I shall do the same."

Darkness came while the two men paced the room like caged animals, their keen minds fighting silently for some method, some way out of their problem—a problem threatening not only their lives but the free existence of their people.

A palace slave entered and threw the switch which exposed the radiant stones set in walls and ceiling, flooding the room with soft light. And later other slaves came silently and set up a table and placed food and drink thereon, then as silently withdrew. And so great, so complete was the concentration of those two men that neither noticed the light nor saw the food. In the great city encircling the palace lights sprang up along the streets and avenues and in thousands of homes, and the people of Atlantis and the people throughout all Atland loved and lived and argued and died and were born while these two men struggled to find a way to keep those people free of slavery from another power.

It was Ashtoth who first broke the silence—broke it with a sudden shout of triumph and exultation that caused his companion to stare at him in startled wonder and dawning hope.

"There is a way, Clat-Ron." He came over to the high priest and shoved him into a nearby chair. "A way that has only a bare chance of succeeding. If it should fail there will be no hope of a second attempt, for Mentanek will fill the skies over Atland with dyarks within a few hours afterward—should we fail."

"Tell me," pleaded Clat-Ron. "For the love of Ammon-Re, tell me!"

"And so simple… No wonder the idea didn't come to me sooner. Listen…"

AT THE sound of the quiet voice from behind him Reed McGurn whirled about, huar leveled, to come face to face with a tall, dignified man of middle age who evidently had stepped into the corridor through one of the doors lining it. For a moment the two men eyed each other in silence, then sudden doubt crossed the expression of the older man.

"You are no guard," he said sharply. "Who are you?"

McGurn's thoughts were fixed only on one subject—Lua, daughter of Yortak. He thrust the muzzle closer to the triangle-studded belt of red material about the man's waist. "No," he growled. "I'm not a guard. You can put me down as an Atlandian if that will help you any. Now where is she? And don't keep me waiting for an answer or I'll burn a hole through that pretty red belt."

The man averted his eyes and shook his head. "I cannot help you. I do not know where she is."

"In that case," McGurn said grimly, "you're no further use to me. So I'll just send you on to Ammon-Re and find her myself."

His forefinger came down lightly against the firing pin on his huar…and the red-belted priest cried out in sudden surrender. "Don't! I'll take you to her… If you promise not to kill me afterward!"

"I'll promise nothing," snarled McGurn. "Get moving before I change my mind."

"Very well," agreed the priest resignedly. "Come with me."

"I'll follow you," corrected McGurn softly. "And there'll be this huar pointed at your back all the way. The first wrong move and you will no longer be with us."

"…As you wish."

The priest led the way through the hangings McGurn had been investigating a moment before, across a large room empty of life and through one of several doors leading off it. This led into another corridor, along which they moved to a flight of steps leading down to the next floor. Descending, they entered a third corridor lined with doors barred from the outside. Halfway along this hall, the priest stopped before one of the barred doors and said:

"She is within. Now I expect you to keep your word and release me. I pledge that I shall not betray you if you will leave the temple at once."

"That trusting I am not," said McGurn. He motioned at the door with the barrel of the huar. "Remove the bar, friend; let's see how good you are at telling the truth."

His face empty of all expression, the priest did as commanded and swung open the door. The room beyond contained a bed, two chairs and a small table. A girl was lying on the bed, face down and apparently sleeping. But where McGurn had expected to see blonde hair and a stained panther skin, were dark curls and a white tunic. After a single glance the American swung his eyes angrily to his guide.

"What're you trying to pull?" he said sharply. "This isn't the girl I'm looking for."

The priest was taken aback. "But I don't understand... What other girl is there you—?"

"Reed! Reed McGurn!"

THE eyes of both men swung to the girl on the bed. She was sitting up now, staring at McGurn, her eyes alight with joy and thanksgiving, and an instant later she was across the room and in his arms.

"Athora!" McGurn pushed her gently aside that he might keep his huar covering the bewildered priest. "So this is where they put you. Come on, we're getting out of here."

"But what of him?" She nodded toward the watching priest.

"Yeah." McGurn eyed the man speculatively. "Can't let him go or he'd have the whole works on our necks before we got ten feet... Here." He handed her his huar. "Keep him quiet a minute. I'll tear some strips off the bed clothes and bind and gag him."

"But he may be found before we can get away," she protested. "It would be better to kill him, Reed McGurn."

"Hell, I can't shoot down a man in cold blood." He turned and took two steps toward the bed when a brief hissing sound reached his ears, followed immediately by a heavy thump. He whirled back—to find the priest dead on the floor, a seared hole in his forehead, and Athora looking at him with a faint smile on her lovely lips.

"He can no longer betray us," she said lightly. "I do not share your reluctance to kill an enemy, Reed McGurn."

"So I see." He reached out and took the huar from her hand, only then releasing his breath. "Come on; we'll find Lua and blow this place."

Some of the warmth went out of her face and her lips narrowed. "There is no time for that, Reed McGurn. Our only hope of escape is to get to the roof of the temple and seize one of the dyarks there."

"I'm not leaving without Lua."

"But we don't even know that she's here," the girl protested. "Why must you peril my safety, and yours, by this senseless desire for a Klysan?"

"She's here, all right. You heard what Atim-Lek said about Fargolt being a Clyrusian spy. There's no other place he could go. Besides; we can't leave without taking along the Golden God, can we?"

She came close to him and slipped her arms about his neck, bringing her flushed, lovely face close to his own. "I don't care about anything but you, my prince. Forget Lua, forget the Golden God—forget everything except that I love you and you love me. Let us find a dyark and leave this horrible place and go far away together—perhaps to your own land, Reed McGurn."

None too gently he disengaged her clinging arms. "Sorry, baby, but it's no dice." Her bewilderment at the strange words reminded him he had spoken in English. "I mean—no. I'm going to find Lua. Do you come with me or do you want to make a break for it—alone?"

Athora bit her lip. "I will not leave you, Reed McGurn. I will never leave you."

"Fine. Now listen to me. The quicker we find her and the gold statue, the quicker we can leave. You're used to the kind of life they live in these cities...where would they be likely to put Lua and that Golden God?"

She thought for a moment. "The Golden God is probably here in the temple—doubtless in the Altar Room itself. If that is so, it would require an army to get it."

"What's so tough about getting into the Altar Room?"

"None may set foot within that holy chamber except the high priest himself. Even a king may not enter. It has but one door and no windows—and that one door is forever guarded by a score of heavily armed priests who know that should anyone enter, other than the high priest himself, their lives would be forfeit and their souls forever be doomed to the awful torments of Oruzal."

"Is that the setup in Atland, too?"

"It is."

"Yet somebody got into that one and made off with the Golden God."

"I know. It is impossible—and yet it was done."

McGurn changed the subject. "What about Lua? Where would they be likely to put her?"

"I imagine she's somewhere in the palace. If Fargolt actually brought her and the Golden God to Clyrus he would be welcomed and great honor would be his for placing within Mentanek's hands the power to conquer Atland. For that reason he—and his woman—would be given an apartment within the palace itself."

MCGURN caught the deliberate sting in the words, "—and his woman—" but ignored it. "Where is this palace?"

"But, my prince," she protested, "only a fool would attempt—"

"Okay, I'm a fool. Where is this palace?"

Athora gave up her efforts to dissuade him. "It was on the palace roof that you escaped from them. I was brought here immediately afterward while the king and Sar-Gath, the high priest, could decide what was to be done with me."

"That doesn't matter now," McGurn said impatiently. "We've decided for them. Can you lead me back to the palace?"

"Yes. I'm sure I can. If we are able to reach the streets."

The American rubbed his chin thoughtfully. "Yeah. There's that, of course. Can you remember the way to the front door of this place?"

"I think so. We came up one flight of steps and through one door into the corridor outside this room."

"Anybody around when you came in?"

"Only two guards just within the entrance itself. The hour is late and most of Clya is sleeping."

"All the better for us." He stood there for a moment, mapping a course of action, his eyes fixed unseeingly on the corpse at their feet. Then: "Only thing we can do is just walk down to the main entrance and on out. If the guards try to stop us I'll have to shoot it out with them."

Athora was shaking her head in patient negation. "It would never work out, my prince. The moment those guards saw us coming down the stairs their huars would be covering us until you could prove to them your right to leave. The people of Clyrus—or Atland, for that matter—do not come and go from the temple as they please."

"That leaves only the back way or the windows."

"Temples, my prince, have only one entrance, and all the windows are barred."

"Well, good lord, we can't just stand here…"

He began to slap a fist lightly against his palm, his forehead furrowed in thought. His roving eyes swept the room, past the furniture, the corpse, the windows and back to the corpse again…

"Hey!" He caught his companion by one softly rounded forearm, a sudden light glowing in his eyes. "How many priests are there in a city this size?"

She gazed at him, wide-eyed. "There are many priests. The rites of worship demand it."

"Are they all pretty well known to everyone by name? I mean would any one temple guard, for instance, know every priest by sight?"

"I don't think so. Oh, a few of the older guards, but even that seems hardly likely. Priests are stationed all over the city."

"Are they free to come and go about the temple?"

"Of course."

"Now we're getting some place," said McGurn triumphantly. He stopped and with quick movements of his hands removed the triangle-studded red belt from about the dead man's waist and fastened it in place about his middle. "I am now a priest," he announced pompously, grinning at the girl's startled expression. "At the order of—of— What's the high priest's name?"

"Sar-Gath," she said in a dazed voice.

"—Sar-Gath himself I am bringing this girl to the palace." He gestured with burlesqued lordliness at a pair of imaginary guards. "Out of my way, scum! Dare you stand in the path of Nabisco, priest of Omahanebraska, himself?"

She was watching him with mingled wonder and admiration in her lovely eyes. "It might work out, at that. You are a brave and resourceful man, Reed McGurn."

"That's what I've been trying to tell you. Let's go…"

SIDE by side they moved along the corridor and around a bend to where a heavy door barred their path. "It was through this door," Athora whispered, "that they brought me. There is a wide flight of stairs just beyond which lead to a great hall. There is the door to the street and there are the pair who guard it."

"Let's hope this one isn't locked," McGurn grunted. His forefinger found the catch and silently the door swung open.

A carpeted continuation of the hall lay beyond, with the top of a flight of steps visible at its end. Moving with neither haste nor reluctance they walked to the steps and down them, side by side, McGurn's hand swinging idly near the huar at his belt.

They were nearly to the floor below before one of a pair of tall, dark-faced men in tunics and with a brace of huars in his belt, glanced up from where he was stationed at one side of massive double doors and saw them. He muttered something to his companion and both men stiffened to attention.

It was not until McGurn and the girl were nearly abreast of the two guards that the one who had first seen them—a sharp-eyed, stern-featured man somewhat older than the other—gave Athora a startled glance of recognition and immediately stepped forward to bar their path.

"Your pardon, noble *tian,*" he said humbly, "but this appears to be a matter I do not understand."

McGurn felt his heart increase its already rapid pounding, but nothing of his inner feelings appeared in his face. He assumed a lofty, rather condescending air, which he felt, was, in keeping with his role as priest, and said:

"I have no time to waste. What is it you want?"

"This woman is the princess Athora, of Atland. She—"

"I know that. Stand aside that we may pass."

"She," the guard went on doggedly, holding his position, "was brought here only a few yads ago and was to remain under guard until Sar-Gath himself arrived to question her."

"Those plans have been changed. Sar-Gath has decided to question her at the palace and I was sent here to get her. Out of my way!"

There was open suspicion in the man's face by this time. "You were sent here by the high priest?"

"That's what I said."

"Strange," murmured the other, "that I did not see you enter the temple. I've been on guard here for over a lat."

"I came in the back way. Now move before I move you…"

The man's eyes narrowed into slits. "There is no back way, *tian!*" His hand flashed for the huar at his hip.

Reed McGurn, however, had recalled Athora's earlier statement that temples had only one entrance the second he saw the man's eyes narrow. As a result his fingers were already closing about his own huar as the guard's hand started to move.

In one single smooth motion Reed McGurn drew and fired pointblank at the man before him. Voicing a startled shriek the guard clutched at his breast and crumpled to the floor. His companion, galvanized into belated action, clawed for his own weapon, only to have it drop from nerveless fingers as McGurn drilled him through the head.

Across the huge hall a door banged open and several red-belted priests, evidently aroused by the first guard's cry, came racing into the room, huars in their hands. Realizing the range was too great for his weapon, McGurn grabbed the girl by one hand and broke for the front door.

He was reaching for the knob when one of the heavy portals swung back, disclosing three white-tunic clad men who were on the point of entering.

CHAPTER SIXTEEN
The Power of Ammon-Re

WHEN Lua, daughter of Yortak, had first been thrust within a small room on one of the palace's upper floors and heard the heavy bar drop into place on the other side, she was aware only of being utterly weary. There was a huge bed near the barred windows—a bed so much larger than the room deserved that only a small amount of open floor remained.

Dispiritedly she crossed to the bed and dropped face down on its yielding surface. What was to become of her? She thought of the incredibly fat man who had sent her here—remembering his final words even as a picture came to her mind's eye of how he had shot down with cold efficiency those helpless men back in that luxuriously furnished throne room.

Lua was hardly more than a savage at heart—accustomed to violence and sudden death and seldom moved by sight of them. But useless and callous murder was strange to her and filled her untamed heart with loathing for anyone capable of such an act.

Because she was completely alone in an amazingly new and frightening world, tears came unbidden to her eyes. Even as they began to roll down her cheeks she was sleeping soundly…

She awoke with a start, to find darkness had fallen outside her window, leaving the room in total blackness. She was conscious too of being very hungry and thirsty but there was nothing she could do about that. Rising she went to the barred window and looked down into the shadowy gardens below. Water from the numerous fountains made a soothing sound against the night and the widely spaced lights atop metal poles made the entire view a thing of beauty.

The sound of the bar outside her door being lifted brought her around quickly, and she watched in helpless fascination as the heavy barrier swung slowly back. In the dim half-light from the hall outside she saw, framed in the opening, a huge hulking shape monstrous and evil. A clicking sound followed and abruptly the room was bathed in light from a number of radiant stones set in recesses in the ceiling.

Mentanek, ruler of Clyrus, stood revealed in the doorway, a small smile on his lips lost in that vast expanse of face. He was forced, because of his immense height, to lower his head to clear the entranceway, and he stalked in and drew the door shut behind him.

Like a bird hypnotized by the unwavering gaze of a snake, Lua could not wrench her eyes from those unblinking eyes in that great expanse of grayish-white flesh.

Mentanek's lips parted and from that cavernous chest thunder seemed to rise and fill the room—thunder that resolved itself into words.

"You need not fear me, Klysan. There is none in all Clyrus who cannot tell you how gentle and kind I can be. Come nearer to me."

Despite herself Lua felt herself moving toward him, compelled by some horrible fascination. She stopped finally directly in front of him but he made no effort to reach out and touch her.

"What is your name, Klysan?"

"Lua."

"What a beautiful name it is—a tribute to your loveliness."

He put out a hand the size of a boulder and passed it lightly over her hair, his touch strangely gentle for a man of his dimensions. The fingers dropped lightly to her bare shoulder, tightened there almost imperceptibly, then fell to his side. "I regret it was necessary for me to kill your lover this afternoon, my dear. But you see he was a very evil man and I dared not let him live."

"He was not my lover," Lua said tonelessly. "I hated him."

"But you came with him to—"

"I came here because he forced me to."

HE TOOK a step nearer, towering over her, those mammoth rolls of flesh that made up his body quivering repulsively with his slightest move. "What a horrible experience it must have been. You are very fortunate that I have taken an interest in you, lovely Lua. You are mine now and I will make you forget how badly you have been treated by that evil man who called himself Fargolt. In return I shall expect you to be…understanding—"

His gross arms slipped slowly about her unyielding body and he bent to bring his moonlike face toward her own. "Tiny, tiny Lua," he murmured. "So alone, so fright—"

And then pure revulsion snapped the spell that had held her helpless and with a snarl that was half sob the cave girl twisted convulsively to free herself of the man's slimy embrace.

To no avail; those immense arms only tightened their hold and the pendulous lips came yet closer. With a single movement Lua raked her nails across that bloated face bringing lines of blood, while her teeth sank through a coating of blubber covering his shoulder.

Mentanek cried out and drew back, releasing her so suddenly that she almost fell. He raised a shaking hand to his torn cheek and an expression of infinite sadness came into his face. "Why?" he said, and for a dazed moment Lua thought he was about to burst into tears. "Why do you repulse me, beautiful Klysan? Can you not understand the things I can give you? All Clyrus can be yours if only you come to me willingly." Again he raised his arms to embrace her. "You must not be cruel to me, Lua. How can one so lovely—"

With a quick turn of her body Lua avoided his grasp and retreated to the far wall, the huge bed between her and the king. Mentanek stood there staring at her, arms still half-lifted, while seconds passed. And then his pleading expression faded gradually, replaced with an ugly anger.

"You have made your choice," he said in a voice like distant thunder. "What you refuse willingly I shall take by force. And when I am through with you, my guards shall enjoy the little loveliness I leave for them..."

Moving with slow, ponderous steps he came toward her, seeming to fill the entire room. Frantically Lua's eyes darted about the chamber, seeking some avenue of at least temporary escape. Between her and the unbarred door loomed that nightmare figure; the wall and the bed hemmed her in on either side.

As the mammoth hands came out once more to seize her, Lua threw herself on the wide bed and sought to roll across it to the open floor beyond. But Mentanek, despite his bulk, was too fast. One hand snaked out and wrapped thick fingers about her slim ankle and she felt herself being drawn to his embrace.

A hand caught her by one shoulder and as he drew her close, the stench of his breath beat against her nostrils. "You might have shared a kingdom," he muttered; "instead you shall—"

A heavy knock sounded at the door.

Without loosening his hold Mentanek turned his heal. "Go away!" he thundered.

"Open, noble Mentanek," called a voice from the corridor. "I must speak with you at once!"

FOR a moment Lua thought he would ignore the summons; then with an abrupt sweep of his arm he threw her into a heap on the bed and turned to cross the room and go out the door.

He did not close the portal completely and Lua was able to hear the conversation that followed.

"I regret disturbing you, noble Mentanek, but Sar-Gath, high priest to Ammon-Re has just arrived from Atland in response to your summons. He asks that you do him the honor of coming at once to the temple where he is already closeted with the commanders of your armies."

"Tell him the matter will wait. A lat or two either way will not ruin his plans."

"I was instructed to inform the noble Mentanek that every yad counts. There is a report that a member of your own guard, wounded in some unknown manner, fled Clyrus in a dyark earlier today and headed for Atland. Sar-Gath, upon being told of the incident, feels the man was a spy and that he may have reached Ashtoth of Atland by this time and told him that the Golden God is being held within the Altar Room itself."

"Why was I not told of this before?" thundered Mentanek.

"As to that I cannot say."

"It would seem I am being served by fools and traitors. Only a lat ago the man who was captured with Atland's princess escaped from my guards with unforgivable ease. Have they found him yet?"

"Not to my knowledge, noble Mentanek."

"Not to my knowledge," mimicked the king angrily. "Once this business of taking over Atland is out of my way I shall make some changes here. Very well. I shall go to the temple. But my stay there will be brief; I have an important matter here to dispose of."

The door shut and Lua, still huddled on the bed heard the heavy bar thud into place and the sound of feet retreating along the hall.

Minutes dragged by and she made no movement—only lay there trembling with relief at her narrow escape and growing horror of what his return would mean.

Despite the turmoil within her she began to sink once more into the blessed relief of sleep when a sudden stealthy sound in the corridor outside brought her bolt upright on the bed.

A moment later she heard the bar being lifted slowly from its place.

ONLY because McGurn's nerves were keyed to expect danger from every quarter was he able to act more quickly than any of the three men who had opened the temple door. Too, his huar was already within his hand, while the newcomers still wore theirs at their belts.

And so it was that McGurn's weapon was spitting its lance of fire while the men outside were still slack jawed at finding him barring their way. Two of them died before realization came; the third, a tall, hawk-nosed individual who wore the familiar triangle-encrusted belt about his waist, caught one of his sagging companions by the belt and held him as a shield while he drew his own huar. McGurn, seeing there was no time to angle for a crippling shot, lifted a foot and, planting it against the limp shield, shoved with all his strength, upsetting the living enemy behind it and sending him sprawling.

All this took place within seconds, and McGurn and the girl were gone into the darkness of the surrounding gardens before those within the temple were able to gain the door.

When the hoarse cries from behind them could no longer be heard, McGurn and Athora slowed their headlong pace to a walk; and soon thereafter the winding path they were following ended at one of the building-lined streets forming the bulk of Clyrus.

Spaced at regular intervals were metal poles some twelve of fifteen feet high and tipped with the strange, light-giving balls of rock common to both Clyrus and Atland. These, however, were far enough apart to furnish no more than a ghostly radiance sufficient to prevent collision with other pedestrians but not strong enough to permit close scrutiny of any chance passerby.

They covered two full blocks before regaining breath enough to waste on conversation. Several times they passed other white-tunic clad figures on the street, but without attracting any undue attention or interest. Then McGurn said:

"Okay, we've reached the streets. Now how do we go about getting to the palace?"

Athora took a deep breath. "Are you still determined to go through with your mad attempt to rescue that Klysan?"

"Her name," McGurn said promptly, "is Lua. And I am!"

"Very well." Athora lifted her head and looked beyond the one and two-story edifices lining the street. "Over there," she said, pointing to a four-story structure whose outlines were lost in darkness but from windows of which lights marked its location. "There is the palace of Mentanek. No other building in all Clyrus is so tall."

"About four streets over and three ahead," mused McGurn. "That's where we're going."

They covered the distance without incidence, reaching one of the unguarded paths leading into the palace gardens. Here the darkness was more intense and they threaded their way past clumps of bushes, half-hidden benches and whispering fountains until the path ended at the outer perimeter of a circle of open ground bordering the white walls of the palace itself. Directly across from them was a side doorway, closed by a heavy wooden portal, in front of which stood an armed guard.

McGurn drew the girl into the concealing shadows of a bush at the path's edge. "What are the chances that door is locked or bolted from the inside?"

"It probably isn't locked," Athora replied. "Else they would not have stationed a guard there."

"Fine. There's where we're going in."

"But…the guard…"

"Yeah. The guard… Look, you're used to these palaces and their routines. What would be the reaction of a guard in Atland who was watching one of the entrances to your father's palace and somebody came walking up to him. Would he shoot first and ask questions later, or what?"

"He would not fire at once," Athora said. "He would demand to know why we were trying to enter by a side door when all visitors must go into the palace by the principal gate. Because of the many spies and possible assassins in both countries none may enter without proving the right to do so."

"But we could get close enough to talk to him?"

"Yes. But the moment he sees us he will draw his huar and cover you until we are permitted to enter or have left."

"Cover *me*, huh?"

"Why yes. The only possible danger to him would be from you…" At his meaningful silence comprehension lighted her face. "Of course!" she exclaimed.

"Smart girl," McGurn said approvingly. "Here," he added, drawing his huar and handing it to her. "Stick this under your belt, pretty well toward your back so he can't spot it as we come up to him. While I'm talking you sort of sidle away until he can't watch you too well. Then pull out the huar and tell him to put up his hands."

"But what if he shoots you anyway?"

"Are sentries around palaces that fanatical?"

"The chances are they're not," she admitted. She tucked the gun into her belt as McGurn had designated, and together they stepped into the expanse of open ground and moved toward the guarded doorway at a brisk walk.

THE armed warrior caught sight of them while they were still twenty feet away. Instantly his hand shot to his belt and came up with a huar, which he leveled at McGurn.

"Halt where you are," he commanded crisply.

"A thousand pardons," McGurn said easily, still moving ahead but at a slower pace. He appeared relaxed and friendly and a trifle ashamed. "This young lady and I made—"

"Halt or I'll fire!" There was no mistaking the ring in the man's voice.

McGurn stopped immediately, but the space between them was now no more than ten feet, Athora being a pace or two further back.

"Who are you?" snapped the guard, "and why are you approaching this entrance?"

The American spread his open hands, more to indicate their emptiness than anything else. "We've run into a little trouble," he said placatingly. "My companion is a daughter of one of the guards stationed at the palace entrance. He has forbidden me to see her…" He was aware that Athora was moving little by little to one side. "…and she fears to pass him. Of course, he has no reason to dislike me, but for some cause of which I am in total ignorance he refuses to allow his daughter—"

"What is the name of her father?" demanded the sentry suspiciously.

Even a moment's hesitation might get him a streak of fire through the head, McGurn realized. "Hitler," he said the first word that popped into his mind.

"Hitler?" The man's forefinger jerked toward the huar's firing pin. "There is no such name in all—"

A lance of flame glinted briefly in the night and the guard crumpled and fell, the huar dropping from nerveless fingers.

McGurn's sigh of relief was an unashamed gasp. He darted forward and caught up the dead man's huar. "And just in time," he said to the coldly smiling Athora. "There are times you come in handy."

Because he spoke in his own tongue she did not understand his words but the tone made her beam with happiness at having pleased him. McGurn was already at the door and an instant later it swung back, revealing a softly lighted hallway.

Nobody was in sight along its length. Quickly Athora followed him in and McGurn was about to swing the heavy door shut when he caught a glimpse of an open doorway a few feet along the hall. The room beyond was dark. Quickly McGurn caught up the dead body of the guard and pushed it within the darkened room, closing the door upon it.

"That may keep an alarm being given too soon," he whispered in explanation. Then he said, "Well, I'd say we've done pretty good, everything considered. Now where is it likely that Lua would be in this place?"

Athora said, "It is unthinkable that you should have come this far without losing your life—and mine in the bargain. But beyond this I cannot help you. The Klysan might be in anyone of the palace's three hundred rooms…"

McGurn scratched his head with the muzzle of his huar. "Like that, hey? All right. We'll find somebody who *can* tell us."

"But you'll be killed on sight."

"Maybe," He gave her a grin he was a long way from feeling. "We'll see. Come on…"

Together they moved along the hall, side by side, their manner relaxed, their progress casual, their hearts in their throats. Through a door—and into a large, overly furnished room crowded with men and women grouped about a table loaded with food. Others were standing and there was a buzz of conversation.

The fact there were so many undoubtedly saved them from being noticed particularly. The triangle-studded belt about McGurn's middle attracted the attention of one of the men in the room; for as he came toward them McGurn saw he wore a similar belt.

Athora saw another door, open, off the room and only a short distance away. Lightly she slipped an arm through that of her escort and, smiling engagingly up into his face said, too low for any of the others to hear:

"Don't let him catch your eye. Look at me! Turn to your right; there's a door only a few feet from us."

AT ANY moment McGurn expected to hear the priest call upon them to halt; then they were through the opening and moving along another hall lined on either side with doors.

McGurn whistled soundlessly and slowed his steps. "That was close. Wonder why he singled me out?"

"It was a dinner in honor of some court noble. At such affairs it is customary for any priest who attends to call down Ammon-Re's blessing on the principal guest." She laughed a delicious little giggle of amusement. "I would have loved to hear you invoke a blessing from Ammon-Re!"

The American glanced at her approvingly. What a woman she was. Stealing through the corridors of an enemy stronghold, with probable capture lurking at every turn, and she could still laugh. He caught himself comparing this girl with Lua, and this time Atland's princess did not suffer quite so much in comparison…

"We can't waste much more time," he said. "Let's get our hands on somebody who knows where Lua is and coax the information from him."

"It will not be easy."

"So few things are."

Through another door at the corridor's end—this time into a reception room, to judge by its furnishings. It was deserted; but at the far end an open doorway revealed a flight of carpeted steps leading to the floor above.

Up they went, feet soundless on the thick piling, McGurn in the lead. Another corridor lined with doors. Here, however, the rug was more deeply piled, the walls were hung with rich tapestries depicting scenes of court life and battles magnificently done, the doors were decorated with intricate scrollwork.

"It would seem we are in the palace wing that houses Mentanek himself," whispered Athora, glancing around. "Such as this is found in Atland's palace."

"Then Lua may be behind one of these doors?"

"Perhaps. But it would take hours to investigate them all, for the quarters of a king take up a great deal of the palace itself. No, we must find—"

Suddenly a door almost abreast of them swung back and a short, thickset young man stepped into the corridor. At sight of McGurn his eyes went wide and his hand darted for the huar at his belt—only to freeze an inch from its stock at sight of the muzzle pointed at his heart.

"Who are you?" the newcomer muttered, "and what are you doing in Mentanek's apartment?"

"My name would mean nothing to you," McGurn said. He smiled thinly. "You might put me down as a friend of the family's. What's your name?"

"I am called Ceodmak, noble of the court of Mentanek," was the sullen reply. "I demand to know why you are here. Unless you have an excellent reason I shall report you for trespassing."

McGurn's mind was racing. "Perhaps *I* should be the one to do the reporting," he challenged. "What right do you have being here?"

Ceodmak drew his not very considerable length stiffly erect. "Now I know you have no right to be here. There is none in all Clya who does not know that I, Ceodmak, am Mentanek's personal attendant, that in these quarters I am second only to the king himself."

"Is that true?" McGurn allowed the other to see that he was impressed. "Why, a man in your position must know everything that goes on around here—no matter how trifling."

It was a trap—but Ceodmak was too bent on adding to the impression he was making to sense it. "Exactly," he said. "It is my business to know. Now hand over that huar at—"

"I'll hand you fire from its muzzle," growled McGurn, "if you don't tell me where Lua is."

Ceodmak's jaw sagged at the abrupt change in the man who had been so visibly impressed only a moment before. "L-Lua?" he stammered. "I know nobody by that name."

WITH a single rapid motion McGurn struck the Clyrusian across the face with the huar's barrel. "Don't give me that," he snarled. "Where is she?"

The man staggered back, a shaking hand lifted to his cut cheek, fear flooding his eyes. "But I don't know who—"

"The Klysan girl who was brought here earlier in the day," interposed Athora, satisfied the stricken man was being truthful. "An Atlandian traitor named Fargolt owns her."

Ceodmak's expression cleared. "That one? Fargolt owns her no longer. In fact, Fargolt is dead…"

"Dead, hey?" McGurn's eyes lighted up. "I owe something to whoever killed him."

"Mentanek killed him and his body was thrown to the beasts."

"What happened to the girl?"

The other looked away. "As to that I do not—" At sight of the huar lifted to strike him again he shrank back, lifting his hands as a shield. "Mentanek took her for himself as she is very beautiful for a Klysan."

"Where is she?"

"I—I assure you I do not know," This time McGurn made no effort to strike. Instead he leveled his weapon at the man's head and his finger hovered close above its firing lever. "Then you're no good to me," he said between set teeth. "This is where you leave us, friend; I'll find somebody who can be of help."

"Wait!" The king's personal attendant cowered back. "Don't kill me. I will take you to her but you must not let Mentanek know I did so or he will put me to death."

"And if I don't find her I'll do the job for him. Get moving…"

"B-But Mentanek is with her now. How will—"

McGurn, his face suddenly white, thrust the huar's muzzle hard against the man's middle and sending his breath *whooshing* between his lips. "Move!"

They went on down the hall to a door at its far end. Ceodmak hesitated, his hand on its knob. "The room beyond," he whispered, "leads into a corridor off which is the room where the Klysan was put. Four guards are on constant duty beyond this door."

"It's up to you to get us past them," McGurn said flatly. "And the first wrong move on your part, or theirs, and you'll be the first one to get it."

Ceodmak nodded, appeared to brace himself, then pushed open the door as McGurn, unnoticed, thrust his huar into the belt of his tunic.

They went into a large square chamber, its furnishings more severe than those of the other rooms of Mentanek's quarters. Directly across from them were four guards, two on either side of a pair of closed double doors. As McGurn's party entered, the sentries reached automatically for their huars, but at sight of Ceodmak in the lead they relaxed and their hands fell to their sides.

"Open!" snapped Ceodmak imperiously, gesturing at the door. Wordlessly one of the guards obeyed and McGurn and Athora followed their captive through.

The instant the doors had closed behind them McGurn's huar was back in his hand and prodding Ceodmak onward. The hall along which they now passed was wider than the others they had found, and lined with doors—all of them barred—*from the outside!*

Halfway along its carpeted flooring their guide halted and pointed at one of the doors. "She is within," he whispered, almost too low for them to hear. "Mentanek is in there with her now. I beg you…do not let him know that it was I who brought you here."

"I don't see any way to keep him from know—" McGurn was suddenly silent, his keen eyes fixed on the indicated portal. "Wait a minute, guy. What are you trying to pull?"

Both Ceodmak and Atland's princess blinked at him uncomprehendingly at sound of the unfamiliar words. McGurn took a deep breath and, in their own language, said, "If Lua is in there and Mentanek is with her—*then why is that door barred?*"

The Clyrusian stared open-mouthed. "But I don't understand. He went to her only a few yads ago…"

VOICING a muttered curse McGurn stepped forward on soundless feet and slowly and stealthily removed the heavy bar, then motioned for Ceodmak to open the door and precede them through. The man's hand was shaking as it closed about the knob, then with a quick motion he flung back the door.

Sitting upright in the center of a huge bed within the room was Lua, daughter of Yortak!

With a single bound McGurn shoved his guide aside and was across the threshold, huar ready to blast in case Lua had not been alone. And then Lua was off the bed and in his arms, tears of joy and thanksgiving streaming down her cheeks. "It is you, Reed-mcgurn! You came for me! Now do I know that you…that you…"

Her voice faltered and was still as she noticed the princess Athora staring at her with eyes flashing a mixture of pain and hatred, and she drew slightly away, her face flaming. In the silence that followed, McGurn motioned for Ceodmak and the princess to enter and close the door.

"Our next step," McGurn said tersely, "is to gain the roof and get hold of a dyark large enough for the three of us." His narrowed eyes went to their unwilling guide. "Where's the nearest way to get there, friend?"

"Continue on along the corridor outside," was the prompt reply, "then enter the chamber beyond the end door. Four entrances lead off that room. The one on your extreme right gives on to a flight of steps leading directly to the palace roof."

"Fine. Lead the way."

"But—but I have given you directions. You no longer need me. You have only to…"

"You gave directions a little too readily," McGurn said sharply. "Quit stalling and start moving…"

His gesture with the huar was more lucid than his words and Ceodmak obeyed with alacrity. When they reached the chamber he had mentioned they found it deserted of life. The Clyrusian went without hesitation to one of the four doors and reached for its knob.

"Hold it," the American said. "You said the extreme right. That one's the extreme left."

Ceodmak shrugged and tried a wry smile, which failed to live up to its name. "I know," he admitted. "But that was before I learned you were taking me with you."

McGurn grunted. "I ought to slug you one."

The four of them filed up the winding steps and a few moments later were standing just within the dome-like structure masking the exit onto the roof. Some distance beyond them was the first of three dyarks—all of them sufficiently large to carry them safely from Clyrus. Other dyarks, most of them the smaller type used for scouting, lined the roof's edge, faint radiance from the light poles giving an atmosphere of ghostly gloom to the entire scene.

Escape lay not more than thirty to forty yards away. But between them and that escape were the dim forms of several landing field guards moving restlessly about the crushed-stone surface.

"Looks like we're going to need you again, Ceodmak," the American pointed out. "Lead the way to that first dyark, and no little signs or unnecessary words if anyone stops you. Otherwise you earn yourself a hole in the head."

"I cannot help you now," the Clyrusian said resignedly. "These guards will take no orders from me. Their pantar is answerable only to Rythark, or to Mentanek himself. Your break for freedom ends here, my friend."

"You sure discourage easy," McGurn grumbled. He stood there for a moment, gnawing his lip and gazing longingly at the distant dyark. Abruptly he turned to Athora.

"Give me your huar."

"But you cannot hope to shoot down every—"

"Give it to me."

Wordlessly she reached within the folds of her tunic and brought out the huar McGurn had taken earlier from the dead body of the guard outside the palace.

"How," McGurn asked, "do I fix this thing so it won't work?"

"But why would you—"

"Come *on!* Tell me!"

"Remove the round ball set just ahead of the stock. A twist to the left will free it. Within its opening you will find a bit of stone and a small rod of creonum. By removing that rod the huar will be rendered useless."

MCGURN was following her directions as she spoke. With the designated rod removed he snapped into place the round ball and handed the worthless weapon to the astonished Ceodmak.

"Here's what you do," he told the Clyrusian. "Keep that huar pointed at us while we cross to the dyark. We'll walk a few paces ahead but I'll be off to one side just far enough to keep an eye on you for tricks. My own huar will be in my hand but concealed by the folds of my tunic. If any of those guards stop you your story is that we are prisoners being taken by you to the temple at Mentanek's orders. That huar you're holding will probably convince 'em you're telling the truth. Understand what you're to do?"

"I—think so."

"Think so, hell! You mess this up and Mentanek will need a new boy."

Again the American's words were unintelligible but his meaning was crystal clear. Ceodmak nodded and they started boldly across the faintly lighted roof, the Clyrusian a pace or two behind them.

For a delirious thirty seconds McGurn thought they would reach the dyark unchallenged. Then from the surrounding gloom two white-tunic clad guards, huars in hand, barred their way.

"What is the meaning—" one of them began, then recognizing the man with the huar, stopped uncertainly, adding: "Your pardon, noble Ceodmak. I failed to recognize you in the faint light."

"Of course."

The guard hesitated. "I—ah— It will be necessary for me to report this matter to my pantar, noble Ceodmak. You will be kind enough to inform me of the details?"

"I understand." Ceodmak was carrying out his act with superlative finesse, undoubtedly because his life depended on doing so. "These are prisoners I have been ordered to take to the temple where Mentanek awaits them for questioning."

"I am grateful for your gracious explanation, noble Ceod—"

Suddenly the speaker's eyes were fixed sharply upon McGurn's middle and the huar he had lowered flashed up to cover the group once more. "There is something wrong here!" he exclaimed. "This man is wearing the belt of a priest…"

Athora, understanding too late the blunder she had permitted, felt her heart sink. Priests who were prisoners of the State were not permitted to retain their holy badge of office. Another second and the entire plan would collapse into ruin.

But Ceodmak, the memory of that huar hidden in McGurn's tunic, was equal to the crisis. "This man is no priest," he said boldly. "He was captured while masquerading as one and the belt was left in place to prove his guilt of that charge."

"I see," Three breaths of relief released in unison, were faintly audible. "Forgive me for acting thus hastily, noble Ceodmak. I was but doing my duty."

He bowed and retreated back into the shadows while the taut-nerved group of four moved on toward the dyark. From the corners of his eyes McGurn saw their questioner join two of his fellows and saw all three were staring after them.

The dyark loomed before them now, its entrance hatch ajar. Another problem confronted the American now—in what order should they enter. Normally a guard would send his prisoners ahead lest one of them break for freedom the moment his back was turned. But for them to go in first, leaving Ceodmak behind even for a moment would give the Clyrusian an opportunity to sound an alarm.

But a glance at the man's face convinced McGurn he was thoroughly cowed and would dare not give them any trouble. And so it was that as the second of the two girls entered the dyark's cabin, McGurn went up the three metal steps ahead of Ceodmak, meaning to turn and cover him the moment he was out of sight of the other guards.

But the wily Ceodmak was not so frightened as he had appeared. The moment McGurn turned his back, the Clyrusian dived nimbly beneath the sheltering bulk of the ship, setting up a simultaneous shout of alarm that echoed across the landing field and brought guards racing from all directions.

MCGURN slammed the heavy door and threw its catches. "Quick!" he shouted to the dazed princess. "Get this thing out of here!" A horrible thought crossed his mind. "Good lord, don't tell me you don't know how to fly it..."

Athora was already on her way to the pilot's chair. "Of course I can fly a dyark," she flung over her shoulder. "Every child in Atland can do so."

McGurn, at the nearest window, made no reply. He aimed his huar at a guard dashing toward the ship and sent a streak of fire into his body. The man fell, skidding head foremost across the crushed stone, and McGurn ducked back suddenly as a lance of fire from another quarter melted the metal window frame inches from his head.

And then the heavy ship lurched abruptly, rising steeply into the night as Athora's fingers darted along its instrument panel. Below a cluster of guards became swiftly dwarfed as the distance grew greater and tiny streaks of flame fell impotently short as the dyark moved out of range.

"We made it!" shouted McGurn, his spirits soaring with the ship. In an ecstasy of relief he threw his arms about the blonde cave girl beside him and crushed her to him until she cried out in pain. "I guess we showed 'em what happens when they fool around with—"

Suddenly a searing wave of heat seemed to pass along the ship's entire length and it staggered sickenly, then rolled at right angles in midair, throwing both McGurn and Lua to the floor. Before they were able to regain their feet Athora managed to right the dyark somewhat, but already the craft was slanting earthward in a steep dive.

"What happened?" McGurn cried wildly, clutching at one of the seats to maintain his balance. "Why are we going down again?" He raced back to where Athora, her face a white, expressionless mask, was wrestling with the controls.

"A ray from one of the big huars hit us," she exclaimed, her voice curiously flat. "I hadn't expected they could get one in use so quickly. We are out of range now but that one blast melted away most of our power, leaving us just enough buoyancy to keep from falling like a stone."

McGurn's eyes were fixed on the vision screen, intent on the scene below. They were floating slowly but steadily down on a slanting path, the buildings below swimming slowly up to meet them.

A glimpse of a white, flat-topped building just to the left of their course and not far ahead struck a responsive chord in his memory. "What building is that?" he cried, pointing at the image on the screen.

She hesitated. "I'm not—why, it's the temple we left only a short while ago!"

"I thought so. I can see several dyarks on its roof. Can you set this thing down on that landing strip, Athora? It's our only chance."

"I can try." Her slender fingers thudded against two of the buttons on the panel and sluggishly the heavy craft swung left. As the temple roof swam slowly beneath them, McGurn indicated a large dyark resting there only a few feet removed from one of the rounded domes masking a stairwell.

"Try to put her down right next to that dyark. I'll have our door open and my huar ready to cover you and Lua while you make a dash for it."

"The odds are against us," the princess said matter-of-factly, nodding toward the images of a score of white-tunic clad guards converging at the point where the injured ship was about to land.

McGurn grunted. "I'm getting used to being on the short—and dirty—end." Huar in his hand he ran swiftly to the passenger hatch and threw back its catches, one hand flat against the section of metal, ready to thrust it open the moment their craft grated against the crushed-stone surface of the temple roof.

CHAPTER SEVENTEEN
Defilers of the Temple

WITH a breathtaking lurch the dyark struck the rooftop, then skidded forward in an uncontrolled half circle. An instant later there was the sound of tearing metal as the injured dyark crashed full into the side of the parked craft in which McGurn had hoped to make a fresh break for freedom.

The American had flung open the door a second before. Unprepared for the sudden impact he was flung violently forward through the open hatch and full in the midst of a group of guards.

Three human forms went down beneath him, cushioning his fall, and before the remaining pair could grasp what had taken place, he was on his feet and the huar in his hand had cut them down.

The two girls were already descending the dyark's three steps to join him. McGurn, after a single kick that reduced to unconsciousness the only guard showing signs of life, whirled about and discharged his huar at four men racing across the roof toward him. These paused as the fiery impulses crackled about their heads, then retreated momentarily as Athora caught up a huar from the hand of an unconscious guard and added her fire to McGurn's.

It required only a moment for the American to size up their hopeless position. "These wrecked dyarks cover us from two sides," he pointed out to his companions, "and we can probably hold off any attack until dawn. But after that they need only to send a dyark or two at us from above and—" He left the rest unsaid.

"If only I could have kept from crashing into that dyark," Athora said sadly.

"You did a big job of getting us down here without breaking our necks," McGurn pointed out cheerfully. His roving eye caught sight of the opening into the stairwell only a few feet distant. "Look, there's no point staying here where we can be picked off like clay pigeons. Let's try making a break for it through the temple itself."

"If not that," Athora said, "we may be able to find a hiding place somewhere below, remaining concealed until a better opportunity comes for us to steal a dyark."

McGurn stooped and caught up another huar and handed it to Lua. "Think you can work this?"

"Of course."

He glanced at her quickly, noticing her subdued, almost sad expression and remembering she had said but little since her rescue. "Anything wrong, Lua? Other than the fix we're in?" he added, grinning.

"Nothing is wrong, Reedmcgurn."

"We'll lick this thing yet and spend the rest of our lives laughing at it together."

The tenderness in his tone, the unmistakable meaning in his words, caused her to reach out impulsively and touch his bare arm in a brief caress. But the sadness in her eyes did not disappear.

"I think," Athora's quiet voice broke in, "they are preparing to rush us again."

McGurn nodded. "We're not waiting. Come on; we'll make a run for that stairwell."

Crouching to lessen the chances of being hit by enemy fire, they broke suddenly across the open stretch of roof between the dyark and their new goal. A chorus of angry shouts told them their move had been observed and fire streaks cut apart the night in their direction.

McGurn entered the doorway last, pausing to return the fire and bringing an abrupt halt to any enemy advance. Then he turned back and, motioning his two charges to precede him, hastened down the narrow flight of steps.

At the first landing McGurn brushed past the girls and threw open the door, only to jerk back and slam it shut as a dozen lances of fire burned as many holes through its metal.

"A roomful of them!" he yelled. "Come on; we'll try the next floor."

Down they went, sandals clicking on bare metal. At ground level now, McGurn opened a door off the landing a crack and peered through. Directly above them feet thundered on the steps.

"Empty," he whispered harshly. "Follow me and keep those huars ready..."

THEY filed quickly across a wide, richly furnished room and on through a door McGurn selected at random in the far wall. This gave on to a corridor similar to others the young American had traversed this night, and along it they raced past several doors all of which were closed.

The corridor forked ahead of them, and even as McGurn was debating which of them to follow, the decision was made for him as a door at the end of the left-hand fork was thrown back and several guards swarmed through. At sight of the escaped prisoners they uttered an exultant shout and bore down upon them, only to fall back in confusion as McGurn's fire-spitting huar cut down the leading pair.

"To the right!" roared McGurn. "We've got to reach that door before they get to the fork…"

Both girls proved even fleeter of foot than McGurn; and the door was opened by the time he reached it. He slammed it shut behind them and then went down a long carpeted ramp at headlong speed—down and down until the man from the Twentieth Century realized they must be well underground by this time.

Twice the incline turned sharply left passing room after room lining the way; those whose doors were open apparently empty of life.

When McGurn was no longer able to hear sounds of pursuit he called to Lua and Athora to slow their pace that they might save their strength. "Any idea where this can be leading us, Athora?"

"None," was the prompt reply. "There is nothing like this in Atland's temple so far as I know."

The ramp's downward slant ceased abruptly, at the same time splitting into three separate tunnel-like corridors. In the ceiling small bits of illuminated rock cast rays of light on the scene. Each corridor appeared to turn after a short distance, making it impossible to see where any of them led or ended.

As they stood there debating which avenue to follow, faint sounds reached their ears from a long ways behind them.

"We've got to keep going," McGurn said. "Let's take the middle path. But first…"

He drew the red, triangle-adorned badge of priesthood from about his waist and cast it a dozen feet further along the winding corridor to his left.

"That may draw them into the wrong way for a while."

Moving at a brisk but soundless pace they hurried down the center corridor, hesitating briefly before rounding each turn. After progressing a hundred yards in this manner they followed an abrupt bend and stepped squarely into a small circular chamber, freezing to an abrupt halt as four surprised guards, fully armed, rose to confront them.

McGurn was keyed to expect trouble; the guards were not—the sole reason why his huar was spitting soundless lances of death before a weapon could be raised against him and his companions. Within seconds four lifeless bodies lay scattered about the chamber and McGurn was crossing to the single huge door on its opposite wall.

He had it open and was well within the chamber beyond, huar ready for instant use, before six men seated about a giant black wood table occupying most of the floor space were aware of his presence.

For a long breathless moment no one spoke or moved. McGurn was staring at open-mouthed wonder at the gargantuan figure seated at the table's head…the most fantastically fat, fat man he had ever seen.

The others were the usual lean, hawk-nosed, dark-skinned men he was accustomed to meeting in Clyrus, although three of them wore the red, triangle marked belts of priests, and each had about him that indefinable air of authority that marks all leaders of men.

McGurn spoke first. "Sit still," he commanded. "And I mean still. The first one who moves so much as his eyebrows gets himself killed."

His words, in English, meant nothing to them, but the savage gesture with the huar he was holding spoke recognizable volumes. They remained glued to their chairs, hands resting on the table before them, eyes fixed unwaveringly upon the young American and his two companions.

SLOWLY McGurn let his eyes drift about the room. Across from where he stood was a mammoth door of solid creonum, two dials similar to a safe's combination knobs set in its surface. The rest of the room was richly, although austerely, furnished, and its only other door was the one through which he and the girls had entered.

It was not until his eyes came back to the table and the men about it that he saw two objects, side by side, on the wood's polished black surface. Both he recognized instantly—one the long-barreled xorth taken from him by Atim-Lek earlier that same day; the other was the golden image of Ammon-Re, its strangely pulsating light partially concealed by one of Mentanek's tremendous hands.

"All right," McGurn said tersely. "On your feet—all of you. And the first man who moves his hands any direction except straight up will never move them again."

Wordlessly the six Clyrusians rose from their chairs, hands lifted shoulder high as evidence of their peaceful intentions. "Now your noses against the wall," the American ordered, "and keep your hands raised."

When his command had been obeyed, McGurn gave low-voiced instructions to his two companions to keep their huars trained on the six while he removed their weapons. Carefully he moved along the row of stiffened backs, one hand holding his own huar ready while the other snaked a fire-pistol from each belt add tossed it onto the table. This accomplished without untoward incident, he spent a few, precious minutes removing the tiny metal rod from each huar, rendering them useless.

With the fangs of the enemy drawn, McGurn restored his own huar to his belt and caught up a world's most terrible weapon—the xorth. An uninhibited smile—his first in several days—crossed his lips and he flourished the xorth in a gesture of airy nonchalance.

"This is what will get us out of here," he said to the watching girls, "—and with us goes this!" and he caught up the figure of the Golden God.

There was no warning—no hurried footsteps, no excited voices. Suddenly the chamber door burst open and before McGurn could wheel about five Clyrusian guards had crossed the threshold, huars ready in their hands.

Their leader proved quicker of wit than most of these men McGurn previously had encountered; for even as the American was turning, the guard struck a swift blow with the muzzle of his huar, knocking McGurn's xorth to the floor. A moment later the huars fell from the paralyzed fingers of both girls in response to a sharp command.

"Me," said McGurn in tones of pure disgust. "I'm the guy who thought of everything. I took all their guns. I got hold of the Golden God. I had the one thing in my hand that would get us out of here. Yes, sir, I thought of everything—except, by thunder, to lock the door! Old hero McGurn—that's me!"

Only the girls were listening to his self-castigation and neither of them understood any of the rush of foreign words.

Now came the monstrous Mentanek, his button eyes alight with supreme satisfaction. "Well done, Lebardat," he said to the leader of the guards. "You arrived not a moment too soon. I am curious to learn how you knew these three were in here."

"Four dead men lie outside your door," replied Lebardat. His face was very grave and there were lines of worry deep in his brow. "I bring disquieting news, noble Mentanek. Only a few yads ago a host of Atland's dyarks, carrying hundreds of her fighting men, crossed Clya's walls and landed on the streets and roofs bordering this temple. Already they have overcome most of the guard on its upper floors and are steadily working their way downward."

"The fools!" roared Mentanek. "They are throwing away their lives. Within a lat there will be thousands of our own warriors surrounding them on the ground and in the air."

"But that will require another lat—perhaps two," Lebardat reminded him grimly. "Meanwhile they may put to death everyone within the temple. Your own life is in grave danger, my king."

UNDERSTANDING dawned on Mentanek's colossal face. "I see it now!" he thundered. "The Golden God! They hope by means of this insane raid to regain possession of it, then flee to Atland before we are able to muster enough warriors to repulse them. That is why their attack has been centered here—the logical place for the Golden God to be."

His face darkened. "They shall not have it." With a quickness that belied his bulk he bent and scooped up the fallen xorth at McGurn's feet. "Before I permit the Golden God to fall again into Atlandian hands I will turn the rays of this xorth upon it and blast it into nothingness…"

Every face in the room other than that of McGurn, to whom the idol was no more than a symbol of superstition, and Mentanek's, whose anger drove all else from his mind, blanched at the king's awe-inspiring threat. One of his red-belted companions stepped quickly forward, panic twisting his expression.

"Recall your words, noble Mentanek," he cried. "Recall them, I beg of you, ere Ammon-Re, himself, strike you dead where you stand…"

He reached a trembling hand for the holy image, only to have the crazed king strike it aside. "Don't be a fool, Sar-Gath," he bellowed. "You know, as do I, that the Golden God was fashioned by no holier a hand than yours or mine. It is no more than a token, an emblem fashioned from insensate metal by the hand of some ancient artisan long forgotten and longer dead. Ammon-Re," he went on contemptuously, "—what is Ammon-Re but a figment of some other dead imagination…?"

"I will not listen to such blasphemy!" screamed Sar-Gath. He sprang at the king, arms outstretched to claw the glowing statue from the other's hand. "Give it to me! Give it to me, lest I call down the righteous wrath of our God upon you."

"I'll give it to you!" roared Mentanek. The xorth in his hand flashed up, there was a sudden almost inaudible crackling in the air, and Sar-Gath was gone—gone as completely as though he never had existed.

There was no semblance of sanity left in those black button eyes as Clyrus's king turned his attention to the fear-stricken guards and his own companions. "Here is my god!" he screamed, brandishing the xorth. "Get out of here—all of you. Aid the soldiers of Clyrus to hold back the enemy until help comes, aid in the protection of your king and your country and Ammon-Re himself…"

The room emptied—and no room was ever emptied more quickly. When all were gone other than McGurn, the two girls and Mentanek himself, the king bolted the door and turned back to his captives.

"They will never get me," he muttered, more to himself than the others. "I know where I will be safe." Moving with short, heavy strides he went to the huge metal door in the opposite wall and began carefully to turn the two calibrated knobs set in its surface, muttering to himself the while.

A minute later the heavy barrier swung silently outward, revealing its tremendously thick layers of creonum and gold. Beyond yawned a lighted chamber, the walls of which appeared to be the same mixture of the two metals.

"Enter!" Mentanek thundered, motioning with the xorth's fluted muzzle.

Silently McGurn and the two white-faced girls stepped within ahead of the crazed monarch, and at the touch of a button the door swung silently closed. Dials matching those on its other side were set on the heavy portals' inner surface, and these Mentanek spun with two sweeps of an incredibly huge hand.

His eyes came back to his silent captives and a smile, more horrible than his darkest scowl, curled those tiny lips. "Now let them come," he gloated. "Let them try to batter their way through that door. Ten thousand men could not more than dent it in as many days."

Brushing the other aside he strode to the room's center where a smooth-sided pyramid of solid gold rose some five feet from its base resting on the floor, its apex flattened to form a square surface perhaps a foot across.

WITH a dramatic flourish that was wholly cynical, Mentanek placed the two-foot statue of the Golden God atop the pyramid and stepped back to study the effect. "There stands the image of Ammon-Re," he sneered. "Molded in his likeness by his own hands, according to every sniveling priest since Egyptus, himself. Look at it…"

Obediently they looked…and in looking felt their pulses stir and an unfathomable awe steal into their hearts and minds. Glowing with a strange, eerie radiance, which appeared to swell and wane and swell again, it held their eyes with almost hypnotic fixedness, while those miniature features, handsome beyond earthly standards, seemed almost to come alive.

The spell was sharply broken as Mentanek's ear-shattering bellow filled the small chamber. "Down on your faces, you worthless clods. Down on your faces at the feet of the Golden

God. Yours is the honor of being the first sacrifice to him whose own hands fashioned his likeness in cold metal. Prepare your souls for Ammon-Re, for only seconds remain before this xorth disintegrates your unworthy bodies…"

Again that spine-chilling, mocking laugh boomed out. Helplessly, realizing any protest was utterly useless, McGurn and the two girls sank to their knees before the golden pyramid supporting the holy image of Ammon-Re and bowed their heads. From the corners of his eyes the American could see Athora's lips moving in silent prayer, her lovely face strangely serene. As for Lua—her expression was largely bewildered, but there was no fear there for the eye to see.

As for his own reactions—they were too chaotic to be classified. He was conscious of being very frightened—more because of his complete helplessness than the thought of death itself. To turn and attempt to wrest that horrible weapon from the ham-like paws of this inhuman travesty of a man was worse than useless—it would only hasten his own end.

And so it was that Reed McGurn braced himself for the rays that would bring instant and complete disintegration…

Heavy blows began to rain against the door.

McGurn, his senses reeling under the shock of the sound, heard Mentanek's harsh breathing catch in sharp alarm. Then came the slither of sandaled feet and he turned his head in time to see Mentanek moving toward the door, the xorth tightly clutched in one hand.

"Who is there?" shouted Clyrus's king.

"It is I, Ashtoth of Atland," came the reply, clearly audible despite the heavy portal between. "Hand over the Golden God, Mentanek, and your life shall be spared. Refuse and you die…"

McGurn fastened his fingers on the shoulders of Lua and Athora. "Quick," he breathed, close to their ears. "Crawl behind the pyramid. It's our only chance to gain time enough to be rescued."

"There is no Golden God here," shouted Mentanek. "Who should know that better than Atland's king? How dare you violate the sanctity of Clyrus's Altar Room? Go away lest Ammon-Re strike you down for your blasphemy…"

Cautiously Reed McGurn drew his feet beneath him and turned in a slow half-circle, his body crouched like a lion in ambush.

"You lie," came Ashtoth's reply, clear and ringing. "The captain of your own guards is my captive and he has told me it is in there with you. Open this door!"

Carefully McGurn measured the distance between him and the fat-sagging expanse of Mentanek's shoulders and back. With infinite stealth he sidled forward.

"Go back to Atland at once!" screamed Clyrus's king. "Unless you do so immediately your daughter shall die…"

There followed a momentary silence more eloquent than many words. "My daughter!" called Ashtoth, incredulity plain in his voice. "My daughter is dead! What lie is this, Mentanek?"

"She is here, within this room. Shall I have her call out to you to leave lest she dies in shrieking agony? Wait. I will—"

It was then that Reed McGurn launched himself at that hulking figure…

AWARE that his greatest danger lay in the xorth Mentanek was holding, McGurn aimed his attack accordingly. With unerring certainty his two hands locked about that mammoth wrist even before the fat man was fully aware what was taking place, and with all his strength sought to force it back into such a position that Mentanek would be forced to drop the weapon. And so completely was the element of surprise in his favor that he came within inches of success.

But there was considerably more to Mentanek than fat. Beneath those sagging lumps of soft flesh were muscles equal to those of a bull elephant. Bellowing curses, the king lifted his imprisoned arm high despite McGurn's solid weight—lifted it and shook it violently, the American's body whipping crazily in midair like a branch in the path of a hurricane.

Fingers, no matter how strong, could not hold under that strain. With a despairing shout McGurn felt his hold torn away and he fell, landing solidly on the balls of his feet, helpless before the gargantuan madman who deliberately lifted the bell-shaped muzzle of the xorth, took aim, and fired…

Even as that immense finger closed on the firing button McGurn was throwing himself to one side, the crackling air exploding almost in his ear.

And then Reed McGurn witnessed a sight unlike any ever before, or since, vouchsafed the eyes of man. He saw the Golden God rock in the path of those unseen rays meant for him, saw its radiance dim almost to blackness as the metal statue resisted impulses no other matter could ever resist, saw it topple heavily to the floor. And in the instant those rays bathed the image of Ammon-Re, Mentanek, king of Clyrus, cried out in terrible agony—cried out as both the xorth and the hand that held it utterly and completely disappeared into nothingness.

But even that miracle won no more than a brief glance from the wide-eyed American. He saw the Golden God touch the floor in an upright position, and as it did so it began to glow again—glow with a radiance so intense McGurn felt his eyes burn in protest, yet some power beyond his seemed to hold them open.

And as that radiance increased, the golden figure began to enlarge, to grow, to swell, to increase in size until it was no longer a tiny figure carved into the likeness of a man—it was a man!

STRAIGHT and strong and of incredible beauty was the Golden God—standing inches beyond McGurn's six feet. And the once stiff and lifeless metal now was transformed into muscles and sinews and flawless skin…a completely naked man—a man whose body was of the perfection no human body might ever hope to attain.

Mentanek, the stump of his severed hand dangling as his side, could only goggle with bulging eyes at the Divine Presence before him, fear rippling over his gigantic body in tiny waves.

Those golden arms lifted slowly…and suddenly McGurn's eyes could bear that awful light no more and he sank to his knees, burying his head in his arms.

Moments passed. Dimly at first, then very clearly, McGurn could hear the sounds of shouted words from beyond the creonum door. A soft hand touched his shoulder from behind and he cried out suddenly, lifting his head to learn who stood beside him.

It was Athora. Dazed, he swung his glance about the small chamber. Gone was that unearthly radiance, on the golden pyramid stood the two-foot figure of the Golden God, its soft emanations of light normal once more—metal instead of living flesh.

On the floor in front of him was a horribly mangled mound of grayish-white flesh, emptied of all life, its once mammoth bones evidently reduced to little more than powder. Mentanek of Clyrus was dead.

Reed McGurn got shakily to his feet and reeled drunkenly across the room and leaned his head against the door's cool surface. "Let us—out," he cried weakly. "For God's sake let us out of this awful place…"

"Open the door, Mentanek," came Ashtoth's voice.

"Mentanek is dead," called McGurn. "Your daughter is here with me. I don't know how to open the door. You'll have to force it open."

A brief pause followed, then Ashtoth shouted. "Get into a corner as far from the door as you can. Hurry!"

Through a dim haze that seemed to grow increasingly thick, McGurn drew Lua and Athora aside as directed. A long moment dragged by—then that creonum barrier vanished magically and through the opening, a giant xorth in his hands, came Ashtoth of Atland, a crowd of his own fighting men at his back.

Suddenly the room appeared to spin in a slow circle—then blackness poured into McGurn's overwrought mind and he knew no more.

CHAPTER EIGHTEEN
Conclusion

"REED…Reed McGurn! Open your eyes, my prince."

The soft, wondrously sweet voice seemed to be calling to him across a limitless void, through an opaque wall of shimmering blackness. And then the blackness began to fade, replaced by a swelling green light that became more and more intense…

He opened his eyes, blinking in the sunlight streaming across his bed from an open window.

A face hovered above him—a face of blood-warming beauty…a face framed with soft strands of blue-black hair.

"Athora," he mumbled, then stopped there to marvel at the weakness of his voice. His lips seemed dry to the point of cracking, and he put out his tongue to wet them. "Athora. What are—" Suddenly the gates of memory opened and he sat quickly erect and groped wildly at the covers. "We've got to get out of—"

Her hand came up to cover his lips with tender pressure, forcing him gently back against the pillow. "We are safe in Atlantis, my prince. We brought you here over a moon ago."

He stared at her uncomprehendingly. "A moon? You mean a month ago?"

She understood the strange word he used and nodded. "When you fainted in the Altar Room of Clya's temple we were unable to revive you, discovering then that you were burning with fever. My father bore you in his own arms to one of our dyarks on the temple roof and brought you here, where men skilled in the treatment of jungle fevers fought to save your life. You came very near to dying, my prince."

He thought that over for a little while. "…The Golden God?"

She smiled. "Back where it belongs—in Atland's temple."

"You saw—" his voice faltered, "you saw what happened to Mentanek?"

"Only when it was all over. The Klysan and I were crouched behind the golden pyramid until it grew quiet within the room. Just before that a great light seemed to fill the chamber and we were forced to hide our eyes against it… Your rage must have been very great to crush Mentanek so terribly. Even with the evidence of his torn body we found it difficult to believe any man could possess sufficient strength to do *that* to him."

"But it wasn't…" His voice trailed off. She would never believe him—none of them would believe him. They would become alarmed and call in the doc's again and maybe keep him in bed longer than necessary, figuring the fever had left him on the balmy side.

And then the memory of another girl—a girl whose hair was golden and whose beauty was no less than Athora's herself—

pushed into his mind. "Where," he asked eagerly, "is Lua? Did you rescue her? Is she all right?"

An expression the American could not analyze passed across Athora's face and she lowered her eyes. "You must rest now, Reed McGurn. I should not have allowed you to speak at such length. I will come and visit with you tomorrow."

"But what of Lua?" he protested. "Will you bring her with you when you come again?"

She patted his shoulder and stood up. "We'll see, Reed McGurn. Go to sleep now."

He would have pressed the point but a wave of weariness seemed to sweep over him then and he closed his eyes. Instantly he was sleeping soundly.

ON THE following day the princess Athora came again, and again he asked about Lua. But when he saw such questions appeared to pain the girl, he desisted, telling himself she was made unhappy by his interest in the cave girl.

In the days that followed, strength came slowly back to Reed McGurn, and when a week had passed he was back on his feet and his old self again. Athora and he walked often in the palace gardens where sunlight and fresh air restored the color to his cheeks and tone to his muscles.

On several occasions Ashtoth came to see him, and a strong friendship built on mutual admiration and respect formed between them. At times the king's remarks disturbed McGurn secretly, for he spoke as though the American would someday rule Atland with Athora as his queen. Always those remarks were made as though such a marriage was a foregone conclusion; and McGurn held his peace for this was not the time to bring matters to a head.

Always his thoughts were filled with Lua, daughter of Yortak, although he refrained from speaking of her to the others. Yet, as the days passed in the comfort and beauty of his surroundings, he found himself thinking more and more of Athora—comparing the gently bred princess of Atland with the untamed girl of the jungle. Gradually he began to wonder—to doubt that his feelings for Lua were truly the love he believed them to be. And when, in parting each day, Athora held up her lips for a farewell kiss, he felt an increasingly stronger impulse to crush her to him and pour out his pledge of love.

One bright sunny morning he rose from his bed with the knowledge that he was completely cured and his full strength had come back to him. He dressed leisurely and was on the point of summoning a slave to announce his readiness for breakfast, when his door opened and one of the palace guards entered.

"His majesty, the noble Ashtoth, sends his respects," the guard said formally, "and wishes to know if you will honor him and his daughter by eating the morning meal with them."

"Why not?" McGurn said with alacrity. "Lead the way; I'm starving."

They moved along the corridors and through lavishly appointed rooms, and many were the friendly greetings the American received from members of the court in passing. Finally they entered a small room bright with sunlight through its many windows, and here, grouped about a small table spread with food, were Ashtoth and a smiling Athora and a stern-faced man of about his own age whom he recognized as Clat-Ron, high priest in Atland, who had called on McGurn during the early stages of the latter's convalescence.

They greeted him warmly and conversation lagged until the food was gone and all sank back in their chairs in the expansive mood that follows a good meal.

Ashtoth was first to speak—and he wasted no words. "For some time," he said soberly. "I have noticed the growing attachment between you and Athora. That she loves you I am sure you know; she told me of it on the very night we took the two of you from Clyrus."

McGurn shot a glance at the princess. Her eyes were lowered to study the tips of her fingers and a slow wave of red was rising in her cheeks.

"But," Ashtoth continued weightily, "during my talks with you I detected an uneasiness on your part whenever I purposely turned the conversation into such channels—a reaction which caused me to doubt that you returned my daughter's love. And so I waited, watching the two of you when together."

He smiled suddenly. "Unless I am a blind old man, Reed McGurn, I would swear that you are very much in love with

Athora—and are hesitating to ask for her only because of her position as Atland's future queen. What do you say to that?"

"Where," McGurn blurted out, "is Lua?"

ONE AGONIZED gasp broke from Athora's stricken lips and the two most powerful men in Atland stiffened in their chairs, their faces suddenly stern. But when Ashtoth spoke his voice was courteous and kindly.

"She is no longer in Atland, Reed McGurn."

"No long—" The young American stared at him, disbelief strong in his eyes. "Where is she, then? What has happened to her?"

"Soon after we brought her to Atland with Athora and you, she came to me and asked that she be permitted to return to her own people in Afrota. She was not happy here, she told me—only in the caves of Mosat would she feel at home.

"Because in your illness you spoke often of her. I asked Lua if there was anything between the two of you. I shall never forget the way she lifted her head proudly and said, "I owe him much, for he was very good to me and he tried to rescue me from the Clyrusians. But it ends there for he is not my kind and his heart belongs to another."

He sighed. "And so I granted her request to return to Afrota. The following day a pantar of my Air Fleet flew her back to the land of her people."

" 'His heart belongs to another,' " repeated McGurn softly. "How could she be so sure?"

His eyes came to rest on Athora's suffused countenance, and as she looked up and saw his troubled expression, all self-possession failed her.

"I told her that, Reed McGurn," she cried out, tears of anger and hurt pride spilling on her cheeks. "She is not for you—she is a Klysan—a beast-woman! You belong here. In Atland. Beside me. Here you shall have power and beautiful surroundings and—and me, Reed McGurn. Forget her, my prince. I will make you forget her…"

For a long time McGurn sat there, his eyes fixed unseeingly on his hands. When at last he raised his eyes to the silent Atlandians, Athora knew that she had lost and she buried her face in her hands.

To Ashtoth he said, "Will you summon the same pantar who took Lua back to Afrota and instruct him to fly me to the same place he left her?"

"Are you sure this is what you want, Reed McGurn?" the king asked tonelessly.

"It is."

Athora's father bowed in acquiescence. "When do you wish to leave?"

"At once, if you will."

Both rose to their feet. "The man you want is, I believe, on duty at the roof landing stage at this time. If you will accompany me there…"

Reed McGurn hesitated for a moment, then placed a gentle hand on the girl's bowed head. "Will you come and say goodbye to me, Athora?"

She lifted her dark head, tears sparkling in her cheeks, and said brokenly. "As you wish, Reed McGurn."

The silent Clat-Ron rose with her, and together the three men · and the girl mounted a flight of circling steps to the roof. Ashtoth called over the officer in charge of the guards stationed there and ordered that a dyark be readied for immediate flight and that Lua's pilot be found and put at the controls.

Within a few minutes the giant aircraft was ready, the pantar at its instrument panel.

Just before mounting the three metal steps to the dyark's cabin, McGurn turned to say his farewells. Both Clat-Ron and Ashtoth made the sign of the holy triangle; but the princess threw her arms about his neck and kissed him lingeringly on the mouth, the tang of tears remaining there.

"Goodbye, my princess," he whispered. "Who knows—some day we may meet again." Gently he loosened her hold and her father stepped forward and drew her away as the American entered the cabin.

From the window, as he took his seat, he saw Clat-Ron's hand reach out and close about one of Athora's…and she did not resist. McGurn's lips parted in a slow smile…

The dyark rose vertically, turned its nose toward the east in a sweeping half circle and sped toward Afrota—and lovely Lua.

THE END

If you've enjoyed this book, you will not want to miss these terrific titles...

If you've enjoyed this book, you will not want to miss these terrific titles...

If you've enjoyed this book, you will not want to miss these terrific titles...

If you've enjoyed this book, you will not want to miss these terrific titles...

Made in the USA
Middletown, DE
02 December 2020

25741196R00130